whispers of *Hope*

ALSO BY CHARLENE CARR

A New Start Series
When Comes The Joy
Where There Is Life
By What We Love
Forever In My Heart

Behind Our Lives Trilogy
Behind Our Lives
What We See
The Stories We Tell

Standalone
Beneath the Silence
Before I Knew You

Whispers of Hope

A New Start, Book 5

Charlene Carr

Published by Coastal Lines, 2019.

Published in Canada by Coastal Lines
www.coastallines.ca

Library and Archives Canada

Whispers of Hope
Book Five of the A New Start Series
ISBN: 978-1-988232-19-5

Typography by Coastal Lines
Cover Design by Coastal Lines

Second Edition, November 2019

This work is also available in electronic format:
Whispers of Hope
ISBN: 978-1-988232-00-3

To all the women who are mothers, and will always be mothers, even if you never hold your own child in your arms.

Your hope makes you a mother. Your love. Your daily sacrifices in an effort to bring into existence the children of your heart.

CHAPTER ONE

The hospital walls are bright and cheery. In the hall outside Dr. LeBlanc's waiting room, lions frolic in meadows while butterflies soar overhead, because, of course, lions frolic. Just above Dr. LeBlanc's head a monkey swings on a vine—a banana in its hand and a smile on its face. I stare at it as Dr. LeBlanc's words echo in my mind. The cysts have tripled in size.

I hold my back tall. From outward appearances, I know I look poised. I draw my gaze from the monkey's almost manic smile and focus on Dr. LeBlanc's mouth and the words it speaks.

"This kind of growth, it's, uh, not unprecedented, but…"

She should be the one to look poised. Doctors shouldn't stutter. Doctors shouldn't twirl a pen while delivering news like this.

She sets the pen down. "I've never seen anything like it. Not personally. Tracey, this isn't severe endometriosis, this is beyond severe. It was severe fourteen months ago."

My focus drifts from her words back to the painted walls, the happy scenes. It makes sense. The doctors here don't just deal with women who have no hope. They're gynecologists. They regularly see women whose joy and excitement grows bigger with each passing day. The friendly murals line up with the hopes and dreams of those women, of the children they eventually bring with them, excited to be big brothers and sisters, to see their families grow.

For women like me there should be a different hall, a different office. *Tripled in size.*

The doctor smiled right after saying those words, as if a smile would make it hurt less, could change words that tore apart the hope I've held as long as I've understood what hope is. "It's not impossible," she says. How plucky. "With surgery and then in vitro, there is a chance. A slim chance." Her smile drops then brightens again, as if her lips need a break from holding their upturned position. She reminds me of a ventriloquist's doll.

"What are the stats?" I keep myself poised. Calm. "The success rate of surgery, of IVF afterward?"

Dr. LeBlanc sighs. "The stats look at all women who have endometriosis. There are four stages and you're beyond the fourth, technically within the fourth—it's so rare we don't even class…" Her voice trails off again. She shrugs, another smile pushing through. I want to slap it off her face. Instead, I smile back. This is not her fault. I know none of this is her fault. She reaches a hand toward me, doesn't touch, just reaches. My body quivers. "If these options don't work, there is always adoption."

OUTSIDE DR. LeBLANC'S OFFICE the happy walls seem to go on forever, just like the months and months of often obligatory, often painful sex, of people telling me not to worry, to be hopeful, it just takes time. Easy for them to say. They're not broken. The act every woman is supposed to be capable of, to do so easily we spend most of our sexual lives trying to prevent, I'm failing at, over and over again.

Just as I approach the hospital doors Adrian bursts through them. "Tracey." The harried grin I fell in love with greets me. "I'm so sorry I'm late. Are you just—" He stops. "You're done, aren't you? You're leaving?" I don't answer. I try to, but my lips won't work. "It's bad."

This time my answer is a nod. His arms circle me. "Ahh, baby. What is it?" He leads me through the hospital doors and out into the bright sunshine. I squint at the light, wanting to hide from it, from him, from my own body. We sit on a bench near the entrance and he pries Dr. LeBlanc's words out of me. He holds my hand.

"I'm sorry I wasn't here." He rubs his other hand through his tousled hair, his green eyes frustrated and almost furious. "I was held up at the studio and then there was an accident. The highway was grid locked." I squeeze his hand back, letting him know it's okay. His eyes soften. "But this is not all bad, right? You can have the surgery. And she said your tubes could be blocked, right? The dye test, it was inconclusive?"

"Yeah."

"So maybe that was the problem." Now his eyes brighten. "She'll clear those tubes up and it'll be smooth sailing. That fertilized egg will just fly through to where it needs to be."

"That *could* be the problem. *Could.* It doesn't mean—"

"Let's be hopeful."

I stare at him, smile, because I know that's what he wants from me. What he deserves, too. I hold my voice as steady as I can. "Even if that's not the problem, inflammation could be, pressure from the cysts. If that pressure and inflammation is reduced, she said it could make a difference."

"Exactly." He grins. "We'll whip this endometriosis's ass!"

We'll?

He puts his arm around me, draws me near. "So what's wrong?"

I shrug.

"Trace."

"It's scary. Overwhelming. Surgery. People die from—"

"But not this kind. It's pretty standard, right? The…" he hesitates, "laparoscopy. We were reading up on it and—"

"Every surgery has risk."

"Life has risk." He pauses. "Trace. This is what you want, what we want. You have the surgery. We try for a few more months. If it doesn't happen, then we talk about artificial insemination or in vitro. We've got options here. We're lucky."

Lucky? I hold back the yell inside me. Lucky? Options? We? It's me. All me. He's not risking a thing.

"Okay." He squeezes my hand again. "You're scared. I get it. So our other options: Try IUI right now or IVF. Before the surgery. What about those?"

"The doctor thinks it'd be a waste of time, money, health. She said if my tubes aren't clear, and with all the endo inflammation I have, there'd be such a slim chance."

"She said it's a waste of time?"

"That's the impression I got from her words, her demeanour."

Adrian nods. "You know I'm open to adoption."

"You know I'm not."

A long pause extends between us. "We should at least start the process, put our names on the list."

My head shakes back and forth. I rest a hand on his, wishing he understood.

"It could be an eight to nine year wait for a baby. Your feelings could change in eight to nine years."

"So you're saying we should give up hope?"

He closes his eyes, his breath making his nostrils flare. "I'm saying we have options and maybe the best way to see hope realized is to explore all the options we can. And even if we got pushed up the list, received a child sooner than expected, we could still have our own."

I draw my gaze to the bright flowers nodding happily in a large earthenware pot next to the bench we're on. Their existence is so simple. I turn back to Adrian, lacking the energy for a conversation we've had too many times before. To do to a child what's been done to me, to have them always feel like they were second choice, the consolation prize…

"You need to let go. You can't let your adoption define your life."

My chin juts out. "I don't. It's not like I wake up in the morning, look at myself and think, I'm adopted." Adrian roles his eyes. "It doesn't affect everything, but it affects this. I can't help but have it affect this."

He sighs, sits back, and draws his arm away from me. "You can try."

"How did the interview go?" I ask, my voice light. "The source pan out?"

He sits forward. "Excellent. Should lead to some new contacts, girls still caught in the cycle." He pushes himself upright. "Oh! And I can't believe I didn't tell you, the producer is pretty sure the documentary will go national. Some of Toronto's head honchos got wind of it and they're really interested."

"Adrian, that's amazing."

He grins. "I know." He sits back. "Sometimes I'm excited about what we're doing here. Exposing such corruption, showing people how easy it is for things like bullying, manipulation, domestic abuse to lead to prostitution or trafficking." He shakes his head. "But then there's the other side of it. Before this all began I had no idea what was going on, right here in Halifax." He lets out a sad laugh and gestures around us. "It looks so nice. So quaint. These girls, though, they're living in an entirely different world."

I graze my fingers along the back of his neck, my heart swelling for him. "I'm proud of what you're doing. I don't say it enough."

"I know." He draws me back to his side and grins. "Was this your way of diverting the conversation?"

I grin back. "Did it work?"

He laughs. "You don't need to make a decision today. But you do need to make one. What's that Einstein quote? Insanity is doing the same thing over and over again and expecting different results. Each month we're doing the same thing. Each month…" he pauses, "not that I don't like the copious amounts of sex. I do." That smile. "But I know it's painful for you a lot of the time." He rubs his thumb against my hand. "Will the surgery help that?"

"It could." I look down. "The doctor said she has an opening in three weeks. The next one after that is three months away."

"When do you have to tell her?"

"She put my name down to reserve the spot but asked that I get back to her by Monday if I don't want it."

"Okay." The look I love and hate, depending on the circumstance—excited, eager, determined—covers Adrian's face. "I think you need to do this."

"It's not just surgery then all is well. I'll need someone to take care of me. I'll be on bed rest for at least a week. Maybe more."

"Your mom will take care of you."

"Maybe."

"She'd be excited to. It'd be like giving her a present."

I chuckle. "Maybe."

Adrian looks at his watch. "Speaking of your mother, we should get on the road. Don't want whatever glorious meal she prepared getting cold." He places his hand on the small of my back as we walk to the car, an action that still makes my stomach flutter. He gives my back a rub. "And maybe after dinner you can talk to your mom about the surgery. See if she'll take care of you?"

"Maybe." Talking about the surgery with my mother means talking about a whole lot more than Adrian realizes, and more than I'm sure I'm capable of.

CHAPTER TWO

When we enter my parents' house, the familiar smell of baked goods mingling with the scent of sizzling garlic greets us. Lulu and Reggie propel themselves upon Adrian, who scoops them into his arms. Neveah, running on tip-toe, darts behind them but veers as she reaches her arms to me. I hold her close and she cradles her head against my neck, always the cuddler.

Mom's voice floats from the kitchen. "Is that Tracey and Adrian?"

"Yep." Adrian shouts above the twins as they batter him with question after question: "Can we play out back? How old are you? Did you know Mommy's twenty-seven? Can we play out back?"

"Leave the man alone." My mother darts toward us. She wipes her hands on her blue polka-dot apron then pulls me into an embrace, her soft arms wrapping around both me and Neveah. Neveah climbs out of my arms and into her Grammie's. "Adrian." He gets a one-armed hug from Mom as the twins slither off of him. "Come in. Come in."

"Smells amazing, Mrs. Sampson. As usual."

Mom waves Adrian's comment away. "Just a little something. But I hope you'll like it."

"Where's Jojo?" I ask.

Something flickers across my mother's face; I'm afraid I know what it is. "She's lying down." Mom keeps her smile firm. "Wanted a bit of quiet, that's all."

"Quiet." Adrian chuckles as a twin pulls on each of his arms. "What would she want that for?"

"Oh, I have no idea!" Mom laughs. "Tracey." Mom sets Neveah down. "Help me in the kitchen a moment." I follow behind her and the smells intensify.

"What are you making?"

"Garlic roasted potatoes and mushrooms with almond asparagus and honey glazed chicken breasts." She glances to the back deck. "Though your father's doing the grilling. For dessert, red velvet cake."

"Sounds amazing." Out the window, Adrian and my dad chat as Dad tends the BBQ and the kids run circles in the yard. "What's the ladder for?"

"Oh, that." Mom sighs. "Here, I'll get you to squeeze this for me." She passes me an icing bag and coupler. "With my arthritis, I just have no more power." She shakes her head. "Yep. Just hold steady. Squeeze, nice and easy."

As Mom rotates the cake beneath my hands I ask, again, "The ladder?"

"He's building a deck out of our bedroom window, which means, of course, building a door where the window is." She pauses a moment, her tongue sticking out the corner of her mouth as she concentrates. I smile. Has anyone ever told her about this little quirk? I doubt it. She'd probably stop. "He says it'll be a nicer place to read in the morning and offer some shade on the back porch. Why we need shade on the back porch is beyond me, but if we wanted it, why not get one of those big umbrellas? And if he doesn't want shade while he's reading, then simply put the umbrella down." Her hair bounces as she laughs. "Unless he just wants to read in his knickers."

"You know Dad can't sit still."

I look away from the window, surprised at the intricate design Mom has managed to create while guiding my hands.

"Nice and steady," she says.

"Sorry."

Her head tilts in concentration. "It's not so bad for him to have something to keep him out of my hair." Her hand rests on mine to pause the squeeze as she surveys her creation. After repositioning my hand she taps for the squeezing to resume. "When he's not working a project, I admit, I go a little crazy having him puttering around all day." She grins, her eyes still on the cake. "I just don't know why all his projects have to bring dust and disorder into my house."

"Maybe he needs to find somewhere to volunteer. Habitat for Humanity?"

"You know something," she turns the cake one final time then motions for me to stop squeezing the icing bag, "that's not such a bad idea."

Dad, Adrian, and the kids enter, along with the grilled chicken. Mom sends Lulu to wake her mother. When Jojo enters the room, it strikes me how different she looks from the woman I introduced Adrian to two-and-a-half years ago. That woman looked like she'd stepped out of a hippie commune. The woman today is more like the Jojo I remember pre-Damien and the kids. She's wearing torn jeans, an old Dirty and the Derelicts t-shirt, and her long flowing hair is pulled back into a messy bun. Every detail of her must grate upon my always perfectly-presented mother's nerves.

"Hey, Sis." Her smile is beautiful. Tired looking, but beautiful.

"Happy Birthday."

"Is that what we're here for?" She laughs almost caustically and turns to give Adrian a quick hug.

"Twenty-seven," I say.

She shrugs and ruffles Reggie's hair. "Surreal. I still feel nineteen."

"Who doesn't?" Dad winks.

"Let's not let it get cold." Mom ushers us to the dining

room where the food, unsurprisingly, is amazing. With the kids' help, after dinner we sing a robust round of Happy Birthday, complete with a chorus about farts, courtesy of Reggie. The cake is so moist it practically melts in my mouth. I've only taken a few bites when the doorbell rings.

Jojo groans. "That'll be Damien. An hour early." She pushes from her seat as the kids yell, 'Daddy.' "It's like he doesn't know how to read a clock."

"He can join us for tea and cake." Mom pops up, her brow creased and her smile on. "We have plenty."

Jojo rolls her eyes and walks to the door. Jojo and Damien's voices are a low rumble: his easy and light, Jo's getting tighter and angrier with every exchange. I hold back the kids, uncertain whether this conversation is one they should hear.

When Jojo and Damien walk into the room, there's no holding Reggie and Neveah back. They run to him. Lulu stays next to me. Damien embraces the kids as if he really missed them, is happy to see them, but something is not right. Damien motions to Lulu, who shuffles over then hugs him tightly.

"Can we finish our cake first?" asks Lulu.

Reggie pulls a spare chair from against the wall, his smile wide. "Grandma says you can have some."

"Oh." Damien, who, unlike my sister, still looks as if he's stepped out of a hippie commune, turns to Jojo. She averts her gaze. "Well…"

Jojo crosses her arms. "I'm not doing this for you."

Damien looks toward the kids. "I'm sorry, but," he pauses, "I can't take you tonight after all."

Lulu steps away from Damien and returns to her cake. Reggie stares at him. "But Mommy has a party with her friends. And we're having a party with you."

"Not tonight."

"When?"

Jojo sits. "Yes, when?"

Damien shifts. "Well, that's the other thing I wanted to talk to you about. Maybe not here though, not now."

"Whatever you have to say," Jojo tips her chin, "you might as well get it out. What's the reason for you bailing this time? Are the stars aligned? Must you meditate in the wilderness?"

"No." He leans on the chair Reggie pulled out for him. "I'm leaving."

Jojo doesn't even try to mask the derision in her voice. "Just tell us what it is, make up an excuse. Don't run away."

"No, I mean, I'm leaving. Me and…" he hesitates, "Crystal. We're going on a spiritual journey."

Mom swallows. Dad's fists clench. Jojo pops out of her chair. "A spiritual journey?" Her voice catches. "Like the one that brought us Neveah?"

"Are we getting another brother or sister?" squeaks Reggie.

"Shut it." Jojo turns to Damien. "Where this time?"

"We'll start in Asia."

"How long?"

"Jojo," his voice holds that sleazy ease I've always hated in Damien, "you know these things don't run by a calendar. When we feel sufficiently self-actualized, we'll come back."

Jojo's voice is low, shaky. "Your children don't need a self-actualized father. They need a present father."

"Jojo," he holds his voice equally low, as if doing so will prevent the rest of us from hearing his words, "you're the one who left me."

She laughs.

Mom stands. "I think, umm…" she motions to the kids, "Reggie, Lulu," and grasps Neveah's hand. "Why don't you come onto the porch with me? Won't it be fun to eat your cake out there?"

Lulu stares at Damien, her feet planted firmly, stares until mom pulls her away.

"You're a selfish bastard," says Jojo, not looking at him.

"Jojo, baby. I know you're mad. But I've always been honest with you. I was honest with you about Crystal from the start."

"From the start?"

"Well, about the potential." The ease vanishes. Damien's posture becomes spindly, like an earthworm before slivering into its hole. "Should we go somewhere more private? We can—"

"Talk right here."

A half sigh, half groan escapes him. "I need this, okay. We need it. To be off the grid, away from distractions. Crystal feels my focus has been on you and the kids more lately, it was damaging, having you leave, and—"

"What?" Jojo's eyes widen, her mouth hangs open. "She's jealous? Jealous of your children? Your children, who you abandoned?"

"I didn't abandon them. You moved out."

"Because you were living part time with another woman!"

"Crystal, she just needs—"

"What about what your children need, Damien? Your children?" She steps forward, as if ready for a fight. "Not that it really matters, anyway. You hardly see them."

"I see them."

"Once a week, twice, if something more important doesn't get in the way."

"I'd see them more if you hadn't moved so far away."

"And if one of them gets sick? You'll be off the grid. No address, I'm guessing. No cell. Free, right? Free to not know about your own children."

"I'll know if something happens."

"Sure you will."

"Jojo."

"Just leave already."

Dad stands. "Maybe that would be best."

Damien steps from the chair. "I'd like to say goodbye to

the kids."

"Go ahead." Jojo spits the words, her arms crossed.

He takes several more steps. "You can have the apartment over the store if you want. If it's eas—"

The tendons in her neck flair. "I have my own place."

"Okay."

"I suppose that child support you've been saying was coming, it'll have to wait?"

"Things have been tight."

"Oh, I understand." She grabs her tea, sips it in a way that would make Mom proud. "So tight you can pay for a flight to Asia."

"Jojo." Damien walks toward her, lays a hand on her shoulder, which she jerks away from him. "The universe will provide. It provided those tickets and it will provide for our children, just like it always has."

"I provide for them." Her face tightens. "Fuck you, you and your free love and your *spiritual* journey."

"Jojo." Dad shakes his head. She ignores him.

Damien steps back. "I'm disappointed in you." He raises his hands, as if brushing off the air that surrounds her. "All of this negative energy. You're not the woman I thought you were."

"Me, not the woman you thought I was?" She laughs that caustic laugh again. "Well, isn't that rich."

He nods as his characteristic ease returns, "I hope you find your peace, your centre," and backs out of the room.

Adrian and Dad look the way I feel—at a loss for words. At last Dad makes his way over to Jojo. He wraps an arm around her shoulder. "You'll be all right, sweetie. It will all be all right."

"Yeah." The caustic tone remains but, to my surprise, Jojo doesn't slip out of Dad's embrace. "It'll be better. None of us need him."

Dad squeezes. "You've got us."

Jojo's face screws up, as if she's battling a slew of

emotions trying to break through. She loses the battle and tears leak down her still tough looking face. She turns into Dad's chest. "I was supposed to have a night out with the girls from my program. It's stupid, I know, but…"

Dad makes a tut-tut noise. "We've got it. No worries. You go have fun."

"I was so stupid." Her voice is muffled into Dad's shirt, thankfully. She'd die if Damien heard these sobs. "I should have listened."

"You were young." Dad's arms wrap tighter around her. "And now you've got the three most amazing kids ever."

She laughs.

I rise from my seat and motion for Adrian to follow. Leaving Dad and Jojo to their moment, we make our way to the backyard where Damien seems to be finishing his goodbyes to the kids. Mom stands off to the side with Lulu against her legs. Both Reggie and Neveah are in their father's arms. He looks happy, excited, and it's hard to tell whether this is for the kids' sake, trying to prevent tears, or if he's actually able to feel excitement as he leaves his children for weeks or months or more. Anger seeps through me. It would feel good to knee this man in the balls. He has three children, three children who love him, and he's walking away.

When the door closes behind Damien, we gather back at the table. The twins ignore their cake and beg to be excused. I try to eat mine, but the flavour seems less. Glancing around the table, I see that no one but Dad and Adrian are still eating. Mom pushes the pieces around on her plate. Jojo stares at the wall, her clenched jaw twitching.

"You still have your party to look forward to," says Mom with a lilt to her voice. "That should be fun."

"A blast." Jojo pushes away from the table. "Mind if I take off?"

Mom looks to her watch. Jojo's not supposed to leave for another forty minutes.

"That's fine." Dad reaches over to squeeze Jojo's shoulder. "Go ahead, sweetie. Have fun."

When Jojo leaves Mom stands and clears the plates. She doesn't ask if I'm done and whisks the plate away from Adrian, whose fork is poised in the air, about to pierce another piece.

"I'm going to go work out back." Dad gestures to Adrian. "You want to help?"

"Well," Adrian looks to me and then back to Dad, "it's such a nice evening, I thought I might take the kids to the park, get them out of Joanna and Tracey's hair as they clean up."

"Good man."

I know what the look Adrian gave me meant, and what he wants me to say in the kitchen with Mom. It seems a bad time, with Mom's mind so full of Jojo and all her woes, but who knows when a good time will arrive? Silence surrounds us as Mom washes the dishes and I dry. She scrubs the cake pan with vigour. "Awful, that man is awful."

"He's still their dad."

"I could just wring his neck." Mom wrings her dishcloth, the force of the action a shock to us both. She lets out an embarrassed laugh.

"Jojo will be all right, Mom. She's tough."

Mom smiles at me. "That she is."

I take the cake pan and dry it. I look at her, perhaps a moment too long, then back to the pan. With a final swipe of my cloth I deem it finished and place it in the cupboard. When I turn back to Mom, she's staring at me.

"Something is on your mind tonight. Something more than this ugliness with Jojo."

I take my time drying a mixing bowl before answering. "There is."

"Care to talk?"

I glance toward the breakfast table. "Can we sit?"

CHAPTER THREE

At the kitchen table I finger a place mat before starting. Mom's eyes are wide and attentive. "So," I pull the edge of the place mat through my fingers, "you've probably been wondering about Adrian and me, when we'll have children."

"You've always wanted a family but," she pats my knee, "no rush."

No rush? I expected excitement, urgency, questions about whether I'm pregnant now…but my mother's not stupid or unobservant. She must know this is not a happy conversation. "We've actually been trying for over a year now."

She nods.

"It turns out I have endometriosis. Severe endometriosis."

Her lips press together, turning into an even thinner line than they usually are.

"The doctor thinks I should have surgery, that other methods won't be worth much without it."

"Oh, Tracey." She shakes her head. "I don't think so, unless…unless the pain is unbearable. Surgery is so dangerous."

"There are risks. But usually it's fine."

Mom looks to her hands in her lap. "Why are you just talking to me about this now? You knew…you know my struggles, that I…"

"We've never really talked about it. Not really."

"Yes, but—"

"We don't talk about these things." I look away from her. "We talk about happy things, positive things."

"Is that what you think?"

I shrug.

"You're right." Her gaze falls. "I've never talked to you about it, not in detail, but the surgery I had, it was two years before we got you, and it almost killed me." She stops, pain crossing her brow at the memory. "They're risky. One little mistake and I had a colostomy bag for weeks. The pain from the endometriosis was even worse afterward. Not better. I wouldn't wish that on anyone."

"But it worked, right?"

Mom seems to pull into herself. "I don't know about that."

"But Jojo."

"The surgery was years before Jojo. I can't imagine it had much to do with her at all. Jojo was—"

"A miracle."

She makes a little noise of affirmation. "Just like you."

It's hard not to laugh, but I hold it in.

"Adoption is a beautiful thing, darling. You know that. If I had known, I never would have had the surgery."

"You would have been fine with never having your own child?"

"Tracey," Mom reaches for my knee, "you *are* my own child."

"Mom, please. You know what I mean."

"You're my child."

"I'm not asking for your advice or your blessing or anything, anyway. I'm just asking if you'll stay with me during recovery. Adrian's so busy with this investigative piece, he can't be with me full time and I need someone there in case. Especially in case—"

"There are complications?"

"Yes."

"I don't know." I follow her gaze to the family photo on the wall, taken when Jojo was just a toddler. "I'm watching Neveah while Jojo's at work. You know that. And I pick the kids up after school. It'll be even busier now that Damien will be gone. He didn't help out much, but it was something. A backup."

I pause, considering. "I could stay here, I suppose."

"With yelling kids and a screaming toddler? You'll need your rest and they won't help."

"They're not monsters. They could be quiet if need be, if we explained."

Mom shakes her head. "I don't think you should have this surgery. If something happened…"

I take several breaths as her voice trails off. "So this is your refusal then? You won't take care of me because you're against the surgery?"

"No, of course not. It's just…if you're at your house it would be carting the kids, all that driving, and if you're here…would Adrian make the drive every day?"

"What about Dad? To take care of me or the kids or—"

Mom's face lights up. "That may work. It would be a different kind of project for him. But maybe."

"I doubt I'd need around the clock care. I'm healthy and—"

"But you might. You said it's severe?"

"Cysts the size of oranges in my ovaries."

Mom's eyes widen and her mouth makes a little 'o'. "Baby."

"It's okay."

"No." She shakes her head. "The pain. Is it bad?"

I let out a little laugh. "One night I was lying on the couch home alone with my hands underneath me. I had to stay like that because I was so scared if I stood up, if I let my hands free, I'd grab a butcher knife and try to cut the pain right out of me."

"Hmm." She smiles gently. "I understand that. I remember."

A pressure wells in my throat. "Anyway," I push a smile, "it is what it is."

"And the doctor thinks the surgery will help with the pain?"

"Some of it." I shift in my seat. "We've decided she'll only operate on the cysts and adhesions that directly affect fertility. It lowers the risk of complications. But based on my symptoms, some of the pain may be stemming from other areas."

The room is quiet for so long it feels weighted. "I'll try to make it work, but Tracey, if this isn't about the pain, I just think…it can be a long and torturous journey. It takes a lot out of a person, a lot out of a marriage. There are other options. Wonderful options. You're proof of that."

"Mom."

"No, honey. I know aspects of being adopted were hard for you. I understand that. But we did the best we could to give you a good life. Your adoption doesn't define you."

My anger flares. First Adrian, now Mom. "Well, it feels like it defines me. Aspects of me at least. It defines this."

"Trace—"

"Mom." I stare at her, throw up my hands. "Maybe I am really messed up. Maybe I'm damaged. Scarred. Maybe you should have had me in therapy so I wouldn't be like this. But I am like this."

"Therapy?"

"Don't you remember what it was like, how I'd get so sick and worried every time you left? How at camp I couldn't handle being away from you, how I was so terrified you'd never come back I threw up everything I ate? Desertion. Adoption. It defined that."

"Tracey." Mom laughs. "That wasn't homesickness, honey. It was food poisoning. Dozens of campers were sick. You were just more upset about it than the rest, so you came home. I'll admit, you seemed more nervous when we left after that, and you didn't want to go back to camp. But you didn't get sick when we left."

"But…"

"Sometimes children blow events up, make them bigger than they were, believe some traumatic thing happened more often than it did…But that was a one-time thing. I promise."

"Only once?" The narrative I'd written for myself threatens to unravel…could she be telling the truth? I'd always thought I couldn't handle being separated from them, that my body couldn't handle it…

"Maybe we should have had you see a counsellor. You'd been through a lot. But you seemed so well adjusted. You were well-behaved, obedient, you smiled. We thought you were okay."

"I wasn't." I look away from her. "I pretended to be okay. I thought if I didn't, you'd give me back. Just like the others."

"The others were foster parents. That was never our intention. We never—"

"Anyway," I look away, "that's not what we're here to talk about. We're here to talk about my surgery."

"I just think—"

"I want a family." The words rip out of me.

Mom jolts back, as if I've pushed her. "You have a family."

"A real family."

She inhales sharply.

"A blood family." I choke on my words. "I meant—"

Her lips tremble, and though what I said is true, I wish I could take it back the instant the words pass my lips. There's no way she'll understand. She stares at me as if I've just struck a dagger to her heart. "We may not be blood." Her voice comes out thin and tight. "But we're real."

"I know. I—"

A clatter and yell from the backyard snaps our heads in that direction. The ladder is gone. Mom slides the patio doors open with a speed and force that shocks me. "Henry!"

My father lies in the backyard, just past the porch, groaning. His leg lies at an angle that doesn't look possible.

"Call 911," Mom shrieks. I run inside, dial the number, then dash back outside. I answer the operator's questions as best I can and prod Mom for responses when I don't know what to say. Dad isn't lucid through any of this. He moans and groans and then goes silent. But he's breathing. At least he's breathing. The operator tells me not to move him but to get several blankets, ensure he's warm. Now I ask questions. Could he have internal bleeding? What if he hit his head? Will he be okay? She can't answer, of course, but tells me to remain calm. Hold his hand, she says, so I do, taking the one not already in Mom's grasp. We wait.

THE PARAMEDICS APPEAR and it feels like something out of a movie, though less…they don't move with the speed I expect, the amped up intensity. They're calm. It helps me breathe. If they're not terrified, maybe I shouldn't be either. They don't make any assurances as I repeat the questions I asked the operator, but one tells me my father is in good hands. I stand, helpless as Mom climbs into the ambulance beside Dad, and takes his hand again. The doors close and I watch the van get tinier and tinier, uncertain of what I'm supposed to do next. The feel of the phone in my hand brings me back to reality. I call Adrian, tell him what happened, and to get back here fast. Then I call Jojo. "The paramedics said he'd probably be fine, I don't want to ruin your night, but—"

"Are you kidding?" she snaps. "Damn." She lets out a

groan. "I've already had a few drinks. Bring the kids. Come get me." I jot down the address she gives me and wait for Adrian's car to turn up the driveway. At last it does.

"Take your mother's car." Adrian gestures to the Volvo in the driveway. "She may want it at the hospital if this is a long haul."

"She won't be going anywhere as long as Dad's in there."

He offers a smile. "He won't be in there forever."

"Fine. You take the kids. Get Jojo." I hand him the address. He nods. I'm on my way toward the front door in search of Mom's car keys when Adrian stops me with a hand to each shoulder. He turns me to him and pulls me tight.

"Henry's strong. He'll be fine."

"I know." I smile up at him and wipe my eyes. "Just fine."

At the hospital I enquire at the information desk, then make my way to the waiting room. Mom sits flipping through a home and garden magazine without looking at the pages. She glances at me then turns her attention back to the magazine.

"Any news?"

Her posture is stiff, composed as always. "He's lucky." Her voice wavers. "No head injury. At least they don't think so. They're doing extra tests to make sure. His reflex tests were positive. They think no spinal injury either."

"The leg?"

"He's getting a cast now. A clean break. They said that's good."

"Well, good." I take her hand. After a few moments she draws it away.

"Mom?"

"What do you care, anyway? He's not your father."

"Mom."

"Isn't that what you were saying? That he's not your father. We're not your family?"

"That's not what I meant."

"It's what you said."

"I just…" The sound of Reggie and Lulu bickering carries up the hall.

"Well," Mom sets the magazine down and stands, "I certainly can't take care of you now. So if you insist on having that surgery, you'll either have to wait or find someone else. Maybe Lydia. She's your real family anyway, right?"

"Mom. I hardly know her."

Mom gives me a hard look. "But she's blood."

"I—" My protest is cut off as Jojo comes into view and Mom rushes to embrace her.

"Dad. Is he all right?"

"He'll be fine, sweetie. Just fine."

I stand and watch them, feeling as if the wind has been knocked out of me, a feeling I deserve. I should have spoken quicker, told Mom she's my mother, not Lydia, but the words didn't come. Adrian sidles up beside me and rests his hand on my waist. "You okay?"

"Yeah." I keep staring at Mom and Jojo. "I'm fine."

WE SIT IN THE HOSPITAL'S waiting room until Dad is cleared for visitors. In twos, we're able to see him. Mom and Jojo go first, next will be me and Adrian. The twins and Neveah are told they can see him tomorrow, once he's likely to have fewer tubes sticking out of him. The doctor who says this lets his arms wave and screws up his face, making them laugh.

When we step into the room, my father looks all of his seventy-three years and more, but still that smile and calm confidence he wears so often remains firm.

"Guess that deck will have to wait." He sighs.

"Maybe your construction days should be over." I move closer to the bed. "At least construction that requires those kinds of heights."

"Nonsense." He grins at me and reaches for the hand that lingers beside him. "You stop living, and you die."

I let out a laugh and sit beside him. "I'm glad you're all right, Dad."

"Never better." I laugh again. "Your poor mother though—she's got those three kids and now me too. You'll help her when you can? Maybe drive up an evening or two when Jojo's working?"

I hesitate. If I have the surgery, I won't be helping at all. "I'll try."

He squeezes my hand. "That a girl. Now let a man get some rest." He grins. "All this hustle and bustle, it takes a lot out of a fella."

Back in the waiting room Jojo and I try to convince Mom to go home for some rest too, but she's like a boulder, refusing to be moved. When a nurse offers to put a cot in Dad's room for her, we give up. Mom maintains her coldness toward me, which I can tell Jojo and Adrian notice. They don't question. When I offer to drive to the house and get a change of clothes for her, and whatever else she'd like, she says she'll be fine. I want to say more, to apologize again, instead I offer her car keys. "Take these." My hand lingers in the air. "Dad will be fine."

Mom stands tall. She takes the keys and sucks in a deep breath. Her shoulders rise then fall. "He's old. He can't keep taking risks like this."

"We'll help you rein him in." Adrian gives Mom's arm a squeeze.

She smiles at him with a look of love. "Thanks. Go on now." She motions to the twins and Neveah, fast asleep atop some bean bag pillows in the corner. "Help Jojo."

Adrian heads toward the children. Jojo lifts Neveah into her arms then nudges Reggie awake as Adrian picks up Lulu.

I linger near Mom. "About the surgery, I—"

"Tracey," she snaps, "how can you even still think to ask? No. The answer is no."

I step back as if she's slapped me. "I was just going to say I was sorry for putting any extra pressure on you and not to worry, I'll figure it out."

"Oh." Her shoulders slump. The anger she's held these past hours seems to dribble out of her. "Okay then."

I shuffle on my feet, take a quick breath. "And what I said. I didn't mean…I just…to carry my own—"

"Just go, honey, all right." Her fingers brush my upper arm. "We all need our rest." I turn to walk away, but her voice follows me. "You think what you think and you feel what you feel. There's no apologizing for that."

CHAPTER FOUR

Adrian and I drive toward home. I feel his gaze on me and look over. He offers a sad smile. "So I guess your mom can't stay with you after the surgery now."

I shake my head.

"Did you have a chance to talk to her beforehand?"

I nod.

"And?"

"She couldn't have, anyway. She's helping Jojo out with the kids, it'd be too much driving, etc."

Adrian taps a hand on the wheel. "Well, I guess that makes sense."

"Absolutely."

He sighs. "What?"

I look out the window.

"What else?"

I shift in my seat. "She doesn't think I should have the surgery. She had it. It went poorly."

"But she's okay now. She got Jojo."

"Yeah."

"And?"

"And she thinks I should adopt. She thinks the surgery is risky."

"Well," his hand squeezes my thigh, "she got you. She knows that's a good route."

"Maybe you can take some time off from the piece? Just

when need be."

"We talked about this."

"I know, but—"

"What if a big lead came up? If I'm stuck on the other side of town or in another town with a source when you needed me, what then?"

I turn to him. "Your career can't be your life, especially when we have a family."

"I know," he makes a noise of frustration, "and I know I'm the one who wants you to do this now." He taps the wheel again. "If it were a few days, maybe, but it'll be more and Trace, reporters have been dropping off like flies." He stretches his fingers on the wheel then grips it once more. "They're all going into PR or becoming Communications Consultants. That's not for me, and this story, it could be my big break, get my name out there so that never has to be me. I can't just walk away."

"I know." I look to the window, wanting somewhere to direct my frustration, somewhere other than him. "We could wait."

"I'd rather not."

"What about your family?"

"You know that won't work. My parents work full time and then often have grandchildren duties in the evening."

"I don't know what to tell you then."

He squeezes my knee. "We'll think of something."

I let out a little laugh. "My mom suggested I call Lydia."

Adrian glances over. "That's not a bad idea."

I stare at him. "It's a ludicrous idea."

"No. It's not. She's your mother."

"My birth mother."

"She's been calling you. Messaging you. This could be her chance to make up for missing the wedding."

"I've only actually met her once, for a weekend, after thirty years of no contact, but sure, I'll just call her up, casual as can be." I mime holding a phone. "'Hey, Lydia, I know when I was sick as a child it was too much for you, you gave me up because you couldn't handle it, but I thought now that I'm an adult and about to basically be sick again, would you like to come be my nursemaid? On three weeks' notice, no less?'" I drop the imaginary phone. "Easy."

Adrian grins. "It can be easy. She missed our wedding to be nursemaid for her stepchild. She's got experience. And she cared for you for two years until she," he pauses, "didn't anymore."

"Yeah. Great reference."

"She was a kid then, now she's—"

"I was a kid. I was the kid."

"Okay…Give her a call though. Give her a chance. I don't see that you have many other options."

I wrap my arms around my middle, wanting this conversation and car ride to be over. Adrian is right, Lydia has been reaching out. A quick phone call, an email telling me about some art show she went to or tidbit of life she thinks may interest me. But that's where it ends. We hardly have a relationship. Her contact could stem from nothing more than guilt.

Only the radio breaks the silence for the rest of the drive. At home Adrian and I crawl into bed with almost no words exchanged between us. I settle in, frustrated, scared, and, on top of it all, worried about my dad and what damage I may have just inflicted on my mother. Adrian's arm reaches out, landing on my middle and drawing me into him. He's so warm. I scooch closer, spooned perfectly, and sigh, feeling just better enough to slip into sleep. At least I have him.

❧

THE NEXT MORNING I CALL the hospital first thing. Dad answers his room phone. "This mother of yours will not leave."

"Are you surprised?" I ask.

"Not at all." I can hear the grin in his voice. "What can I say, she loves me."

"How could she not?"

"You little flirt." He chuckles. "I need her gone though, at least for a little while. Come keep me company. The two of us can convince her to go home, shower, and maybe make me a little meal. Turns out your mom's cooking spoiled me for anything else."

"Any home cooking would spoil you for hospital food."

He laughs again. "I guess it's a cliché for a reason."

His voice eases my worry. He sounds fine. "You feel better?"

"Right as rain. I'll be running marathons in a week."

"You've never run a marathon."

"But the doc said my leg would be better than ever."

I laugh. "Sure, Dad."

"I know, I know. Marathon running is Jojo's thing. So, will you come?"

"Of course. Two hours all right?"

"Perfect."

⁓

AT THE HOSPITAL MOM GIVES me a quick hug and kiss before leaving. On the surface she's the same as always, but she avoids making eye contact; her hug lasts a second or two less than normal. I settle in beside Dad and make small talk. Something seems off. "Dad?"

"I've never been a good poker player." He pats my hand, as if I'm the one who needs comfort. "Your mother told me what's going on."

I wear a question on my face, though I imagine what she told him was everything.

"About the fertility issues, the surgery." He pauses. "What you said about family."

I look to our hands, clasped and resting on the bed.

"You didn't mean that." He gives my hand a squeeze. "We're your family, Tracey."

"I didn't mean it in the way Mom thinks. Just in the sense that it's a fact. Of course you're my family, but you're not my blood family. I'm not your blood daughter." I look up at him. "There are differences between me and Jojo, no matter what you say, and I want the chance to have my own child. Someone who comes from me and Adrian."

"I can understand that." Another pause. "You really hurt your mother."

"I didn't want to."

"I know." He raises his hand to my shoulder. "You're not that kind of girl. Um…" He coughs. Grins. "Woman. You're certainly not a girl anymore."

I can't help but smile.

"I'm really sorry to hear about what you're going through. I witnessed your mother…it's not an easy thing."

"It's not."

"And this has been going on for over a year now."

I nod.

"And you're just telling us now." He shakes his head. "You don't have to be so strong. You've always been this way, but you don't have to. Share your burdens."

"I tried to."

He sighs. "Your mother just doesn't want to see you hurt, to see something happen and," he gestures to his leg, "thanks to me it's not really the best time."

"How are you feeling, really?"

"Oh," his smile crinkles, "I'm sad to be laid up. I can't imagine what I'll do with myself—stuck inside on my back. I'm a mover."

"And a shaker."

He chuckles.

"Mom will love it. You won't be able to mess up the house."

"Ahh, she likes my messes more than she says." We both smile. Dad tilts his head. "So what will you do about the surgery?"

"I want to have it."

"I may be able to convince your mother. What's one more invalid? If you don't mind setting up at our place."

"No." I let out a deep breath. "She's right. It'd be too much. You, me, and the kids? I don't think so." I'm quiet for a moment. "Both Mom and Adrian thought I should ask Lydia."

"Do you think she would?"

"I have no idea."

"Give her a call."

I let out a laugh, more of fear than humour. "I may."

"I mean right now. Give her a call right now. I'll be your emotional support."

"Are you kidding?"

"Not in the slightest." He gestures to my purse. "Go on, pull that phone out and dial away."

I stare at my father. He's serious. And why shouldn't he be? He's not the one making the call. He's not the one whose mother abandoned him. "She's an Oxford Professor and my surgery would be just before the start of the fall semester. If anything went wrong, if I needed longer care…"

"Maybe she could teach the first few classes on web cam. What's the worst that can happen?"

A smile twitches at my lips. It's a question he's asked me dozens of times throughout my life and one I've used with my students. "She says no, and she's so appalled by my asking that she wants nothing to do with me ever again."

"Not asking is a definite no and if she's so awful she wants nothing to do with you because of a simple question, then I say good riddance and you're better off without her."

He's right, as he so often is. I reach for my phone, my gut clenching. "You want to do it for me?"

"Not at all."

"Maybe an email?"

"Call. It's just a call."

I dial the number. It rings once, twice, three times. I'm about to hang up when Lydia's voice comes on the line. "Tracey, hello!"

"Hi, hello."

"What a nice surprise."

"Is this an okay time? I know it's a bit early."

"Just heading out for a run."

"I can call—"

"Not a problem. How are you doing?"

I picture Lydia standing in her back garden sipping some tea before heading out for a jog. Westin must not be going with her, she'd definitely use 'we' if that were the case. Is he still in bed? Are the kids there? Maybe he's making them all pancakes, and Lydia will come back from her run to sit with her family over flapjacks hot from the griddle, drizzled with maple syrup—the life I should have had. Only I did have that life, just not with her. "I'm good. I'm all right."

"And your family?"

I look to Dad. "There was an accident yesterday, actually. I'm sitting in the hospital with my Dad right now."

She makes a little noise of alarm. "Is he okay, is—"

"It's fine. He's fine. Just a broken leg. He'll be out of commission for a few weeks. That's not why I'm calling though, not exactly." I explain my situation to Lydia: the cysts' growth, the surgery, how, with Dad and Jojo's kids and Damien leaving and Adrian's investigation, none of my family can be relied on right now. I tell her what I'm asking of her and assure it should only be a week or two, so long as everything goes well with the surgery. "I have no expectations," my voice shakes the tiniest bit, "but thought it wouldn't hurt to ask." The line stays silent for several moments after I've finished talking. "Are you still there?"

"Yes. Yes." I can almost see her energy come back into focus. "I'll come."

"You'll?" My thoughts fluster. "I mean, think about it. Won't you need to talk to Westin, arrange things with the college in case something goes wrong and—"

"No, no." She pauses again. "This is practically kismet. I'm on sabbatical this year. We both are. We were going to do some travelling, spend time with the kids. I thought I may come home as well, since I haven't in years. I have a few friends in Halifax still, and we were planning that for the spring, but why not the fall? I'll have Westin fly up once you're feeling shipshape and then we can go on our journeys together."

Now it's me that's frozen. Dad grins at me with his thumbs up. My mother. My birth mother, who I've seen once in the past thirty years, just agreed to fly across the Atlantic to take care of me.

"Tracey?"

"Thank you. Thanks. That's uh…great." I will have the surgery. Hope and fear flow through me.

Her voice is warm. "Thank you. For asking. It means a lot that you thought of me."

We exchange a few more pleasantries before I hang up the phone.

Dad pats my hand. "There now. That wasn't so hard."

A laugh bursts out of me. Tears stream onto my face. Are they elation or trepidation? I'll be cut open. The extent of my disease will be seen and known, and all the pain and effort could make no difference at all, or all the difference in the world. And my mother, my birth mother, will be here for it. "No, not so hard."

CHAPTER FIVE

My mother calls five times in the next two-and-a-half weeks. Her excuse is always to give updates on my father, who's coming along wonderfully. Without failure, each time she manages to work Lydia into the conversation. She says things such as: *Are you sure she wouldn't feel more welcomed if your father and I came to the airport to greet her too?* and, *Perhaps you should reconsider. You hardly know this woman,* and, *To be in her hands, and her hands only, for hours a day…it's risky.*

I remind her that asking Lydia to help me was her idea and say it's too late to turn back now. Though I completely squash the coming to the airport idea, I'm unable to come up with enough legitimate reasons why Lydia shouldn't join my family for dinner the night after she arrives. My mother wanted the night she arrived, but I insisted after all that travelling an hour and a half drive from the airport would be asking too much. When the day comes to make that trip to the airport, however, I almost wish Mom was with me. If anything, she'd be a buffer and ensure the conversation never faltered. Adrian is with me though and, as he assures me and has proved time and time again, if he has a mind to, he can keep a conversation flowing endlessly as well.

His glance catches mine as we approach the terminal. "It'll be fine. Better than fine."

"I know." I grin, my hands pressed so hard on my lap all the muscles in my arms are taut. "It'll be great."

"Are you excited?"

I let out a little laugh. "Don't push it."

"Nervous excitement?"

"I'll give you that."

Adrian parks the car and we make our way to arrivals. After a quick peek at the screen we see Lydia's flight landed fifteen minutes early. If customs isn't busy, she could appear any moment. We stand in front of the doors, waiting. It's surreal, almost as surreal as when I stood in front of her door two years ago: that time, the first time I'd seen her in almost thirty years, I'd had no idea what to expect. This time, all I have to do is look for the face I'll wear in another twenty years. My eyes scan the groups of people who walk through the sliding doors. Many of them smile, wave hands in recognition to others waiting, and then her face is smiling too, her hand lifting along with so many in the crowd.

"Tracey!" She steps forward and her arms are around me, squeezing. She lets go quickly, as if she's not sure it's okay, which I'm not sure it is.

"Hi." I smile at her then turn, my arms gesturing. "This is Adrian."

"I figured as much." She grins, the same smile I've seen in countless pictures of myself. "I saw the wedding photos but you're even more handsome in real life."

She puts out her hand, but he draws her into an embrace. Their hug lasts longer than ours did. "It's so good to meet you." Adrian looks natural around her, happy. He glances to me then back to Lydia. "I saw the pictures in the baby book but you're…you're…"

Lydia holds her arms out, as if on display. "Pretty close to what you'll be waking up to in a couple of decades?"

He laughs. "Well, yeah." He nudges me. "Good genes." I smile a tight-lipped smile.

As we maneuver our way out of the terminal, Adrian's conversational abilities soar. Lydia asks me tons of questions, but I don't seem able to get more than a few words out at a time. With Adrian's interjections, however, it hardly seems awkward. I offer Lydia the front seat on the drive to our place so she can see how the city of her birth has changed. A part of me yells inside, tells me this is what I've always wanted, my mother—my birth mother—here for me, showing she loves me, showing she cares. If dropping your travel plans, your partner's travel plans, and journeying across an ocean to take care of a convalescing patient isn't a sign of caring, nothing is, but still my brain travels over other scenarios for why she could be here, imagines me waking up tomorrow to discover she's vanished or this was all a dream. It feels like a dream. Let it not turn into a nightmare.

"Tracey!" Lydia squeals. I'm broken out of my reverie. "Adrian." She grips his arm. "Pull over. Yes. There. The house with the yellow flower pots." She leans on the door handle as the car slows, reminding me of a cat about to pounce on its prey. The instant the car is parked she pushes open the door, steps out, and waves for me to do the same. I do, though much more slowly. Her eyes are wide. She steps forward: eager yet tremulous. "This was it." She looks to me. "This was our house."

"What?"

"Well, part of it was. We rented the top unit." She laughs. "Try getting up three flights of old wooden steps with a stroller. Not fun. But," she raises her arm and points to a window with a purple curtain fluttering in the breeze. That was our room."

I'm quiet. Staring. Adrian comes up behind me. "Tracey?"

"This is where I lived? This house?"

"Yes." Lydia settles back on her hip, as if seeing something that we can't. "There was a tree in the yard, right there." She points to a flower patch. "A lilac. It was beautiful. And the steps are different. They were wooden, not this stone. But this is it. 1678 Robie Street. You took your first steps here. Said your first word here." She laughs then turns to me. Her smile falls. "What is it?"

"I've been here before."

Adrian gives me a curious look. "We drive by all the time. It's on the main—"

"No." I stop him. "I mean here. At a party in undergrad. It was a bunch of guys renting the place. They had this huge party."

"Oh…" His hand rests on my shoulder.

"I've been here. I crashed on the couch."

"That's amaz—"

"It's not amazing." I squeeze out the words. "It's nothing. It's just…could happen to anyone, right? Who remembers where they lived when they were two?"

"Yeah." Adrian pulls me against him. "It's nice now though, that you know. A little part of your history."

I stare at the house, amazed that a secret to my past has been this close for so long.

"Are you all right?" Lydia turns to me. "I didn't mean to upset you. Would you rather I not mention any more…places of significance?"

"No."

"Okay. I wo—"

"No." I try to push a smile. I want to be smiling. I'm just not quite there yet. "This is what I wanted. To know about my life. I spent years wondering, trying to create a history for myself." I stare back at the house. "And here's a piece of it."

"Something to tell your child one day." Lydia grins. "A little piece of history you can share."

I nod and stare at the woman who brought me into this world, who took care of me for my first two years of life, who seems so relaxed about all of this, who looks at me like she knows me. A tremor passes through my toes, up, and out my fingertips. The upcoming week still terrifies me, the hours I'll spend alone with this woman, but looking at her now, knowing we're standing on the same ground she carried me over countless times in the past, she feels less a stranger.

❧

WE PASS THE EVENING CASUALLY. Thai food ordered in, a walk along the harbour, home for a few rounds of cards before Lydia, wiped by jet lag, calls it a night. Adrian and I whisper back and forth, careful not to disturb her—my birth mother—sleeping in the spare room. The thought is still an unbelievable one.

The next day we travel down more streets that take Lydia along memory lane. For her, the city holds much more than memories of me. It's where she grew up, went through school, learned how hard life could be. After visiting each of her old schools, walking through the Common, which she says is incredibly different yet still so much the same, she asks to visit her parents' graves. The request shocks me, not that she wants to visit them, but that it never occurred to me to ask if this is where they were laid to rest. We walk to Camp Hill, one of the city's central cemeteries, passing through the gates and onto the path I used as a shortcut dozens of times during my university days. I'd even run the perimeter several times to enjoy a trail free of traffic lights.

Lydia leads the way, walking as if she'd been here just yesterday. When she stops, Adrian and I halt just a few feet behind her.

"Good." She kneels. "My money wasn't going to nothing." No moss grows on the graves, as on some of the nearby headstones. Lydia picks up a bouquet of flowers, dried and wilted, but clearly not more than a few months old. She turns her head back to us, the slightest smile creasing her cheek. "I pay to have someone lay flowers twice a year, make sure the plot is tidy."

"You should have told me."

Lydia shrugs. "That would have been a conversation."

I chuckle. "I guess so."

Lydia smiles then turns her gaze back to the tombstone. She sinks to her knees and rests one hand in the centre of the engraved words: Beloved Parents. She's an orphan, even more than me, or than I was, than I believed myself to be.

Adrian, who's remained quiet, clears his throat. "Tracey's told me a little, but not much. What were they like?"

Lydia looks up. "My parents?"

"Yeah."

She turns her gaze back to the stone. "They were happy. At first, anyway. Mom was this petite little woman."

"Like you and Tracey."

"Exactly. She was so…alive. She'd dance around the kitchen. Cook amazing meals. She made place settings at the table for Thanksgiving, Christmas, Easter. New ones every year, every holiday. Domestic. Smart. She could have been a professor or a pharmacist or…instead she was my mom, my dad's wife."

"She sounds great." Adrian gives my arm a squeeze.

"She was…until she wasn't." Lydia drops her hand. "It's awful watching someone, seeing someone. Lung cancer." She looks up at Adrian. "Did Tracey tell you?" Adrian nods. "My dad was always so solid, so together, but it turns out Mom is what kept him that way. He fell apart when she got sick. It was like he was lost in a dark maze. He never really found the way out." She stands, brushes off her jeans, and angles toward me. "In all the mess, all the hurt, you were the one bright thing for Dad."

Lydia steps back from the grave. Adrian and I follow her. We make our way out of the cemetery with no more words said, but the words in my head race and whirl. All these years, even now, my focus has been on me, what my life was like because Lydia chose not to be my mother, how she hurt me, damaged me, I've hardly thought of what hurt and damage was done to her.

As we step onto the sidewalk Lydia turns to us. "So, time to meet the family?"

"Time to meet the family." Adrian chuckles. "You ready?"

"As I'll ever be." She grins, back to the confident, strong woman who looks so much like me. I wear that face too, even when what's inside would tell an entirely different story. As we settle into the car, I can't help but wonder the story that's being told beneath her smile.

CHAPTER SIX

Within a few minutes of entering my parents' house we're all sitting in the living room. The coffee table is strewn with so many appetizers I can't imagine a need for dinner. A mellow music mix, full of Michael Bublé, Norah Jones, and some other, older crooners I can't recall the names of, serves to cut the silences that keep floating upon us. It's Mom, Dad, Adrian, Lydia and me. I wait anxiously for Jojo and her brood to arrive. With the children, silences are impossible. Not that there are long stretches of silence, not at all, but each time one happens, each time one sentence of the conversation doesn't flow easily into the next, the weight of all our hopes and fears and nervousness settles like a hundred gallons of water pushing down on me.

"It is amazing," says my mother for about the third time in the last fifteen minutes, "how alike you are." We all smile, nod. Her voice catches. "You're really her mother."

"No." Lydia leans forward. "You're her mother. You're the one who raised her, who—"

"Thank you for the album." Mom leans back in her chair. "It was amazing. It was such a gift."

"We loved looking through it." Dad nods. How does all this affect him? Surely it's hard, uncomfortable, but it must be nothing compared to Mom's experience. No other father sits here, threatening to take his place. Not that Lydia's threatening…

"Tracey was the real gift though." Mom presses her lips together. "If you hadn't, if we…" She smiles, the most genuine one I've seen tonight. "We can't even imagine what our lives would have been like without her."

My gaze darts from parent to parent. The mother who raised me and the mother who gave me life, only to give me away, four feet from each other.

"Please don't think," Mom's genuine smile vanishes. She wrings her hands in her lap, "that I wouldn't have taken care of Tracey after the surgery if I could have. It's a stressful time for us. With Henry," she motions to Dad, his foot to thigh cast, as if Lydia may not have noticed, "and our youngest. She's going through a rough time." Mom looks at the clock. "She should be here soon with her three."

"Not at all." Lydia waves a hand. "I was in a similar position when I missed Tracey's wedding. We had a sick child at home. I wanted more than anything to be here, but I couldn't." She smiles—a nice smile, the type of smile no one could dislike. "I'm just glad I'm able to be here today." She sits tall, her wavy hair framing her face perfectly, her clothing fitting her slim, trim figure as if it were made for no one else, her makeup so naturally applied I wouldn't know she's wearing any if I hadn't seen the supplies on the bathroom counter.

My mother nods. She has always presented herself as an attractive and put-together woman, which she is, but at sixty-one, twelve years older than Lydia, I fear she's comparing herself, feels inadequate next to this younger, blood mother. "So, Oxford," Mom's smile is large. "A slew of degrees. That's impressive." She looks to me. "Tracey was always smart too. She must have gotten her smarts from you." She pats my hand.

My mother is a smart woman. She runs her household perfectly. She ran much of the business side of my Dad's construction company for years, but with not more than a high school education, does she feel inadequate? She chats with Lydia, stresses how wonderful it must be to spend her life enlightening young minds, making the world a more educated place. Her laugh is like tinkling glass bells. Pretty, but fragile. I want to scoot across the couch, hug her, tell her she's wonderful just as she is. I don't. When we get a quiet moment, perhaps in the kitchen as she preps the final dinner touches, I could tell her she's the only mother I've ever needed, but we'd know it for a lie. I wanted more than her. I wanted the mother who gave me life—I draw my gaze back to Lydia—and here she is.

"This is such a beautiful home." Lydia's arm sweeps across her. "I love the way you've decorated it. Each piece complements and adds to every other." Not a hint of pretension is in Lydia's voice. Mom's smile unfurls like a flower blossoming. "You've created the perfect mix of," Lydia pauses, as if searching for the words, "class, comfort, and a sense of home."

The front door opens. Reggie bursts through it. "Shoes!" Jojo's voice calls from the porch. Reggie kicks off his Roblox sneakers and practically falls into the living room. "Hi, Grandma!" He gives her a massive hug and kiss then races to his Grandpa and is just reaching me when Jojo enters with Lulu and Neveah. She looks worn. She smiles though. "Sorry I'm late."

Lydia stands. The rest of us, except Dad, follow. Jojo sets Neveah down and watches as her girls smother our mom in hugs. She pulls her gaze away and her eyes widen. "Wow." I expect more exclamations of how alike Lydia and I look, but Jojo just shakes her head then steps forward, her hand extended. "You must be Tracey's Mo—birth mom. It's nice to meet you."

"Lydia." Lydia extends a hand to Jojo. "It's nice to meet you too." She crouches down beside Jojo, where Neveah has returned to wrap her arms around Jojo's left leg. "And let me guess, you're Neveah." The tiniest smile lights on Neveah's face then disappears as she crouches farther behind Jojo's legs. Lydia stands and smiles at Lulu, who smiles back.

"Do you know my name?" Lulu bounces on her tip toes.

"Lulu, and," Lydia glances toward Reggie, "Reggie." The twins are pleased.

"You're Tracey's mom?" asks Reggie as he crunches a handful of honey roasted almonds into his mouth.

"Her birth mother, yes."

Lulu sits beside Mom. "What's a birth mother?"

"Well," Lydia keeps her gaze on Lulu, not looking to any of us for help, which impresses me, "she's the mother who gives birth to you, uh, to a person, who welcomes them into this world when they're born, but she isn't always the person who raises a baby. That's the mother."

Reggie looks confused. Lulu looks stricken. She whips her head to Jojo. "Do I have a birth mother? Who's my—"

"No," says Lydia as Jojo shakes her head. "Your mother is your birth mother and your real mother."

I can almost see the questions spinning in Lulu's head, questions that won't be fun for any of us.

"Well," Mom stands, "now that everyone's here, let's move into the dining room. Dinner should be just perfect."

The table is set with Mom's best dinnerware, crystal wine glasses, and an expensive red and white already set on the table. The meal is more impressive than the one Mom made for Adrian's first visit, even more impressive than her can't-be-missed Christmas and Easter spreads. Adrian and Dad do most of the work of keeping the conversation flowing and light. They talk with Lydia about the cultural differences between here and England and the places she's travelled. They chat with each other about Dad's recovery and the home improvements he'd like to make once he's back on his feet (not that anything about this home needs improving). We Sampson women, however, seem laden with unease. Mom wears a constant smile. Jojo looks like a kid forced to sit in her Sunday best when she'd rather be out in the mud.

She has her glass in her hand and her mouth full of wine whenever anyone asks her a question. And me? I'm just trying to remember to breathe. How Lydia is faring I can only guess, though on the surface she's nothing but delightful.

After dinner, Jojo puts Neveah to bed. From the sound of it, there's a struggle. Jojo exits the room looking dishevelled. Next she calls the twins and sets a movie on in the room Mom keeps for them, saying they can watch forty-five minutes and then lights out. Again, grumbles of complaint travel up the hall. When she returns, Jojo pours what I'm pretty sure is her fifth glass of wine. If I had that much I'd topple over. Lydia tells us about a Turner painting recently discovered at an estate sale in Wales. Her face lights up and her hands dance as she says it's one of his earlier pieces. Her eyes glow with the excitement she felt when she first saw it, a treasure at last revealed.

Jojo, who remained uncharacteristically quiet throughout dinner, laughs. "You know, you seem really perfect." We all stare at her. My breath catches. "I mean, obviously you showed some imperfection when you basically threw away your kid—I'm not the best mother and I'd never do that—but beyond that little lapse in character, nothing's really wrong with you, is it?"

My mother's face blanches. Her mouth hangs open before she realizes the faux pas and clamps it shut. Lydia manages a convincing smile. "No one's perfect. And yes, giving Tracey up for adoption, calling that a sign of imperfection would be an understatement."

"Even a perfect response." Jojo pours herself more wine.

"Honey, maybe you should—"

"I know, I know." Jojo looks at Mom. "What can I say? I am not perfect. Not like you. Not like Tracey. And not like Lydia either it seems." She laughs again. "You know, I always thought it was kind of crazy, like nature made a mistake or something. Tracey was the ideal daughter. The one who never disappointed, who made it all look so easy. I thought there must have been a screw up, that she was supposed to be yours and I was meant for some other, less put together woman. Well, I guess I was just the screw up, plain and simple. I obviously wasn't meant for you." She raises her glass to Lydia. "Oxford professor. Perfectly poised. I bet your partner's amazing too, right? A dreamboat with a brain." Jojo looks to me. "That's what Autumn said, isn't it?"

"Jojo," Mom hisses, mortification sprawled across her face.

"It's okay." Jojo stands. "I'm done. Really done. Sorry. Rough day." She stands, steps away from the table, and stumbles somehow. "Really rough day. It's nice to meet you, Lydia, really. I'm glad you and Tracey have found each other."

"Jo." Now I stand, not knowing what to do or say. I should want to hit her, my brat of a little sister, instead I want to hug her. Her eyes say it all. She's crying inside. Sobbing. She smiles a strained smile. "How embarrassing." She laughs again. "I'm going to turn in."

"We haven't even started dessert." Mom rises too.

"I know. I know." Jojo's eyes dart from side to side. "I'm just really tired and have an early day tomorrow." She steps further away and braces herself against Reggie's empty chair.

"You're not driving," says Dad.

Jojo shakes her head. "We'll stay here." She shifts her body toward Lydia. "Don't mind me. I'm just the lost soul. Every family has one."

"We're all lost, Jojo, in some way. Every one of us."

Jojo pauses in her retreat, "Nice of you to say," then turns away. She heads toward the hall without saying goodnight to the rest of us. She stops. Looks back at me. "Your surgery's tomorrow?"

"Day after tomorrow. Tomorrow's pre-op."

"Right." She nods in slow motion. "It'll be fine. You'll

get everything you want. I can feel it."

Unsure what to say, I nod too. "Night, Jo."

She stares at me a moment too long. "Night."

❧

IN THE MORNING, LYDIA joins me for my day of pre-op. This section of the hospital is crowded with people—most older than me. I'm directed from room to room, down one hall and then another. My bloodwork shows no issues. The anaesthesiologist and nurses seem confident all will go well. Their words and body language tell me this is a smooth, easy surgery.

"Forty-five minutes. You're in and out," says a lady who seems to be in some sort of counselling position.

"Forty-five minutes?" I ask.

She looks up from her papers. "Generally. It could be a little longer. An hour. An hour-fifteen."

"My doctor told me several hours. Two, maybe three."

The woman looks at me as if I'm daft. An air of frustration seeps from her. "Perhaps your doctor meant the whole process. Getting to the hospital, seeing the anaesthesiologist, surgery, and recovery. Sure. That could take two, maybe three hours, especially if you're not first."

"She said I'd be first."

Another glance at the chart. "Looks like you are."

The woman tells me not to wear contacts during surgery, to come to the hospital with glasses on. I never wear my glasses in public. Never. A small request, inconsequential, but it makes me feel stripped of control—just like I will be as I lie on that table.

Four hours after we arrive, I'm cleared to leave. Lydia and I try to make the rest of the day as normal as possible. We have dinner plans later with Adrian but see a movie to kill the time in between. The screen is full of action.

Dinosaurs, danger, a rugged Chris Pratt. My mind is full of action too. A shaky hand, a cut where there shouldn't be one, and my life could take a drastic change for the worse.

My mother's words keep travelling back to me. Her face. Her fear. *It almost killed me.* She could have been exaggerating. She probably was exaggerating. A damaged bowel. A colostomy bag. That doesn't equal death. But could it? My pulse races. My throat goes dry. Lydia laughs at something happening on the screen. I glance at her. Our eyes meet. Her laughter stops. She grasps my hand and squeezes, offers a smile. I look at our hands, enclasped, then draw my attention back to the screen. My chest fills with air and I let it out slowly. It's just a surgery. A routine surgery that some women undergo simply for answers, simply for a chance to explore what's wrong with them. Everything will be okay. Everything has to be okay.

CHAPTER SEVEN

T he hospital lights shine bright and menacing. We arrive just on time, follow the floor's painted dots to the correct waiting room, and wait. The large space is eerily quiet, with not another person in sight. I tap the little metal bell at reception several times. No one appears. We sit. I rise again, tap once more.

Five minutes later a woman in her mid-fifties wearing bright pink and purple scrubs walks in. She greets us, apologizes for the wait, and the process begins. Whereas minutes before the world seemed in slow motion, now it races…or perhaps that's just my heart.

The air is chilly in my hospital gowns. Thankfully, I'm wearing two: no bottom on display for me. Adrian and Lydia sit in chairs beside my large, reclinable patient's chair. The anaesthesiologist is young and handsome. Different from the one we met yesterday. At first this startles me, but I knew this. They told me this. It's just the restless night I had, tossing and turning, worrying I'd oversleep and we'd miss the appointment, worried the surgeon would make a mistake. The anaesthesiologist smiles and jokes as he inserts a needle into my hand, attaches a tube, tells me I can imagine the cool liquid flooding my veins as liquid power.

Shortly after he leaves, Dr. LeBlanc arrives. She's a tall, thin woman. The type of woman who probably was envied by her friends her whole life for eating what she wants and never putting on a pound. She looks taller still from my sitting position. I almost always see her in a chair. Her hair, which usually falls to her shoulders with a jaunty little curl, is in a tight bun. She's all business—makeup sparse, smile wide.

"How you feeling?"

"All right." I bite my lip. "Nervous."

"I've got one of my best teams with me today."

"What would you say if you had one of your worst teams?" asks Adrian.

Dr. LeBlanc gives him a wink. "We don't have worst teams."

"Dr. LeBlanc," she turns to me, "how long will it take? One of the ladies yesterday said forty-five minutes, but I thought you said longer."

"Yes." Her look is genuine. Comforting. "You're not a typical case. I'm guessing two hours forty-five, maybe three. I was only allowed to book the OR for two hours, but we'll keep going until we've done everything we intend to do."

I nod. I'm not typical. I know I'm not typical…but hearing it…Dr. LeBlanc talks to us for a few more minutes, answers questions about care, which activities should be okay and which I should avoid after the surgery. At last she crosses her arms and gives me a little nod. "You ready?"

I want to say something chipper, spunky. I only manage a close-mouthed smile. Adrian wraps his arms around me as I stand. My lip quivers. He holds on tight, whispers in my ear. "It'll be fine. I'll see you soon."

I turn to Lydia. We pause a moment, staring at each other. I reach out and she pulls me to her. I try not to let myself think the thoughts I'm thinking. This is routine. This is normal. People have this surgery every day. But those people are typical. Me…not so much. Each extra minute on an operating table is another minute for things to go wrong. My mother's words again; *It almost killed me.* But this won't kill me. Everything will be okay. And even if it isn't, my mother is fine now. It didn't kill her.

I follow Dr. LeBlanc down the hall, feeling exposed, vulnerable, with my bare legs and cotton booties. I've left my glasses with Adrian so the world around me is a blur. Shapes. Movement. But no true form. A mix of foreign smells and sounds. I hold onto the IV stand as if it's all that's keeping me upright. The room Dr. LeBlanc leads me into is even brighter than the hall. I want to see it. I want to know where I am. But it's just more shapes, colours, figures. White. Blue. Silver. I can't even tell if the figures are male or female until I get close. When I am close their facial features still blur. I prop myself up on the bed and lie back, wanting to push forward, wanting to say no, wanting to feel in control. The figure beside me starts talking. It's the anaesthesiologist. He tells me to relax, to think of a beautiful Caribbean beach, palm trees swaying in the breeze, waves lapping against the shore, warm sand beneath me.

"Are we starting?" I ask, but already relaxation flows like a hug enveloping me.

"Sure are. Do you smell that ocean air?"

No, but I see it, the beach, the brilliant turquoise ocean glistening in the sun, the…

I hear moaning and shift. Pain courses through me. Another moan passes through my throat. Just seconds ago the anaesthesiologist was talking about the ocean. Fear settles over me. *Did something go wrong? Am I awake too soon?* But no. My eyes open and slowly adjust to the light. This room is different. I see a fuzzy haze of peach that must be the walls. Far less bright silver glistens. A voice above me smiles. "There we go, finally rejoining us."

"What?" My voice sounds low, gravelly. My abdomen burns like it's been slashed open.

"Hmmm," the voice is kind, sweet, "still in a lot of pain?"

I groan in response.

"I can give you a bit more, but that's the max."

Like a fog lifting, the pain dissipates until it's more a pressure than the sharp intensity I woke with. The owner of the voice makes her way around the bed. I think she smiles, but her face is a blur. "My glasses?"

She reaches away and comes back with my glasses open, poised to settle on my face. I lift my arm to guide them along.

"It took you a long time to wake up. They really had you under."

"It feels like I just went in."

"That's how it goes. You were in there for over four hours."

"Over…what?"

This time I see her smile clearly. Her face matches her voice. Kind and sweet. "There were complications." She pats my arm. "But you're just fine."

"Compli—" Something rests against my thigh. I reach down. A bag. "My bowel? My—"

"Not as bad as that. A little bladder nick. That's all. It'll make recovery a bit harder than expected. A bit longer. That's all." Another pat.

Normally my mind would be swimming with questions, ping-ponging around, but the bounce seems muted. The balls tumbling slowly over questions I can't fully form. At last one question feels solid enough to speak. "Adrian?"

"Your husband? Oh yes. We'll wheel you to recovery in just a minute. We needed to monitor you until you woke up. He can see you there."

Moments after I've been transferred to another room, Adrian and Lydia are by my side. Adrian pulls his chair as close to my bed as he can maneuver it. He rests his cheek on my hand. "You had us worried."

"Things went wrong?"

He grins. "Just a little. To add excitement to the day. Amp the dramatic tension, you know?" His green eyes glisten. He squeezes my hand tighter.

"Where's the doctor? You see her?"

Lydia nudges her chair closer. "We did, but they had to keep you under longer than expected, which extended the time to wake you up. She needed to get to the next patient."

I take a breath. "So I won't see her?" Already my cognitive functions seem to be returning. I want to ask Dr. LeBlanc questions. Was she able to shrink the cysts? Are my tubes clear or smushed? Did she find other cysts and adhesions on my bowels or bladder? Why the nick? Why this bag at my side?

"No," says Lydia. "Not until your next appointment. But she said outside of the complication with your bladder the surgery went as well as she could have hoped. Your tubes are clear. So that's good."

"And?"

Adrian and Lydia look at each other. "Not much else," says Adrian. "Make sure you take it really easy, take your painkillers religiously, let us care for you. They considered having you stay overnight for observation, but all your vitals are strong. You're strong."

"The bag, will it…"

"A nurse is coming to let us know how to care for it."

As if on cue, a man in scrubs arrives with a clipboard. I try to pay attention but keep zoning out. He's talking to Lydia and Adrian anyway, giving them the directions about my bandages, my catheter, what I should and shouldn't do and for how long.

He directs his gaze to me. "Some ladies find the bladder nick and bag a blessing in disguise." I raise my eyebrows. "We'll give you a bigger bag for night, so you won't have to deal with the pain of getting out of bed to relieve yourself. The pain of that sometimes keeps people awake for a long time."

I ease myself up. It hurts but is nothing compared to the torture on the days my endometriosis really starts to flare. "The pain's not that bad."

"Oh." He gives a little laugh. I like him less. "It will be. You're on morphine now. The narcotics you're being sent home with are strong, but not that strong. The pain's coming."

I'm wheeled out of the hospital and up to the car door, which, somehow, is waiting by the curb with Adrian in the drivers' seat. Isn't he behind me, pushing? I crane my head back. Lydia. In the car the world feels and looks loose, like nothing is tethered down as it should be. We stop and start and stop and start and I can't understand why. The next thing I remember clearly, I'm on the couch, ashamed at the sight of the soup that's just come back out of me, of the fact that Lydia, this woman who rejected me, is cleaning it up. And then sleep. Blissful sleep. When I wake another woman is kneeling in front of me.

"Mom?"

"Hi, sweetie." My mother's face is close to mine. Her eyes are moist and pink, a little puffy. "You gave us quite the scare. We called and…well, looks like you'll be all right though, doesn't it?"

"I'm fine." I start to prop myself up then fall back in agony. The pain hits like a baseball bat to the gut.

"Stay still, honey."

My eyes close, an extended blink, when they open both women are before me. My mothers.

"It's time for your next round of painkillers." I nod. Misery floods my senses. *What if this doesn't work? What if I go through all of this and*—a hand caresses my forehead as another holds a palm out with three pills. A third presents a glass of water with a straw. I can't quite figure who the hands belong to.

But then it's my mother's voice. "This was so foolhardy." Is she talking to Lydia? Adrian? Me? "All this risk. And now a catheter.”

“It’s not that bad.” Adrian’s voice. “The doctor says—”

“She’s lucky it’s not worse. Lucky. People die on that table.”

“Based on what she’s told me, don’t you know…” Lydia’s voice, “don’t you understand her urge to have a child who—”

“You,” my mother’s voice, angry and sharp, a tone I’ve only heard a handful of times in my whole life, “you stay out of it.”

CHAPTER EIGHT

Throughout the next day the world seems a blur of faces and words and uncertainties. I am wholly disoriented. The first time I try to empty the catheter myself the tube slips, covering me in urine. The stench wafts up and I hurt so badly: every step, every turn feels as if my body is on the verge of tearing apart. The thought of bending down, wiping the shameful liquid off of me, rinsing the cloth, all that motion, is too much. Whimpers escape me, despite my effort to keep quiet. Tears slide down my face. I don't know what to do.

Footsteps make their way to the door. I will myself to calm my tears, to take control. A soft voice. "Tracey?"

"Yeah, umm. Just a minute." Extra towels are in the hall closet. Why would we keep them in the hall closet? "Just a—"

"Are you okay?"

"Uh…"

"Do you need help?"

"Umm…" The tears are back, accompanied by choking sobs that wrench through me, doling out sledgehammers of pain with every convulsion.

"Tracey."

"I spilled. It…I didn't mean—"

"Tracey, unlock the door."

I turn the lock and shuffle back. The door opens to reveal Lydia, a smile on her face and washcloths in her hand.

"Not to worry. It happens." Her tone is light, as if I've done nothing more than spill a bit of milk. But milk doesn't smell like this. I expect a turned up nose, a look of disgust. Instead, her smile remains firm. "Here. Let me help."

She eases me onto the edge of the tub, helps me wriggle out of my pyjama pants, wipes down my legs with an ease that cuts through my embarrassment, all the while talking casually about the story she just heard on some talk show. Once the clean-up is done she looks up with that smile again. "You hold this." She passes me the catheter bag. "I'll be right back." Moments later she returns with fresh pyjama pants and socks and, yet again, helps me ease into them. She offers a hand as I stand. "You're still a bit shaky," she says. "I'll help you the next couple of times, just until you get your strength back." I nod as we make our way to the living room, me leaning on her for support. A feeling like love trickles over me.

By the next day I'm feeling more like myself. The surface pain is easing, but it makes the shock of that deep inner pain more intense whenever I turn or twist certain ways, so I move as little as I can. I'm not used to such laziness: hours on the couch, watching movie after movie or show after show. I try to read but can't finish a page before I've forgotten what it said and need to scan up to start again.

The drone of the constant motion on the TV is better than the alternative though, sitting and wondering what's happening within my body. *Are the endometriomas so small now they're inconsequential? Will the inflammation settle down with those huge cysts gone or will it increase, centring around the fresh scar tissue? Have I done this for nothing or will it be the best choice I've ever made? Will it fulfil my dreams?*

Another question that plagues me is that of my mother. I know she didn't want me to have the surgery but to just abandon me, to not take a few hours away from Dad and

Neveah to come see me—it seems heartless. More evidence, I suppose, that just like I always suspected, I'm more her daughter in name than in actuality.

"What's for dinner?" Lydia looks at Adrian like I've just asked something ridiculous or concerning. "What? I'm hungry." The look intensifies. The two of them have been doing this a lot lately, looking back and forth, whispering, as if they know something I don't.

"Pho," says Lydia.

"What?" I question as Adrian talks to Lydia, not me. "It's the Dilaudid."

"What's the Dilaudid?" I press as Lydia questions, "It causes memory loss?"

"Yeah. Sometimes." Adrian nods, completely ignoring me. "I called the nurse this afternoon. She said it's not a big deal unless she needs a particularly keen memory right now. They run out in a few days anyway and then it's just the ibuprofen and acetaminophen."

"Why are you talking about me like I'm not here?" I push myself up, groan, then keel over, gasping a bit. "What's going on?"

"You've been having trouble remembering things." Adrian's smile is soft. "We just put in an order of Pho for dinner about a half hour ago. You don't remember."

"No, I…" I hesitate. "Of course I remember. Pho, right, from that new restaurant?" Adrian nods. "Wow, I…" I take a deep breath, laugh, then cringe at the pain. "What else have I missed?"

"Oh, not too much." Adrian laughs too. "You'll be fine soon."

OVER THE NEXT SEVERAL DAYS, as the stitches heal, my inner pain seems to intensify. An early visit to the doctor, after the pain progresses to the point even breathing hurts, lets me know in addition to the bladder nick, there was more to be done inside me than she's ever experienced.

"What do you mean?" I ask, wishing I hadn't entered her office alone.

Dr. LeBlanc twirls her wretched pen again. "The cysts, the adhesions and scar tissue, they pushed your ovaries and tubes out of place, adhered organs together that shouldn't be together, in some cases shouldn't even be beside each other. I fixed what I could, what directly relates to fertility, but I couldn't fix all of it without taking greater risk. You're still a bit of a mess in there. You'll be in pain for a while most likely."

"A while?"

"A couple of months I imagine, before you feel fully whole."

"A couple of months…" my voice wavers, bordering on anger. "I was told a week. Two tops."

Dr. LeBlanc nods. "That's typical, but your case wasn't—"

"Wasn't typical. I'm not typical. I get it."

I stand to leave.

"A couple of months until you're one hundred percent," she says. "Get back to your life. Just ease into it. No marathons, no weightlifting competitions." She's trying to joke. I'm not laughing. "Don't drive until you can twist and bend without those blasts of pain."

Lydia seems to sense my anger as I enter the waiting room. She keeps her voice calm and even as I rehash the doctor's words, as I limp through the halls toward the car. I want to stride, an angry retreat, but standing straight is still a challenge. Sympathy passes through me for the elderly who have their ability to make an enraged exit forever stripped away. Lydia, who matches my pace without complaint, stops just outside the passenger door. "How about yoga?"

"What?"

"To ease you into movement again, keep you from just sitting around all day with nothing but your walks."

"Yoga?"

"Yes," she smiles. "I've had a practice for years now. I could show you."

I pause, my hand on the door handle more for support than to open it. "I've read it's really good for fertility."

"Well, there you go."

"Yoga."

With the unexpected bladder nick and organ repositioning, Dr. LeBlanc recommended I stay home from teaching at least five to six weeks. On the day I was supposed to return to school, two weeks after the surgery, Lydia and I decide I'm ready to try some yoga positions beyond lying on the floor and breathing. So far, learning how to breathe is all we've done. Breathing. Not an activity I was aware had to be learned.

After a session of simple, low pressure stances, I prepare for another post-surgery first: guests. Once the introductions between Eloise, Sheila, Allison, and Lydia have been made, Eloise sits beside me. "Still feeling pretty rotten?"

"Pretty." My cat, Toulouse, purrs on my lap. Tiredness seeps over me. "But each day is better." I fill them in on the surgery, the misplaced organs, briefly mention the surgeon's slip and my subsequent catheter. Sheila shifts in her seat as I mention this last part. "So," she takes a sip of the tea Lydia made, "once you're healed you can start trying again?"

I nod. "As soon as I'm feeling well enough to…you know."

"Oh, we know." Allison's voice drips with teasing and innuendo.

I smile back, as if in on the joke, I can't tell her how it really is, how I never know whether our efforts will be full of pleasure or deep, slicing pain. "I'll be seeing the doctor in a month. I'll get more details then."

My friends smile, say words of encouragement and hope. I smile back, wanting to tell them how it really is, how the unknowns of this disease, the wish it would all just go away, consume me. It would seem like whining if I explained a typical day: I eat granola for breakfast—*Are the cysts growing?*—sip a cup of coffee—*are they expanding right now?*—take my multivitamin—*are they marbles still, or large as grapefruits?* I sit and smile, ask Adrian about his day, connect with Lydia, talk to these friends right here in front of me, and wonder—*Is my body amping up to fail me yet again? Am I broken, irreversibly broken?*

⋖

AS THE DAYS PROGRESS, Lydia and I keep up with the yoga. The concentration it takes is the one thing that calms my raging, self-destructive thoughts. Slowly, the breathing turns to sitting poses, light stretches. By the end of the week I slowly transition into moves such as child's pose, cat and cow, and even attempt a modified downward dog. We try a balance pose but quickly learn I'm not there yet. All the moves are tough. I'm shaky. A ten to fifteen minute session leaves me dripping sweat, but Lydia stands beside me always, her hands there to guide, support, to catch if I fall. On the morning I hold downward dog for a full minute, her hand smooths along my back, encourages my body to go deeper into the stretch. I relax onto all fours and glance at Lydia. "Why were you with him?"

"Hmm?" Her hands motion for me to pull back into child's pose.

"My father. What—"

"Oh." She sits back and I rise into a simple cross legged pose, my gaze on her. She hesitates before continuing. "I was young."

"Lots of people are young. They don't—"

She stands. "How about we try warrior?" I rise, go through the motions I've learned to get to this position, slide my foot forward, raise my arms (but only midway), and sink into the stance as Lydia guides me. She adjusts my front foot, taps my shoulders down, rests her hand along my back arm. "I was sad too. My mother had died. I felt lost without her. And seeing her through those last few years…no one should have to see that. Breathe in."

I do as she says, letting the breath flow through me, revelling in the strength it brings. I still hurt, bad, but it's a pain I can push through; in this moment, the pain in her voice seems worse. I turn my gaze to her.

She lets out a small sigh. "My father was so consumed by his own grief that it became his world and he, Sebastien, he paid attention to me. He made me feel wanted, needed." She guides me to turn, try the pose with my opposite foot forward. My body shakes. I try to imagine what it would have been like, watching your mother die, losing her and in that same moment, essentially losing your father as well. I step out of the pose, the pain too much.

"It sounds so cliché." Lydia shrugs. "It is cliché. My father was absent. I wanted to feel absent. I wanted…Here. Rest in mountain." Lydia does the pose and waits until I've mimicked her. "I wanted an escape." She pauses again, this time in thought. "Sebastien gave me that escape. What we did, it was so foreign, so unlike anything I'd ever imagined. It helped me let go of the pain, for a time at least."

"Was he your first?"

She makes a noise that tells me yes. I tilt side to side. I want to stretch up but know the pain will be too much. I consider Lydia's words. It's hard not to judge, but really, the judgement should be on Sebastien. Lydia was seventeen. She was practically a child. "Will you see him when you're here?"

"No. Of course not. No." Lydia steps out of her pose, as

if I've said something appalling. "The last time I saw that man was when I told him about you, when he denied…No." She shakes her head. "I have no desire to ever see him again."

I'm quiet as I study the mat she bought me, the swirls of turquoise that grow into a tree. At last I look up. "I've thought of seeing him, even gone to his office." Lydia watches me but offers nothing. "Not in a long time. Not since before my marriage."

She steps to the couch and sinks into it. "That's fine, Tracey. It's different. If you want to see him you should, just know you may be disappointed."

"You don't even know what I want out of it."

"Whatever you want, you may not get it, unless it's simply to see his face."

I settle on the couch beside her. "That may be all I want."

She smiles as old pain flits across her face. "I'm sure you could at least get that." She stands. "Any requests for breakfast?"

I shake my head. "Whatever you come up with will be perfect."

A few minutes later Lydia is back with a plate full of fresh fruit, Greek yogurt, and homemade granola: all foods to speed my healing. After breakfast we take our daily walk. The pain is less than the day before and the day before that, but each step sucks my energy as if it's not just me my legs are carrying, but three of me, one on top of the other. The blocks in my neighbourhood are small, and we add an extra one to the walk. When we make it back home I feel as if I've walked three hundred blocks, not three. I want nothing more than to lie on the couch, but my artificial bladder needs emptying—the stupid thing. It should be out by now, was supposed to be gone five days ago, but, of course, I'm not typical. I shake with exhaustion. Beads of sweat pop up along my forehead. I pushed too hard. Far too hard. Lydia follows me to the bathroom and stands outside the door. "Just let me know."

I shake my head, smile, and close the door. But my hands tremble. My legs feel like jelly. Everything within me wants to push past this, to not need help, but help now would be better than help after creating another mess. Pride tries to prevent me, but this is what Lydia is here for. I rap on the door. Three little taps. It opens. As Lydia helps with the catheter I look away, knowing my shame is unjustified but feeling it anyway.

She speaks softly. "This is nothing. Okay? Nothing. I changed your diapers as a baby. Trust me, this is way better." She laughs. Sensing she's finished, I turn back. Her smile is subtle. "I missed out on a lot. So much I didn't do…couldn't do. But I can do this. I'm happy to do this."

I nod, letting my resistance fade.

CHAPTER NINE

The day passes when Lydia is supposed to leave for her travels with Westin. She stays. I argue she's done enough but she brushes off my words. "You're not ready yet. Are you supposed to do the dishes and make dinner and—"

"Adrian can do that."

"When he's here. But what about when he's not?" She pats my leg. "I'm not leaving you on your own throughout the day."

Should I protest more? Fight? No. She's made her choice and it feels good having my mo...Lydia. Having her here. That night, while Adrian is out covering some political something or other, Lydia and I settle down on the couch with the first photo album my mother made for me after the adoption. Lydia laughs as I share the stories Mom passed on to me. At the final page her smile fades. Silence builds around us until I have to break it. "What's wrong?"

"It's just..." She draws her hand along the cover of the album. "The missing years."

"The?"

"We have the album I made you. This one. But the years in between? Years you were learning to talk in full, comprehending sentences, to read, maybe to ride your first bike, they are completely lost. No one knows a thing about them except some group home workers we'll never meet."

She's right. It's a truth I've wondered about, wished

could change, dozens of times. Part of me wants to assuage her guilt, another part knows it'd be pointless. Nothing can take it away, just like nothing can take away the anger I still feel toward her for letting those years be lost.

She caresses the cover again, her eyes closed. "I still remember so much. Your first smile. First burp. First laugh. The first time you rolled over." She laughs. "That was a big one. I called Dad at work, told him to get home as soon as he could so he could see it." She looks over at me, her eyes glowing with the memory. "I may have been even more excited about that than your first step."

"Well," I try to pull back the words but they leak out of me, "by the time I had my first step I was sick, right? More of a burden than a joy."

She nods, her gaze toward the floor. "I wouldn't phrase it like that, but it made it harder." I regret my words, but not enough to take them back. My insides are at war: Love this woman. Hate this woman. Exist with no idea of the place she holds in my life or the place I want her to hold.

"Your first word was pretty original." Her smile is back, though smaller this time.

The urge to love rises up. "What was it?"

"Pretty."

"Pretty? Why—"

"I used to call you my pretty girl." Her gaze falls again. What battle rages within her? "I loved you, Tracey. Really loved you. I've never stopped."

It's not the first time she's told me this. But something is different this time, the words don't feel like a lie. After these past few weeks: her cleaning up my messes, helping me bathe, cooking food to aid my healing, just being here— how could I not believe her?

I lean over, for the first time in my life feeling nothing like an orphan. Lydia wraps her arm around me. What exists between us is complex, it probably always will be, but she's my mother. If I'm ever blessed enough to become one I'll never put my child through the fear, the feelings of rejection that she laid on me, but this love she's giving now, this devotion, that's a lesson I'll pass on.

FIVE WEEKS AFTER MY SURGERY, Westin arrives. We spend two days introducing him to the city before he and Lydia leave for the rest of their travels. It's hard to fill the hours with her gone. The house feels empty. At her suggestion, over the past few weeks I started looking into alternative treatments for endometriosis: Traditional Chinese Medicine, specific foods to eat and foods to avoid, yoga, of course, meditation, visualization, and an array of blogs and testimonials of women swearing by each of the methods with pictures of their babies—the proof—in their hands. Though many movements still bring deep pain, I've been well enough to make my own meals and do light housework for over a week now. If I'm well enough for that, I'm well enough to actually start putting some of these new methods into practice. Being with Lydia amplified my desire to have a baby, my own blood baby. In five weeks, even after three decades apart and all the hurt and anger in between, I feel as close to her as I've ever felt to my mother. Closer. If a biological connection can do that, it's something I will not miss. And if these women I read about can make changes and see their dreams realized, I can too. I will.

"What do you have there?"

I look up from my newest self-healing related purchase as Adrian enters the room. "A book on eating to cure endometriosis."

He sits beside me. "I thought all the fruits and veggies and fish was to help you heal from the surgery."

"That's where it started." I grin. "I've been researching. Apparently diet can make a huge change with the disease."

"I thought your doctor said—"

"My doctor was trained with Western medicine. The world is much bigger than that."

"Okay." He rises. "So I should expect some changes?"

"Yeah." I draw my gaze back to the book. After a few moments I realize Adrian is still in the room. I look up. He's staring at me.

"Work was good."

I keep my gaze on him, my hand marking my spot on the page.

"Work's been good all week."

His tone isn't his usual one. He sounds almost caustic. "That's great." I smile. "You've been interviewing the shelter workers, right?"

He takes a moment before responding, his gaze still heavy on me. "That was last week. This week I'm interviewing a group of runaways. Double runaways. First from their homes, then from their pimp up in Montreal, and now they've made their way to Halifax. Kind of operating their own ring."

"Really?" My eyebrows raise. "That's, wow, I—"

"I told you about this two days ago. I told you all about it."

Did he? I scour my mind, trying to recall the conversation. He was talking about work over dinner the other night. I remember that. He said filming had gone well. I was cramping and wondering what it meant, wondering if the cysts were coming back. "Right." I chuckle, as if remembering. "Sorry. Brain fart."

"You've been having a lot of those lately."

"Latent effect of the Dilaudid perhaps?"

"You've been off of it for almost a month."

He keeps staring. We both know it's not the Dilaudid. It's the supplements and yoga positions and mental lists of specific foods to eat during my period, before ovulation, and after implantation. Mess it up and I could be sabotaging instead of helping proper hormonal balance. Intense. It's the fear. The fear that despite all I'm doing, despite everything I've already done, none of it will make a difference. With all of that, there isn't room for anything else.

I keep my smile on, wanting Adrian to say something or leave, wanting to get back to my book. He crosses his arms and leans against the wall. "The girls are hesitant to talk. I don't know if they'll end up in the doc, but the information they're giving me, the insight, it's good."

"That's good then. Great."

"I might go down in a week or two and try to search out and connect with some of the people they've mentioned. People on the right and wrong side of the law."

"Down?"

"To Montreal."

"Oh." My eyebrows arch. "Just a sec." I reach for my phone and swipe to my ovulation tracker. "Next week's not great, but the week after is better, so long as I'm on schedule and—"

"So long as you're on? Oh." He sighs. "Trace, I don't know if I can schedule this trip around when we should have sex. I have other stories and with the network, if it's not an emergency, sometimes it depends on the flight deals and—"

"Everything I'm doing means nothing if—"

"I know. I know." He plops down in the arm chair opposite me. Toulouse jumps on his lap. Adrian scoots him away. "But this is important too. This story represents over two years of my life."

"Off and on."

He looks at me, disappointment swimming in his eyes. "Yeah. Off and on. But of all the stories I've worked on in that time, this matters the most."

"I know."

"Some of the connections I'll make in Montreal could transform the story, make it secure."

"Secure?"

"There've been issues, people who aren't willing to talk, who'll make it difficult to have a well-rounded piece; they don't like the light it casts on the city, but if I have high-ups from other cities, make it more of a national problem, that will go a long way to making this story all it can be, all it should be."

"I didn't know you were having those kinds of problems."

Adrian sighs. "I've mentioned it."

"I'm sorry, I—"

"Anyway," he kicks up his feet, "I'll do my best."

"Thank you." I still hold the book in my hand. He still looks at me.

"You excited to go back to work next week?"

I set the book down. "It'll be rough starting mid-semester. I've missed a lot. Way more than we expected."

He smiles, that charming, boy grin that makes me think I can do anything…that used to make me think that. "You'll be fine. A few days and it'll feel like you never left. You're a pro."

"I've actually been thinking I'll take the rest of the term off."

Adrian stiffens, not visibly, but I can sense it, like a force pushing through the room. "Trace—"

"I called the principal today and it's not such a big deal. The sub they have is doing really well and Sally thinks there's a good chance she'd want to stay for the rest of the term, that she'd be thrilled."

"Are you in more pain than you let on?"

"No." I look away from him. We don't need the money. We have savings. But it won't be about that for Adrian. "I'm tired. Drained. That's part of it."

"Part of—"

"I really want to focus on this. Healing myself. I've been reading so much, and the body can do a lot to…to fix itself. Food and exercise and visualizations, meditations. I think if—"

"What does that have to do with going back to school?"

"It takes time. I'd like to work up to at least a half hour of meditation a day, and then there's the yoga and self-fertility massage and acupressure points. And this way of eating…it means no frozen pizzas, not even frozen lasagnas. Take out would be next to impossible." I give him my best smile. "This prepping my body for fertility thing, it's pretty much a full time job."

He throws his hands up. "A full time—"

"And teaching is more than a full time job." I shrug. "I love it, but you know it takes up all my days and half my nights. I don't think I can do both."

He sets his feet on the floor and leans over, his head down. "I don't know."

"You don't know…"

"I don't know what I think of this." He looks up. "It sounds like you're trying to make fertility your whole life."

"A baby would be my whole life, for a while anyway. At the start. I just…I have to try, right?"

"But maybe everything's fine. Maybe you'll get pregnant next month."

"Not if you're gone."

"Trace."

"Sorry. Maybe. You're right. Maybe. But even if I do you know that's no guarantee. You know miscarri—"

"I know the statistics." He sighs.

"Exactly, and if I could heal my body maybe those stats would change."

Frustration and sadness hover behind his eyes. "Just one more week, then we'll see what your doctor says?"

"You may not believe in this stuff. I get that. But I've been reading a ton and—"

"It's not about that." He sits beside me. "Trying to get pregnant can't be your life."

Why not? I want to say. What's wrong with that? What's wrong with hope? Instead I take his hand and agree to what's been offered. One more week. Then we'll see.

CHAPTER TEN

The day before my six-week check up with Dr. LeBlanc, I head out for my first social event since the operation—lunch with the gals at our favourite café. We're so used to the place we never use menus but seeing as my go-to meal is not approved for my new dietary regime, I search out the menu online beforehand to find my best option: A pumpkin soup or the salad.

I'm the first to arrive and slide into our usual booth. Eloise and Allison step through the door one after the other. "You're looking good!" Allison grins and slides into the seat across from me. "Not so pale."

"I'm feeling good."

She glances around the café, her moves exaggerated, her red hair flashing. "What? I'm not the last one here. Could it be true?"

"Guess so." After hanging her coat on the rack by the booth, Eloise slips in beside me. "I'm sure Sheila will be here soon. She's working a big case right now."

Just as the final word falls from Eloise's lips, Sheila enters, looking dishevelled, for her at least. About two strands of hair are out of place and her shirt and skirt aren't perfectly pressed. "Sorry, I—"

"Big case." Allison practically bounces in her seat. "I love it. I wasn't last!"

"We should order now." Sheila sits beside Allison. "I can't afford more than an hour away." She waves for the waitress, who indicates she'll be a minute.

Sheila sighs and rests her elbow on the table. "How is everyone?"

"Fabulous!" Allison grins. "Eloise and I went on a double date last night."

"Arthur's cousin," says Eloise. "It seemed like the two hit it off."

"I'd say." Allison leans forward. "He's thirty-seven. A widow, so it's not like he's been single the whole time 'cause he's got a bag of all his old nail clippings in the closet or something—what's that from?"

"Some movie." Sheila waves to the waitress once more.

"Anyway, he works at that independent outfitters store downtown so he's all into hiking and rock-climbing and mountain biking—"

Eloise laughs. "Necessary to keep up with you."

"Exactly. And I love that naturally fit look and his dark brown eyes and his dreads. They're wicked cool."

"They're just dreads." Eloise rolls her eyes. "But yeah. He seems like a great guy. Arthur approves."

"And you and Arthur," I ask, "things are progressing?"

"They are." Eloise's smile is small but so content. "Since he first convinced me of that coffee it's been, what, two years?"

"The first year was so sporadic though." Sheila jostles her keys before slipping them into her purse. "You made the man work. I thought for sure you two would end up nothing more than friends, if you even managed that."

"I was cautious. Scared, I guess. But he persevered." She grins. "We've been talking about marriage."

"He proposed?" Allison slaps her hands on the table.

"No. We've just been talking about whether that's something we want, what we think of marriage as an institution, whether it's necessary to define our relationship. We both think it's not, but like the idea anyway, especially in regards to the children we hope to have."

"You're talking kids too?" Allison clasps her hands and

looks up as if in prayer. "Oh, everyone is so grown up."

"What about you, Trace?" Eloise brushes some stray curls out of her face. "Recovery going well?"

"Really well." I smile, hating the thought that shot through my mind at Eloise's words: She could be pregnant before me. She could have the dream she didn't even think she wanted in a matter of months while I, who have wanted it my whole life, may never. "Hardly any pain anymore."

"That's awesome." Allison grins.

"You talk to the doctor yet? Find out more details on the surgery?" asks Eloise.

"Tomorrow."

The waitress sidles up to our table with four tall lemon waters. The girls all order their regulars and then the waitress turns to me. "Is there any dairy in the pumpkin soup?"

The waitress, who knows me and my normal order of an avocado grilled cheese sandwich and Caesar salad, raises her eyebrows. "Yeah, cream."

"I'll take the house salad then with a vinaigrette dressing."

"Sure thing." She walks away.

"You discover you're lactose intolerant or something?" asks Allison.

"No. I've been researching endometriosis. A lot of people believe dietary changes can make a big difference."

"So no dairy?" asks Eloise.

"No dairy. No red meat. No sugar. No wheat. Minimal eggs and other meat. Avoiding processed food, basically anything with chemicals."

"And you'll eat what?" Allison takes a long swig of her water.

"That leaves plenty of foods. It just requires some creativity, some planning."

"That's intense." Allison shakes her head. "I mean I eat well…about ninety percent of the time. Whole foods and all that, but no meat? No dairy? No wheat and few eggs? You'll be living off of beans for protein."

"I don't need as much as you do."

"I guess." She takes another sip.

"This is really good what you're doing though," Eloise rubs my shoulder, "taking control of your own health."

"Yeah. A whole health thing is what I'm focused on." I tell them about the other paths I've been filling my mind with: the yoga, the meditation, all of it.

"You seeing any improvement?" asks Eloise.

"It's only been a week or so since I started, less since I learned about some of it."

"So have you seen any of these alternative health practitioners yet?"

"Not yet."

Sheila, who has remained silent the past few minutes, bites her lip. "Have you looked into your father any more? Your siblings?"

"No." We all turn to her.

"That was quite the redirect." Allison laughs. "All this health conscious talk make you uncomfortable with your Ramen noodles and host of other quick and efficient microwavable food?"

"I cook," she snaps. "Sometimes. No." She taps her fingers on the table. "Your sister. She's a naturopath."

"Jojo?" Allison spurts. "What the—"

"No." Sheila shakes her head. "Of course not Jojo. Saadia's her name. Your—"

"My father's daughter." The waitress arrives with a tray of our food and the conversation ceases. The moment she's out of ear shot I lean forward. "You know my sister now too?"

"No, no." Sheila waves a hand. "I've never even met her. I was working a case with Patrick a few months ago and he mentioned it. He called her his 'quack' sister and so of course I was curious."

"So she's a quack?" asks Allison.

"That's what Patrick said. He says she was en route to becoming an MD, a profession their family approved of, and then right in the middle of her training she changed her mind, started studying naturopathy and then acupuncture. Their parents were not impressed. Still aren't."

I spear a piece of tomato with my fork but don't pick it up. "She does acupuncture too?"

"Apparently."

"And her name's Saadia." I swallow, digesting the information. "You know where she works?"

"I could find out. I'm sure there aren't hundreds of naturopaths in the city named Saadia."

"That would be pretty cool," Allison gives a sideways smile, "if your biological sister helped you have a biological baby."

"Yeah." I stare at the salad. "Could be."

"Are you going to contact her?" asks Eloise.

"I don't know." I look up. "Wouldn't it be weird? What would I do, walk into her office and say, 'Hi, I'm the sister you probably never knew about, the one your father sired with a seventeen-year old. You may know her. She was in the same class as one of your siblings. Maybe you.'"

"That would be weird." Allison picks up her massive double chicken and bacon burger. "Very weird."

"You wouldn't have to tell her," says Sheila. "Not right away. Not until you wanted. You could make an appointment, get to know her, and then decide."

Eloise gives Sheila a look. "Don't you think that's deceptive?"

"Maybe." Sheila rubs a finger along her plate. "But Allison's right, the alternative would be very…awkward."

I'm quiet, and they are too. At last Eloise breaks the silence. "But it's not like you need to go to her. You have options. There will be other naturopaths."

"And other acupuncturists," says Allison.

"Yeah, of course." I finally put that tomato in my mouth. "Of course."

"Anyway," says Eloise, "now that the six weeks are up, I wanted to talk to you about Aspire. The first few sessions have gone really well at all of the schools. The older students are taking over so much of the load, really mentoring the younger girls and—"

"I'm not sure if I'm going back."

"What?" Eloise looks at me like I've just said something crazy. Allison and Sheila stare as well.

I laugh. "I mean, not quite yet. I'll go back of course, but—"

"Why?"

A flush creeps across my cheeks. "I haven't even seen the doctor yet. And it's half way through the semester." They keep staring, questions on their faces. "All this health stuff I've been talking about. It'll take time. It's important, too."

"Of course it's important." Eloise's voice is hesitant.

"Will you lose your job?" asks Allison. "Can you just not go back?"

"I'm on a medical leave right now and getting sickness benefits. I can get it for up to fifteen weeks."

"But you're fine now. Aren't you?" says Eloise.

"Certain moves still hurt. A lot. And I am sick. I have a disease. A very painful disease."

They all stare again. At last Eloise breaks the silence. "A disease you've had for years. One you've always been able to work through before."

"I just think—"

"Scamming the system?" Allison laughs. "I never would have believed it. You with all your work ethic."

"I'm not scamming anything," I snap. "If the doctor thinks I'm medically fine to go back to work I may just ask the principal for a leave of absence."

Eloise inhales sharply, her lips kept closed. "Sally would

give it to you if she thought you needed it. But Aspire. The girls…"

"It would be weird to return to that and not return to teaching, don't you think?"

"I suppose."

More silence. The waitress stops by to ask if we need anything more. Sheila answers for us all. Eloise looks over with a smile that doesn't quite seem to reach her eyes. "If you think you need more time then you need more time. I'll handle Aspire. You take care of you."

"Thanks." I bite my lip, wondering how much of the judgement I'm feeling flows from them, and how much from my own uncertainty. Am I doing the right thing? "Tell the girls I said hello, though. Tell them I'm thinking of them."

"Sure." Eloise takes a bite of her food. "Will do."

"Just focus on you," says Allison, her smile as genuine as they come. "So the doctor tomorrow. You nervous?"

"A little." I pierce another piece of tomato. "But it could be really good news."

IN ADDITION TO THE MURALS of frolicking animals, one wall of Dr. LeBlanc's waiting room is lined with photos of successful, happy families. Usually I avoid them, but today I peruse the faces as I sip a thermos of tea. The number of twins and even triplets is shocking. But I'd take twins. I'd take quadruplets. Four would be better than none. The photos are meant to be encouraging, but instead they mock. I look away, then try to look back with new eyes. It happened for them. It can happen for me. It will.

We wait only ten minutes before a nurse calls my name. Adrian and I follow the nurse to Dr. LeBlanc's office.

After another wait, Dr. LeBlanc walks in. "How are you

feeling?" Her smile is broad.

Get past the pleasantries! I want to yell. "Fine. Great. Almost one hundred percent."

"Almost?"

"Sometimes when I twist or reach a certain way, I get a pain deep inside. It rarely lasts more than fifteen to thirty seconds at a time though."

She rubs her chin. "We did a lot of work in there. It makes sense you're still feeling some tenderness." She looks to her notes. I keep my smile on. "Dr. Watson said everything went well with removing the catheter a few weeks ago. Any problems in that department?"

"Not anymore."

She asks several more questions regarding the catheter and I answer politely, patiently, while inside I'm still yelling—tell me the news! At last she puts her file down. "It turns out your tubes weren't blocked." I raise an eyebrow. "Which, essentially, is a good thing. Only, I was hoping the cysts were squishing the tubes and that was preventing the necessary pathway for fertilization." She removes her glasses and holds them in her hand, the action seeming to signify bad news. It feels as if a huge metal hand grasps my torso, squeezing in. "As I told Adrian and your mother, the surgery itself went as well as we could have hoped. Her words drone on: "…able to shrink the cysts…couldn't get rid of them entirely…organs fused together, remember I told you about that during our quick check-up?…scar tissue, adhesions…inflammation…" Words. "Tracey." Words. But what do they mean? "Tracey, are you listening?"

"Yes." I'm listening. I've heard every word.

"So she still has endometriosis?" asks Adrian.

"Oh, yes." Dr. LeBlanc turns her gaze to him. "The surgery was never meant to change that, couldn't change that. In some cases excision surgery makes it possible, but not for Tracey, not if she wants to keep her eggs. Excision is not performed here, anyway."

"If we went somewhere else?"

"No, not for Tracey."

"Okay." Adrian takes my hand. "So this means?"

"This means we've created a much better potential environment for a baby to grow. Her uterus today is exponentially better than her uterus six weeks ago. Each cycle, though, presents potential for the disease to progress."

"So we should be trying?" I ask.

"Oh yes." Dr. LeBlanc hesitates. "If you feel ready."

"And what about natural therapies?" Adrian leans forward. "Tracey has been doing a lot of research—food changes, supplements, yoga."

Dr. LeBlanc rests her hands on the desk. "I doubt it could do much harm. Most of that research is nothing more than anecdotal, but if you enjoy it, if it helps you feel more in control, it's fine."

"And acupuncture? Naturopathy?"

"The same. Feeling healthy is a positive thing."

Adrian glances at me and then Dr. LeBlanc. "What do you think we should do?"

"IUI—"

"Artificial insemination?"

"Yes. I don't see a high chance for you two. Your sperm and Tracey's eggs seem fine. That's the only real issue IUI addresses."

"Okay."

"If you were to have any chance your best one would be in vitro fertilization. IVF."

"If we were to have any chance?" I ask. "What does that mean?"

"It means I wouldn't want to give you false hope, but it's possible that could be successful for you."

Adrian squeezes my hand again: a reaction more than an attempt at comfort. "So we should do that?"

"I'm not saying that. I'm saying if there were any way I

could help you, that way would be the most likely."

"And so if we don't, you can't help us?" That metal hand grasps so hard, it's difficult to breathe.

"If you choose to do IVF you should do it sooner than later, while your condition is as optimal as it can be."

"It's so expensive." I sip my lukewarm tea, a pathetic attempt to wash away the taste of this news.

Dr. LeBlanc looks to her notes again. "For your situation, and depending on whether you choose to have it done here or travel, you're looking at sixteen to twenty thousand dollars."

The hand is like a vice-grip, crushing me.

"We can work it out," says Adrian. "That's what the low-cost wedding was all about, right?" He rubs my shoulder.

"But even if IVF is successful, a confirmed pregnancy," my voice shakes, "IVF doesn't change the chance of miscarriage, right?"

"The sooner it happens, most likely the less that chance would be."

"But it's still a high chance."

Dr. LeBlanc nods. It could fail. I could fail. Twenty thousand dollars. Dr. LeBlanc hands us pamphlets on IVF, on living with endometriosis—information we already have.

A few minutes later we rise from our seats. We can't leave the office without passing that hall I hate: the frolicking lions, the happy elephants. Laughing. Ignorant to the reality of life. I hurl my thermos at the lion's head. The top pops off and the remaining sips of tea splatter on the wall and floor. Adrian stares at me. My shoulders heave. "It's stupid, having something like that here." He doesn't say a word. I pick up the mug, the cover, and stride the five steps to the nearest trash can, ignoring the part of me that feels badly for whoever ends up cleaning my mess. I turn and meet Adrian's gaze. "At the group home every time I got close to someone, started to feel like maybe the people there, the caseworkers, the other children, could be my family, they were taken away…or left." I brush a rogue strand of hair out of my face. "A child would get adopted or go back to their real family. A caseworker would move on…I don't know where. A better job probably." Adrian steps toward me, his arm out, as if I'm a dangerous animal he needs to approach with caution. "They'd go and yet again I'd be left." My voice cracks. I hate it. "But I thought, one day it'll change. One day I'll have my own family."

Adrian steps closer. "You do, Tracey."

"No."

"You have a mother and father and sister. Two mothers." He takes another step. "You have me."

"That's not what—"

"Tracey." His arms enclose me. "You have a family."

It's not what I want. It's not real. Not real enough. I let him hold me, but he doesn't understand.

CHAPTER ELEVEN

D r. LeBlanc, who seemed so hopeful going into the surgery, who gave me reason to believe, has lost hope. In the hospital hall, just minutes ago, I almost lost hope too. But I can't. I won't. IVF and IUI aren't good chances, so I'll make my own chances. I'll give and do everything my body needs to heal this disease. I'll make life possible, a family of my own, possible. On the short drive home from the hospital I close my eyes and visualize a clean, healthy uterus. I imagine the bright light of the universe—which I never even imagined existed before reading my new books—and envision that light melting away all the spiderweb-like adhesions that pull my organs into positions they have no right to be in. The light then melts away the cysts, calms the inflammation, leaving nothing but healthy, nourishing tissue a baby would love to make its home.

Adrian rests his hand on my thigh. He thinks my eyes are closed in sorrow or frustration. He's got it all wrong. This stillness is pure determination. I squeeze his hand, but that's the most assurance I can give at this moment.

Now that my womb is ready, I visualize a strong egg releasing when it should, making the journey to where it needs to be, welcoming the one sperm that managed what none of the others could. Next, a little embryo burrows into my healthy uterus. Thoughts cloud my visualization. *This is stupid. This won't change anything. The doctor said you had no chance.*

Screw the doctor. She's not God. I draw in my focus again. That little cluster of cells grows and grows. I send all the love I can muster toward it. I put my hands on my abdomen and imagine the way my belly will expand, the inklings of movement that will stir within me: first a flutter, and then a firm kick. It's the last part of the visualization I have the most trouble with. When I hold this baby in the crook of my arm its face is a terrifying blankness. I can't put the face of a baby I've seen in its place, so the emptiness remains. It's okay though. Rather than a vast hole of impossibility, I need to think of this nothingness as potential, the amazing possibility of the child I will one day hold.

As the car pulls into our driveway I open my eyes. "It'll be okay," says Adrian. "We'll figure it out. One way or another we'll have our baby."

"I know." More than he does. We will have *our* baby. Adrian waits for me to get out then turns the car around to head back to work. I sit in the living room and pull out my agenda. Usually by now it would be full of curriculum plans, assignment due dates, tests, and the array of extra-curricular activities I help with, the Aspire program taking up the bulk of that. Instead it's almost empty, waiting…

Before filling in this space I sit up straight, note the shaking in my hands, and wait until it's ceased. On a separate piece of paper I list all the activities and dietary changes that will help me hope. I start planning. I might as well go all in with food, so on each day for the next month I list the name of three endo-friendly recipes I've found and try not to repeat much within a given week. Next comes yoga and acupressure. To start, I'll alternate every day. Then EFT tapping (a technique I just learned about) and meditation/visualization, again, alternating. I make a shopping list for all of the non-hormone disrupting toiletries I'll now use, then open my laptop.

After a quick Google Search, there she is, Saadia Medina. I didn't even search for her, just naturopaths in the city.

She's third on the list and the only one on the whole page who performs acupuncture as well, which means half the expense…I click on her name and her picture pops up. Although I can see the resemblance to our father in her, she must have more of her mother's genes. She looks pleasant, kind. The bio next to her name talks about her training, her degrees, and says she's especially interested in women's health and fertility. It's kismet. The clinic she works at has an online appointment schedule so in less than ten minutes I've chosen a date and time, filled out a short questionnaire, and received a confirmation message. I have an appointment with my sister.

By the time Adrian gets home I've grocery shopped for my meals for the next week, as well as picked up an assortment of natural toiletries. I've done a yoga workout, fifteen minutes of visualization, and an endo-friendly dinner is simmering on the stove. I am well on my way to proving that doctor wrong.

"How are you doing?" Adrian pulls me into a hug, his voice low, an expression of concern on his face.

"I'm fine. Good." I grin. "How was work?"

He steps away from me. "You're good?"

"Yeah. I had a super productive day."

He glances around the apartment. "Doing what?"

"Preparing for our baby."

"Tracey." His eyebrow raises. "You heard what the doctor said…you mean IVF? Were you researching?"

"No. No. Preparing me. My body. Like I told you about."

"Okay." He follows me to the kitchen where I serve our plates. I take mine to the dining room. He follows again. "We having company?"

"No." I sit.

"Okay." He sits.

"I need to connect to my meals more. Be present, aware, focus on food as nourishment. Chew."

"And you can't do that while watching an episode of *The Big Bang Theory*?" He smiles.

"Not as well." I hesitate. "It's one of the things—"

He rubs a hand across his cheek. It doesn't look like he's shaved in several days. "In your books?"

"Yes. You can eat in the living room if you'd like, but I'm going to eat my dinners at the table."

He stares at me and I sit straighter. He's not the enemy, my disease is, but I need him to be on board. I need him to want this. His smile returns. "A good habit, anyway. I've always liked the idea of families eating dinner at the table together. Mine always did."

My shoulders relax. "Us too."

"Will you eat here tomorrow, when I'm gone?"

"Gone?"

I see the flicker of frustration, but he masks it well. "Yeah. My trip. First Montreal, then on to Toronto. I'll be gone for almost four days."

"Of course." I smile, a broad smile that brings to mind the housewives in 1950s television, holding back all their repressed anger at the world, at the life they've always wanted but fear they'll never have. "Maybe I'll play some music."

"That'd be nice." We eat in silence. I count my bites and focus on tasting the food. Adrian's gaze is on me.

"What?"

He opens his mouth, pauses. Closes it.

"Adrian."

"Nothing. It's nothing." He takes a bite. Is it the taste? This isn't the most flavourful meal I've ever prepared. His shoulders are tense, the energy that emanates from him so different from what I'm used to. I make my smile bigger, brighter. Maybe that's what it is, my smile. My fake smile. It could be so many things—the conversation about me going back to teaching, the one we were supposed to have after the doctor's visit. I'm not ready for it, because I'm not ready to go back to school. I have a new job now: healing my body. I try to make my smile more natural, comforting. "Pass the salt, please."

He does, but he doesn't look at me while doing it.

OVER THE NEXT FEW DAYS I store up some freezer meals so I have more time to spend with Adrian when he gets back. The whole making every single thing from scratch thing sometimes means three to four hours in the kitchen a day— cooking and cleaning. It's exhausting, but I tell myself it's worth it. I've just finished the morning's dishes and am getting ready for my first appointment with Saadia when the phone rings.

The voice on the line is eager. "Oh good, you're home."

"It's a cell, Mom. I could be anywhere."

"Right, I know that."

"Mmhmm." I pull out my favourite pair of tights and grab some warm socks. Cold feet mean a cold uterus.

"Tracey, it's awful."

My chest clenches. "What?"

"Jojo."

"Jo—"

"She came stumbling in last night at three-thirty in the morning. Three-thirty! What can you even do at three-thirty in the morning?"

The tension eases as frustration enters. "Lots, Mo—"

"I know what she was doing though. Drinking. Not just drinking. She was drunk. So drunk she still was this morning."

"What time in the morning?"

"Seven. She was supposed to take the twins to school and then go to work. She wanted to go. She insisted on going, driving with her children, drunk."

I plop down on my bed—one sock on, the other in my hand. "Was she actually still drunk?"

"She wasn't slurring her words or anything, but she'd been drunk three and a half hours earlier."

"So what happened?"

"Your father stopped her, that's what happened."

"Good." I pull on the other sock.

"But I doubt this is the first time. She's been drinking more."

"I've noticed."

"You've even noticed." Mom lets out a half sigh, half moan. "You're never even here."

"I haven't exactly been up for travelling."

Silence. "How are you feeling, honey?"

"Much better."

"Good. Good." Mom stops again. "I'm sorry I didn't visit you more."

"More?"

"Well, after that first visit, it was odd. Hard. To be there with you and…Lydia. To see her tending my baby."

"What are you talking about?" My pulse increases. The anger and frustration at my mom's neglect bubbles up in confusion. "You never came at all."

"Tracey." Mom sounds wounded. "Of course I came. The day of the surgery…"

I hold the phone away from me then draw it back. A memory surfaces: soft nurturing hands, too many hands for just Lydia, both sets too feminine to be Adrian's. One set is so familiar—perfectly manicured, finely wrinkled. And a face. Mom. She kneels beside me—smiling, sad, worried.

"Tracey?"

"Sorry, I—" Did the Dilaudid do that? It must have. "I

didn't remember. I…Yes, you came."

"Of course I came." Mom's voice is tight. Hot. "I should have come again. I know that. I'm sorry."

"It's uh…" I look to the ceiling, not knowing what to do with this new information, whether there is anything I should do. Forgive? Apparently there's nothing to be forgiven. "It's okay."

A pause. A puff of air in the phone. "So, what are we going to do about this?"

"What do you mean?"

"Should we have an intervention?"

I yank a t-shirt over my head and grab a sweater. My need for contrition vanishes. "It's been a few drinks."

"And driving, driving with her children after those drinks."

"She drove home last night?"

"A cab, but—"

"I need to leave or I'll be late for an appointment. Can I call you when I get back?"

"Tracey, this is important. Why don't you talk to her? Invite her over. She's always admired you so much."

I laugh.

"No, really. She has. And she needs help, Tracey. She has a lot going on right now."

And I don't? "Yeah. Okay. I'll try to get in touch with her this weekend, see if—"

"What do I always say?"

"Don't try, do. I'll get in touch with her this weekend, okay?" Not that I know what I'll say: Stop drinking? Be happier? So what if Damien left you, move on? All things I'm sure she has no desire to hear. But Mom's right, I should say something. An ache shoots through me for Jojo, how broken she is, how broken we both are. Maybe I don't need to say anything. Maybe I just need to be there, spend time with my sister. My sister. I glance at the clock.

"Tracey, I really think—"

"I have to go now. Love you."

CHAPTER TWELVE

The wellness clinic is painted light grey. Large canvases of woods, waterfalls, and icebergs surround me. The seats are plush, a grey several shades darker than the walls. I'm welcomed by a smiling receptionist and told the wait shouldn't be long. It isn't.

A woman steps out to greet me. Her silky black hair falls past her shoulders, her tan skin is luminous, and her smile makes me think I made the right choice in coming. My sister. The first blood family I've ever met who hasn't abandoned me. She introduces herself.

"Hi!" I jump to my feet. "It's so nice to meet you." She offers her hand and I grasp it with both of mine and then drop it. "Sorry, I…"

"It's all right." She motions for me to follow. "It's normal to be a little nervous. Is this your first time seeing a wellness practitioner?"

"Yes." I step into her office. It's small. Books line one shelf. Another is full of pills and what looks to be baggies of herbs. She motions for me to sit in an armchair and pulls a stool in front of me.

"I looked at your questionnaire, so I know the basis of why you're here. But tell me in your own words."

The story comes out hesitantly at first, then flows. Not just my endometriosis, the almost two years of trying, my irregular periods, the pain that's become an almost constant companion, but before that too. As Saadia nods and prompts, I tell about my birth mother leaving me in a room I'd never seen before with nothing but the clothes on my back and a teddy bear in my arms, how I didn't see her again for almost thirty years. I talk about the two years in a group home, my eventual adoption, meeting Adrian—how I had trouble believing anyone could really want me, love me, with all my faults, and how he helped me work through that. I don't go into detail about my need to have a baby, to have a 'real' family because something in her eyes tells me she gets it. I want to tell her more, reveal all—why I'm in her office and not someone else's—but I hold that back too.

When it's clear I'm finished answering her final question, she brings her hand to her chin, her gaze still locked on mine, and lets the silence surround us. Just as I'm starting to feel so uncomfortable I decide to ask about the baggies on the shelf to end the silence, she speaks. "That's a lot of pressure, Tracey. A lot of pressure."

"Pressure?"

"This is not just a baby you're hoping to bring into existence, it's the healing of a lifetime of hurt, the realization of a dream that extends far beyond being a mother. It's a lot to put on a new soul."

Something in her words and look make me want to crawl out of my skin. The words she says, the way she says them, remind me of Damien, of Jojo several years ago. Only from Saadia the words don't sound fake, they sound convicting. I let my chest rise and fall before answering. "I don't think of it like that."

"I know." She extends her hands and motions to mine. "I'll take your pulses." She lays her fingers on both my left and right wrists, silent as she does so. "Now open wide. Let me look at your tongue." She tilts her head back and forth as she examines, then moves to her desk for the first time since the appointment started. She makes several notes and returns to me. "I'll step out of the room. If you could undress, everything except your underwear, and get under the sheets, I'll be back in a few minutes."

"Umm, sure." I step to an adjustable bed against the wall.

About two minutes later Saadia calls from behind a curtain and steps back in. "Have you ever had acupuncture before?"

"No."

"Expect a slight prick. If you have a stronger reaction, let me know." She pulls back the sheets and starts inserting needles in me. Some I hardly feel, others cause a jolt of pain. She tells me my condition is complex, so to start she's focusing on strengthening my flow of blood and the pathways to my kidney. When all the needles are inserted she stands where I can see her face. "I'll leave for about forty-five minutes. It's a long time for most so I generally put on some music. I encourage you to relax. Take deep breaths. Visualize the blood coursing through your body, strong and nourishing. If you'd like to take it further, you can envision the life you'd like to see grow inside you."

"I've been doing that. I started a few weeks ago." The words come out almost like a child's, hoping for approval. I want approval from Saadia…my big sister.

"That's great. There's a monitor, so if you need me just call. I'll be going over your condition to determine the best herbal formula to start you on." She brings her hand to her chin again. "One more thing to think about. Sometimes we want something so badly that we become terrified we won't get it. That terror becomes a presence in our bodies, almost a life force, and we may not be consciously aware of it, but our bodies are. Because of this awareness, I believe it's possible for our body to manifest the very thing we hope so much will never be." She lays a hand on mine. "Not that it makes it our fault in any way. Not at all. Realizing this is not a cause for guilt but rather for thankfulness. Fear is stressful and stress destroys our bodies; this is scientifically proven. So, knowing that, it makes sense to believe that pure hope and love can do the opposite, can heal. I encourage you to let go of the fear that you'll never conceive, never have this particular family you dream of, and focus on the wonderful things you already do have. Believe that when the time is right, when your body is ready, you'll share this wonderful life you live with the child you've always hoped for, while realizing even if that never happens, it doesn't make the life you're living today less wonderful."

I stare at Saadia, my mouth slightly open. Allison would be questioning whether this woman is for real, maybe echoing Patrick's sentiment that she's a quack. But her words feel real, feel right. When she leaves I lie in the bed, dozens of needles poking out of me, and breathe in and out. I try to imagine the healing force of the universe entering me with each inhalation and the diseased parts of me escaping with each outward breath. The ideas Saadia just presented aren't entirely new to me. I've read similar concepts in the books and articles I've consumed in the past few weeks. When I read them, guilt coursed through me as my mind spun: *I could have created this. It could be my fault I'm in such pain, my fault that after months of trying Adrian and I are still childless, may always be childless.* Today though, no guilt surfaces. Instead, I feel hopeful. Free. Just as she said, if my body could create such damage, it can also heal it. And then fear creeps in…*but what if it can't heal? What if it's too late?*

I draw my mind back to my breathing, to the universe, to joy and hope. Every time my thoughts wander I pull them back. In the next days and weeks and months I'll keep doing it. I'll fight my mind and my body until it lets me experience peace, health, fertility.

Today, at least, it's working. The longer I lie on the table the more relaxed I feel. My breath comes easy. My limbs sink into the mattress. My mind drifts, but it's to a peaceful place, an almost thoughtless place. When Saadia returns I smile at her, groggily.

"How do you feel?"

"Great." I yawn as she pulls out the needles. "Sleepy."

"Mmm-hmm." She grins. Once all the needles are out I push myself into a half-sitting position. My head spins. "Easy there." Saadia rests a hand against my shoulder. "Stay here a moment. Ease up slowly."

"I feel a little loopy."

"That's perfect."

"Hmm?"

She chuckles. "We call it acu-stoned. Just enjoy. I'll be right back. Take your time getting dressed and say the word when you're ready."

Saadia returns with a bottle of pills and a baggy of leaves. She tells me when to take each, how much, what they do, and emphasizes connecting to the treatments, being present as I let them enter my body, believing in the work they will do.

I rise to leave. "Just one moment." I sit. "I was thinking, you didn't talk about your father earlier. Have you met him?"

"No."

"Do you know who he is?"

My throat almost closes but I push the words out. "I do. He works not far from me. I pass his office regularly."

"Wow." She stares at me a moment. "Would you like to tell me about him?"

I swallow. No. Definitely not. What if I slip? What if she knows enough to piece it together? "I'd rather not talk about him."

"That's fine. Do you think of him often?"

"Sometimes."

"Meeting him could be healing for you. That's an unknown in your life. Unknowns often create fear and stress, yet most times the reality of the things we fear are far less scary than our imaginings." She stands. "Just thoughts to ponder."

"Thanks." I lift my purse and jacket off of the chair and shake Saadia's hand like a normal person this time.

"It was a pleasure to meet you, Tracey. If you'd like to come back, it would be beneficial for me to see you in two weeks. The herbs I gave you should be done by then as well."

I agree to return. After paying at the front desk, I step into the crisp fall air. Saadia, my sister, thinks I should meet my father. Would she say the same thing if she knew he was our father? From everything I know about Sebastien, he would not welcome me with open arms. But his daughter has. His daughter is beautiful, strong, loving. Could the man who raised her really be so bad? I shake my head. Thoughts for another time. I slip into my car and go over my mental to-do list for the rest of the day. The acupuncture treatment can wipe meditation off the list, but I still need to do yoga, prepare an endo-healthy dinner, and call Jojo. I can't forget to call Jojo.

CHAPTER THIRTEEN

Energized from my meeting with Saadia, I do a yoga session as soon as I get home, brush my skin—a practice that's supposed to support healthy blood flow—then start dinner. Arms encircle me as I chop sweet potato.

"You're back." I turn into Adrian's embrace and give him a kiss. "How was the trip?"

He stares at me before answering, an expression of tenderness on his face. "Well worth it. My meetings in Toronto solidified that the story's going national." He gives me another squeeze then looks over my shoulder. "What culinary creation is on the menu tonight?"

"Sweet potato and kale salad."

He grins, but a grimace lurks behind it. "Sounds nourishing."

"It will be." I lean against the counter. "I met my sister today."

He leans beside me and scoops up a cluster of Brazil nuts.

"No." I swat him. "One a day. That's all you need for selenium."

"Well this," he holds up his hand, "is exactly the amount I need for a snack. What do you mean you met—" He stops, the nuts inches from his mouth. "Your bio-sister?"

"That sounds so weird." I turn back to the potatoes. "My real sister. My birth sister. Saadia."

He pulls me away from the counter. "I don't get it. Did you run into her or…"

"She's a naturopath. I made an appointment with her."

He stares at me, his mouth half-way open. "So it was a coincidence?"

"Of course not. I found out she was my sister. Sheila told me. And I wanted to see a naturopath anyway…so."

Adrian waves me to the dining room and pulls out a chair. He props his elbows on his knees. "What did she say? You're smiling, so—"

"She gave me some herbs and pills for my condition. She wants to work with me. I had my first acupuncture treatment. It's weird but—"

"No. What did she say about being your sister? Did she already know about you or—"

I shake my head, uncertain at his tone. "I didn't tell her. Not yet."

"Tracey."

"That would be quite the bomb, don't you think?" I let out a little laugh. "She expects someone in for an appointment and that person just comes out with, 'Hey, your father had another kid. It's me!'"

"So instead you lied to her."

"It's not lying, it's—"

"What then?" Adrian stands. "What would you say it is if it's not lying? It's definitely deceptive."

I step away from him. "I'll tell her. I just wanted to get to know her first."

"You honestly think she'll be okay with that?"

"I don't know. She's nice, though. I really like her. She seems kind and passionate and I think she wants to help me. I think she will help me."

Adrian runs a hand through his hair. He looks at me, then away. "Okay." He turns back. "So acupuncture?"

"Yeah." I relay the details of the appointment, the various herbs and what they're supposed to do, and how I'll integrate them into all I'm already doing.

"And teaching?"

"Hmm?"

"We haven't talked about that yet."

I pull out a seat and finally sit. "I don't have time."

"Tracey, it's your job."

"And I'm not quitting. This won't be forever. Just until we get pregnant."

"You said just until next semester."

I pause. That is what I said, but somehow in the past days and weeks my desire to transform my body into the perfectly healed baby-making machine I want it to be has taken over. This is my new mission. My new job. "Hopefully we'll be pregnant by then."

"And if we're not?"

"Be hopeful."

"Be realistic." We stare at each other. My chest tightens, a feeling I'm becoming too familiar with. Lightness, positivity, joy. These are the feelings I want. Why doesn't he get this, support it?

"All this stuff you're doing, it costs money, too. Have you thought about that?"

"Don't condescend." I snap. "You're the one who said just the other day that we could 'work it out' for an IVF treatment. That could be up to twenty-thousand dollars. My herbs and treatments and yoga isn't costing that."

His shoulders tense. His jaw. "Exactly, Tracey. Exactly. Twenty thousand dollars and you're deciding not to work? Instead you're blazing through what money we have."

"I'm not blazing—"

"Your sickness benefit is all up, or whatever the doctor's note cleared you for is up, isn't it?"

I cross my arms.

"Isn't it?"

"That's not the point."

"That's exactly the point." He doesn't yell. But it's close.

My tension rises. My stress. I close my eyes. *Breathe deep. Take your mind somewhere peaceful.*

When I open my eyes Adrian is still staring at me, but his expression has changed. "Let's not fight, okay? You know what I want. You know what I think is important for you. For us. Just consider, you have no idea how long it will take. And if the IVF doesn't work will you keep doing this?"

"We haven't decided about IVF."

"Okay. But will you stop teaching for years? There has to be a point where you return to your life."

I can't look at him. "Like you said. I know what you want, and you know what I want."

He rubs his hand along my shoulder. "We're both stressed. Why don't we go out for dinner, just relax? Those potatoes will save for tomorrow, right?"

I clench my jaw. "I can't just go out for dinner."

"What?"

"Adrian, I can't eat what I need to eat at a restaurant. How do you not know this?"

His arm drops. "You've been doing amazing. Just take a break. I can see that all this…fertility stuff, it's stressing you out."

My shoulders slump. He's right. Not always, but at times, now, the stress is like a wall of fog, threatening to press in on me. But I'm my own sun—I'll burn it off. I am burning it off. "This is something I can do. A way I get to feel in control."

"You're in control too much. Take a night to relax." His voice and grin is cajoling. "We need a date. I know you must be craving some nachos or wings."

"No."

"Fine." He turns. "I need a night out. I'll be back in a few hours."

"Wait." I step after him. "Tell me more about the trip. Tell me—"

"I don't need to talk about the trip."

"But dinner."

"Use my share for your lunch tomorrow." He leaves the room and a moment later the front door slams. I return to my sweet potatoes. The knife pounds onto the cutting board, again and again. I wipe my shirt sleeve across my cheek. I'm doing the right thing. I'm definitely doing the right thing. He'll just have to figure that out.

❧

THE NEXT WEEK THE PHONE RINGS. Jojo. Damn. A wave of guilt flows over me. I never called. "Hi." I make my voice light, excited to hear from her. "How's it going?"

"You know. Life." Mumblings in the background. "You all healed up?"

"I've been feeling good. Yeah."

"Great, uh," the twins' distant laughter travels through the line, "I know it's last minute but would you mind watching the kids tonight? Mom and Dad have some thing, some event or something, and I was offered a chance to take another shift at work."

I've already done my yoga, but I had an hour long meditation and visualization session planned for tonight, and then dinner to make. I could make it early and pack it to Jojo's… "It's important that you take this shift?"

"It would help. Yeah. Besides, you haven't seen the kids in a while. They miss you."

I laugh. "They said that, huh?"

"They always miss you."

"I'll come."

"Great. So can you be here in an hour and a half?"

"That means leaving right now."

"Yeah. I said it was last minute."

I sigh. "I'll be there."

Jojo's new apartment is small. Two bedrooms, a combined living room and kitchen, almost no counter space. I've seen it once before, but it didn't look like this. I step over toys and cardboard boxes to get to the living room. Jojo, who opened the door then left for her bedroom without even a greeting, seems to instinctively know her way around the mess. I have to maneuver. Old pizza boxes and an assortment of McDonald's takeout containers sit stacked in the centre of the table. A large pile of laundry rests outside the kids' room. It doesn't look clean. The scent of stale food and warm bodies fills the air.

"When will you be done?" I ask as Jojo emerges.

"Shift's five to nine. You won't mind if I meet up with a friend after though? Just for an hour?"

I shove some Lego out of the way and perch on the couch. "It's a long drive home."

"You're not back to work yet, right? What's an hour? Stay up late and sleep in."

I give her a look.

"Come on. I just need a break, okay? I'm with the kids whenever I'm not at work."

"I thought Mom and Dad were helping out."

"They help. When I'm at work."

She stands before me in tight jeans and an old t-shirt. Doesn't seem the appropriate outfit for a secretary at a law firm. "You get a new job?"

"Another job. Moonlighting at McDonalds. All the discount McNuggets and Big Macs we could want."

So that explains the excessive takeout. "You like it?"

"The twins begged for Karate and gymnastics this year. That shit's expensive." Her face falls then pushes up in a faltering smile. "But look at me, best mom ever." She rests a hand on her hips. "So another hour?"

I nod. "Sure."

"Great." She grabs her purse. "I should be home a little

after ten. Maybe eleven.”

“Jojo.”

“Thanks so much, Sis.”

She heads to the door. I stand. “Where are the kids?”

“Oh.” She stops and turns, laughs. “They’re in my room watching a movie on the tablet.”

And with that she’s gone.

After the kids are asleep I debate doing my meditation and visualization, but the mess in the room is too distracting. Every time I close my eyes I can see the piles of garbage and clothes and disarray. My mother must never come here. She’d have a heart attack. I tackle the living room first: putting away toys, picking up clothes, and piling pictures and paintings the twins must have brought from school. The kitchen seems overwhelming, but I head there next. In a few minutes I have a garbage bag full of takeout containers and other refuse. When I finish the dishes it’s ten-thirty and still no Jojo. I debate tackling her room next. On the floor I see more clothing than carpet, but Jojo doesn’t have her own washer and dryer and I’m not about to go in search of one with the kids in bed. In the living room I stretch out on the couch. Eyes closed, I start my visualization. When I open my eyes, Jojo’s hands are on my shoulders, gently shaking me.

“What time is it?”

“A bit past midnight.”

I reach for my phone. It reveals it’s twelve fifty-three, a text, and three missed calls from Adrian. Nothing from Jojo. I sit up. “What happened?”

“Nothing happened.” The scent of beer travels on her breath. She looks around the room. “You cleaned up. Thanks.”

“You said you’d be home by ten.”

“A drink turned into several. You were sleeping,

anyway."

Mom was right. Damn. Mom was right, and here I just enabled more drinking.

"Did you even go to work?"

Jojo tosses her jacket on the couch. "Of course I went to work. I just had a couple drinks with a friend afterward."

"Are you drunk?"

"Do I seem drunk?"

"Did you drive?"

"Tracey, lay off."

"Did you drive?"

She stretches. "I have work tomorrow. Should probably get to sleep. And you're obviously tired. You can leave. Or stay if you want. Leave in the morning."

There's no chance I'm leaving. Not now. And I'm not staying just to go to sleep either. "Sit, Jojo."

"Trace."

"Sit."

She plops onto the couch. "Happy?"

"Were you driving?"

"I'm under the limit."

We have a stare down. "How do you know? Are you sure about that?" She looks away from me. "What if you got in an accident? What if you got stopped at a check point? What about your kids?"

"My kids are fine. I'm fine. I didn't get stopped at a checkpoint." She stands. "Thank you for babysitting but it doesn't mean you get to give me the fifth degree."

"It's the third degree."

"No. The fifth."

"Whatever." I step toward her. "I'm worried about you. This isn't you. This mess," I wave my arm toward the hall full of dirty laundry, "this," I tap her chest, "you have to think of your kids."

"Why?" She clenches her jaw and backs away from me. "Why do I have to worry? Why can't I just have some fun?

Relax?"

"Because—"

"Because I'm a mother. I know. But Damian's a father and he's off with his new love toy travelling Asia. It's been months now."

"I know."

"And you know how often he's contacted the kids? Not once. Not once in what, two and a half months? And you know how much money he's sent?"

"Jo—"

"None. Nada. Zilch. So if I want to have a few drinks, if I want to forget all the responsibility and the 'mommy, please' and the 'mommy, now,' for a couple of hours when my kids are safe and looked after at home, I think I have the right."

"I'm just saying—"

"You're saying you think you know better than me. You're saying I'm a bad mom. Well, maybe I'm not the best, but compared to Damian I'm parent of the year. So again, lay off."

"Fine." I grab my bag. "I'll lay off. I'm gone." At the door I turn. Jojo stands in the living room, her jaw still clenched, her arms at her sides, fists clenched too, her chin held high. I've seen this same stance a dozen times: as a kid when she'd done something wrong but didn't want to own up to it, or when she didn't get her way. But she's not a kid anymore. She's a grown woman. A grown woman with three beautiful kids. And it's not just the drinking, it's what she's doing for it—lying, coming home three hours late. My shoulders stoop and I hesitate, tempted to turn back, to take her in my arms. She's not only a grown woman with kids, she's also my baby sister. And she's falling apart. "You're not a bad mom, Jo. I didn't mean to imply that. You're a great mom. But you know you can't keep on like this." Her jaw twitches. "You love your kids too much to let this person be their mother. This isn't you."

"Oh, it's me."

"No, Jo. It isn't." I put my hand on the doorknob. "Are you sure you don't want me to stay? We can talk."

"Just go."

"I'm here if—"

"Go, Tracey." Her voice trembles. Do I go or do I stay? Should I force myself into her life when she doesn't want me there? I turn the knob and step into the dark hall. It's late. And Adrian's probably terrified. I need to call him. This conversation can continue another time.

CHAPTER FOURTEEN

Over the next two months I stick to my fertility practices like it's a religion. Yet, as the Christmas holidays approach, my tension grows, which is not what I want or need. What I want and need is peace. Joy. Hope. They're hard to hold on to. I imagine all the parties, the mother's with babies, the round bellies. Adrian's family alone has eight children under eight: exuberant, rosy cheeked, existing. It's not only the babies and round bellies though, the holidays mean food galore—food that will destroy my efforts.

"Tracey?"

I lift my head.

Adrian steps toward me. "Were you meditating?"

"No, I…" What was I doing? "Sitting. Just sitting." I uncurl my legs from the couch.

"Your eyes were open, so…"

"Can't a person just sit?" My words come out with a snap.

"Yeah, of course." He sits beside me. "What were you thinking about?"

"I don't know. Nothing."

His hand rests on my thigh. I'm not looking at him, but I can hear the soft smile in his voice. "What were you thinking about?"

"Christmas."

"Oh yeah? Getting excited."

"Not really." The words come out lower, sadder, than I expect them to. His arm lifts from my thigh to wrap around my shoulder. He draws me to him but I feel so far away. He plies me for answers, dragging out my fears and insecurities, my frustrations.

"You need to get your mind off all of this," he finally says. "You need to relax."

I pull away. "Off of all what?"

"Obsessing about your fertility. Having a baby. No wonder you're staring at a wall in the middle of the day. It's consuming you."

"It's not—"

"You have to have other focuses."

I turn to him. "This is the focus I have to have. Don't you get it? Every month, every cycle, our window of opportunity gets smaller, unless this is working. I have to believe this is working. I have to devote myself to it so the cysts shrink, not grow. I have to believe."

"We could also do an IVF treatment, the window of opportunity's fading for that too. The doctor said—"

"I know what the doctor said." I shake my head. "I'm not ready for that."

He lifts his hand. "But you're ready for this? This effort to heal yourself, it's all you talk about. All you think about." He runs the hand down the side of his face. Frustration pours from his voice. "Practically all you do is stuff focused on getting pregnant—the food, the reading, the constant meditation. It's getting ridiculous."

"It's ridiculous to try to heal my body?"

"No." He lets out a groan. "But it's ridiculous to stop teaching, something you love. It's ridiculous to never see your friends anymore. It's ridiculous to dread Christmas."

I look to the floor. When is the last time I've seen my friends? Weeks, for sure. When's the last time Adrian and I had dinner out? Months. We went to a movie once, but I hated being able to smell the popcorn and not eat it. Stupid.

Weak.

"I'm trying to be supportive. I really am. I've been eating the food, right?"

My gaze remains focused on strips of old hardwood. "Sure."

"It's great what you're doing. It's impressive. Admirable. But it can't become your life. It's stressing you out."

"No." I look up. "It's about letting go of stress. I'm doing something positive. Important. A good meditation session is relaxing and—"

"You don't seem relaxed. You seem obsessed. Don't you miss your students?"

"Yes, I—"

"Don't you miss me?"

He looks hurt, sad. Scared? I've always been so scared he'd pull away from me, leave, and here he is looking at me like I'm the one walking away from him. "I'm here, Adrian."

"You're not. Not as much as I want you to be, as I need you to be. I want a baby too, but not if it means losing my wife."

I push out a laugh. "You're not losing me." Though I feel like I'm losing myself.

We sit several moments. I don't know what to say. He must not either. At last he speaks. "Is it actually helping? Are you noticing a change?"

"It's only been a few months."

"Go back to teaching, Tracey. Please. You can still do all this. You have it down now. You know the recipes. I'll help out more. I'll take on cooking. I need to see you out of this house. I need to see you doing what you love."

"I'll think about it."

"Tracey."

My phone rings. "It's Eloise."

"Take it." He rises from the couch. "And if she invites you out, go."

∾

"MAN, TRACEY. IT'S BEEN months!" Allison stands to greet me when I walk up to their table in the Latin restaurant she loves.

"You look fabulous!" I hug her, my smile large.

Allison flings her shimmery red hair back. "Thought I'd treat myself to a salon day."

"So your first five figure month at the studio? That's what we're celebrating?"

"It is indeed." Allison plops back into her chair. "Now don't think I'm taking all that home. There are a truck load of expenses: my trainers' salaries, rent, insurance, equipment. But still, it's a milestone."

"Is it ever." I take the seat beside Eloise and give her a quick hug.

"It's marvellous." Eloise squeezes me back. "Our little superstar." She grins at Allison.

"You helped. That marketing campaign you suggested—"

Eloise cuts Allison off. "It was all you." She signals to the waiter. "Three Sex on the Beach." Our traditional celebratory drink. Alcohol is certainly not on my approved list of foods, but I don't stop her. One won't sabotage me.

"Is Sheila not coming?" I ask.

"She'll try to swing by later." Eloise's phone jingles and she swipes it to silent. "That case she's working on is taking so much out of her. Hopefully it's resolved soon."

"I know." Allison lets out a little moan. "I can't imagine what it's like, having to keep such horror in her mind every day."

"She's got a thick skin." Eloise takes a bite of the nachos they must have ordered before I arrived. "But still."

What case? What horror? I'm tempted to ask, but I should know. They suspect I know.

"You've been pretty AWOL too." Allison grabs a nacho

loaded with chicken and cheese. It looks so good. "Still in pain from the surgery? Or is school really intense?"

Eloise gives me a side look. She knows I never returned to teaching or to Aspire. "I'm doing well," I say. "Just busy."

"Would this be finals season?" Allison laughs. "I get all confused with the semesters now. Grade school is really different than Uni was, right?"

My chest feels tight. Why? I'm not embarrassed I haven't gone back to school. It's not like I'm sitting at home doing nothing.

"Tracey's not teaching yet." My head whips to Eloise. "Well, you're not."

"I know."

"I didn't think it was a secret."

"It's not."

"You're not teaching?" The next nacho Allison reached for stops half way between the plate and her mouth. "Still? I mean…Are you okay? You love teaching."

"I know. I just…" First Adrian and now them. No. Allison's just curious. Eloise…concerned? "I thought it'd be a good idea to be one hundred percent first. Not just from the surgery but try to give my body what it needs to heal itself. To heal the endometriosis."

"I thought there wasn't a cure." Allison tilts her head.

"There's not, as far as Western medicine is concerned, but the body can do amazing things. Food can be healing, and focusing on your mind, positive thoughts. That kind of thing."

She stares at me. "Don't tell me Jojo's got you all New Age now?"

"Jojo has nothing to do with it."

"Okay. Okay. Whoa." Allison raises her hands. The drinks arrive and she takes a long sip of hers. "Yummy. What do you mean though? Did you find a naturopath like you were talking about before? That kind of healing?" She looks up, as if remembering. "Sheila said…was it your sister? Did you?"

"Yes, actually." I grin and tell them both about Saadia: Her treatments. Her sweetness. The awful tasting herbs she has me on. How great it feels to see her every two weeks, especially since she's my sister.

"But she doesn't know you're her family?" asks Allison.

"Not yet."

"When will you tell her?" Eloise.

"Soon. Maybe. I don't know."

"Are you scared?"

Am I? I shift in my seat. "I just don't want to ruin a good thing."

Eloise gives me that look she has. The I'm-on-to-you-and-I-know-you-know-better-than-what-you're-doing look. The words she says don't match it. "Maybe if you told her it would turn into an even better thing."

"Maybe."

"And maybe by not telling her you're being really deceptive and unfair and the longer you leave it the more betrayed she'll feel." Those were the words.

I direct my gaze to my drink, not wanting to look at Eloise. "Maybe you should mind your own business and let me live my life."

"Oh, I'm letting you live your life." Eloise leans forward. "And I get that you're having a rough time right now. I get that you're trying to do something great. But that doesn't make it okay to just ditch your responsibilities."

My head snaps up. "What responsibilities?"

"Teaching. Aspire."

"I have a substitute, a substitute who's doing fabulous, and you told me you had Aspire handled. You told me to take as much time as I needed to get better."

"And you're better." Eloise leans back. "That took a few weeks, not a few months. And yes, I have it handled. But it's not about it being handled. It's about a relationship you have with those girls. How do you think it looks to have you just back out of what you started? To desert them?"

"Is that what you're telling them?"

"Of course not. They know about the surgery, though they don't know why. They're concerned and I have to just keep telling them you're not ready to come back yet. They want to know when you will be, and I have no idea."

"They're fine." I brush away her words. "They have other people. They have you."

"Of course they do, but that's not the point."

"Gals." Allison flits her gaze between us. "Ease off, okay?"

"Sorry." I look to Allison. "This night is supposed to be about you."

"That's fine. That's not it." She smiles a half-smile. "Just don't fight. You guys are besties. We all are. Support, right? Being there for each other."

"It's hard to be there for someone when she evades your calls and offers to get together." Eloise rests her hands on the table. "And I mean that in the most loving way possible. I want to support you. I'd check out a yoga class. I'd cook a dinner you can eat. And I get that you're doing something important for you, but that can't be the only thing you do."

"You sound like Adrian."

Allison grins. "Well ain't that interesting. You married a man who sees things the way your best friend does. That's good, I'd say."

I put on a smile, but I'm not smiling inside. Why does no one understand? Eloise should understand. She knows what it is to single-mindedly pursue something…and it lost her the man she loved. But this is different. Entirely different. I'm doing this for love, not career advancement. The only one who gets it is Saadia. She understands. She supports everything I'm doing…not that she knows what I've sacrificed to do it…but still, she understands.

"Anyway," Eloise waves a hand, her jaw un-clenches,

"let's move on to another topic for now. You both going to Jenn's baby's birthday party?"

"I'll be there with bells on." Allison grins.

Jennifer's baby's birthday party. My mind races to put the info together. I know I saw something about it. An evite. Yes. Both Adrian and I were invited. I can't remember when it is…Eloise and Allison look at me, waiting for a response. "Yes. Of course." I smile. "I'm excited." An afternoon around more babies and fertile women. Should be a ball.

I nod at something Allison says, not fully hearing it. Is this how I missed the details of Sheila's big case? I need to check myself. Pay attention. Be present. The party will be fun. Great. I love children and I love my friends. Focus.

"It was so romantic," Allison gushes, "the way he got down on one knee like that. I was actually terrified he was going to propose or something."

"After only a couple of months? That would be terrifying." Eloise laughs and shakes her head.

"But the question he popped was if you'd be his girlfriend?" I ask.

She grins. "Yep. It felt like high school."

I take a sip of my drink, thrilled at the way Allison's lit up. "That's wonderful. You deserve a dose of romance!"

She giggles. Actually giggles. "That I do!"

CHAPTER FIFTEEN

The next week Adrian comes home wearing the broad grin that always makes my heart pitter-patter. "I've got a surprise."

I look up from my yoga mat. "What?"

"Dinner."

"Dinner?"

"That's right. Dinner at a restaurant that has gluten free, dairy free, red-meat free meals."

"Really?" I pick up the mat. "Locally sourced?"

"Whatever they can get local. The reviews are great. So, what do you say? Date night?"

"Uh, yeah. I guess."

He pulls out a bag. "Spiced nuts and roasted chickpeas made at a health food store downtown. A healthy, crunchy treat for the movie we'll go to after?"

Love flutters within me. "Sounds good."

"I made reservations for an hour and a half from now. That all right?"

"Tonight?" My mind travels to the stew bubbling in the crock pot. It'll keep. "Sounds good. Sounds great."

"Wicked. I'll grab a quick shower."

My gaze follows Adrian as he leaves the room. In the past months he's made dinner a few times. At least half a dozen, though I know he doesn't like my new way of eating. He shook his head at meditation and visualization but went to a couple of yoga classes with me. This, though, is great.

This is getting both of us what we want. Not that I don't want a night out with him…I definitely want that. And maybe, just maybe, I'll tell him about the little hope that's been growing inside of me.

The food at the restaurant is amazing. More flavourful than anything I've been creating, and it feels so good to not prep the meal myself and do all the cleanup. Never in my life have I cooked full meals as frequently as I have the past few months. Not a processed or packaged anything has passed my lips. And now this. After a particularly delectable bite of falafel, I catch Adrian grinning at me. "What?"

He leans back in his chair. "You look happy."

"I am happy."

"I know. And you look it. You haven't looked happy in a long time."

"Adrian."

"It's not an insult, okay? I'm glad. Really glad."

I drop my gaze to my plate. "I'm glad too. Thanks for thinking of this. It was a wonderful idea."

He leans forward, his arms resting on the edge of the chair. "There are other restaurants too. I started researching. This is the only one in the city where everything is gluten and dairy and meat free, but several others have options that sound good." He takes a hold of my hand. "I know I haven't been helping out as much as I should, but I want to do better and find ways to make this easier on you."

"And those other restaurants," I smile, "mean you can eat something normal."

He laughs. "That's true, but I won't if you'd rather I didn't. And hey," he scoops up a bite with his fork, "this is pretty good."

"Sure is."

"There's more too. There are people who will cook for you and freeze it up. I know you do that yourself, but it's a lot of work. The service is kind of pricey, not something for every day, but it's something for those days when you're really busy and a way to keep this going. Like when you go back to teaching, if you had a late night of marking we could just pop one of those in. Easy."

I put my fork down. "Are we having that conversation again?"

"No." He waves a hand. "When you decide to go back to school. I'm not saying when."

I let a smile grow. "Next semester."

"I'm not trying to pressure y—"

"No. Next semester. I'll go back next semester. You're right." I tap my fingers on the table. "I need to be doing something more. And that will make a difference—prepared meals, being able to eat out sometimes. Cooking is the most time consuming thing of all the fertility stuff."

"I know."

Warmth spreads through me. I needed this: A night out. My husband looking relaxed, smiling across from me. "Thank you."

"For?"

"This. For taking the time to set this up, for thinking of solutions. I know I haven't been the most present."

"Moody and unpredictable and—" he winks, "fully the woman I love. I just want to see you happy. That's probably equally as important as everything you're doing." He releases my hand. "And I know you say you're focusing on it, but you haven't seemed very happy lately."

"I'll try to do better."

He sighs. "See, it's just that. All this trying. If you could relax a bit more, let go of everything that must be swimming around in your head, maybe it would just come naturally. Happiness, I mean."

Let go of everything? Relax? Easier said then done. But he's right about one thing, I feel happier tonight than I have in a while. "To relaxing." I raise my glass.

He grins. "To enjoying each other. Enjoying life."

After we've finished our meals we make our way to the

theatre. Adrian raises the arm rest between us and I snuggle against him. It's a comedy and, for the most part, I sink right into it, laughing easily. Back at home we make love for the first time in weeks. We've been having sex almost every other day, but this night we make love.

Afterward, as I lay in his arms, I snuggle closer and tilt my head to look up at him. "Adrian?"

"Mm-hmm?" His gaze is on the ceiling.

"Adrian." I nudge him until he looks down at me. "I'm late."

"What?" He props himself up on his forearm.

"I'm late."

"Aren't you always late?"

"Yeah, but based on my temperatures I'm pretty sure I know when I ovulated this month, and based on that day I should have started my period five days ago."

"Five?"

"Yeah."

"Did you test?"

"Both the doctor and Saadia said I should always wait at least a week, two would be better."

Adrian rubs my arm. "You've had a lot of false hopes before."

"But not since the surgery."

He looks back to the ceiling. "Yeah. Not since the surgery." He turns to me. "Do you really think?" His eyes widen. He looks so happy. So hopeful. Just how I feel.

"It's possible." I rise up on my forearms as well. "I've been doing everything, well, everything I should be doing, and my temperatures have stayed high—"

"That's good, right?"

"Very. And my breasts are tender. My sense of smell has been crazy."

"Signs?"

"Could be."

"Wow, Tracey."

I place my hand on my stomach and draw his toward it. "This could be our baby. Right now, we could be a real family."

He lies back and pulls his hand away. "We are a real family."

"Adrian."

"Trace, let's not get hopeful yet, okay? You're irregular. You've told me before, the temperatures aren't a science."

"But it could…"

"Yeah. It could. And it could not. I just…aren't you tired? I'm tired."

"Sure. Yeah."

"Roll over." I do, and Adrian wraps his arm around me, pulling me close. "Hope, but not too much. Okay?" He kisses the back of my neck. "And I'm holding my family. You're my family. Baby or no."

FRUSTRATION FILLS ME AS I try to fall asleep. Of course Adrian's right. The temperatures have fooled me before, but that doesn't mean they will this time. There has to be a time when they don't. I try to let hope fill me instead: it's there, but fear's there too.

All through the next day I hold on to hope, pushing out fear as best I can. It's a good day. During the next night, however, I wake with cramps, low and deep in my abdomen. They're not awful. They could be nothing. Indigestion. Maybe something I ate that didn't settle with me. They could be my uterus contracting in preparation to expand. I roll over and rub my torso, willing the pain to go away. When I wake up several hours later the pain is still there. Worse. It rips through me. In the bathroom I don't like what I see. But it's scant. It could be implantation bleeding. I always start with spotting. And so always, I wonder.

I keep holding on to hope, knowing at any moment it could fly away. Usually before spotting I'll have days of horrible cramps. That's lessened since the surgery. Whether it's the operation or the lifestyle changes, I don't know. After a quick breakfast I do my yoga and meditation. Throughout my visualizations I channel all the love I can muster within me, imagining the life that could be growing, willing it to hold on. Next on my to-do list is calling the school to arrange my return to teaching. Sally is thrilled. She lets me know another teacher is leaving on maternity, so she'll just move my substitute on to that position. The timing's perfect. We chat for a few minutes and I hang up the phone.

Again I imagine there's a life inside of me, will it to be a life. It could be, a little embryo struggling to fight through my body's inflammation and damage, struggling to stay alive. I visualize the meeting I'll have with Sally when it's my turn to tell her I'll be going on maternity leave.

The cramps linger throughout the day. Sometimes more insistent but never truly awful, never debilitating. I want an ibuprofen but I won't take one, not after learning the way they can mess with a woman's cycle. Every time I use the bathroom it's with held breath, hoping the trip doesn't reveal my fears. By the time night comes around again my body still hasn't given me a clear answer. When I slip into bed the cramping has been absent for several hours. Hope bubbles up. In the morning, it's dashed.

"Tracey." Adrian raps on the door. "Tracey, are you okay?"

"Just." I hold my breath in an effort to stifle my sobs, but they burst out again.

"Tracey. Open the door."

"Give me a minute." A moment later I step out of the bathroom, my tears contained, but my sadness still fresh. "You were right." I walk past him.

"Don't say it like that. It's not about being right. I just didn't want this. I didn't want your hopes so high and then—"

"You didn't think it was possible."

"That's not true."

My sadness starts to warp. I turn to him. "Maybe I was pregnant. Maybe it was that drink the other week."

"Trac—"

"It could have been."

"Don't be ridiculous. Women get drunk all the time before they find out they're pregnant. Didn't you just have one drink?"

"Yes, but—"

"Relax. It didn't happen this time but might another. Don't think of it as losing a baby. It wasn't a baby. You can't think of it like that."

"It could have been."

"It wasn't. Okay? Don't ever think of it as a baby. There's no point. Not even with a positive test. It's still a fetus. Until we hold it in our hands it's a fetus you could lose any moment."

"Adrian."

"You can't just fall in love with this possibility every month."

"I don't—"

"It'll kill you."

"Adrian."

"This wasn't a baby." His voice raises. "Okay? Even if we did conceive, it wasn't a baby, just the idea of a baby. Nothing more. We could go through this dozens more times. You can't get emotional with each one. You can't act like—"

"I can act however I want."

"Well, I can't." His hand raises then falls. "I can't." He walks past me and sinks to the couch.

"I need to hope. I have to hope."

"Then hope without me." He grabs a magazine, opens it, tosses it to the coffee table, then reaches for the remote.

"How can you say that? We're in this together."

"Are we?" He turns to me. "You say we're in this together, but you make all the decisions. You decide to upheave the way we live our lives. You decide no IUI, no IVF, no teaching—cutting our income in half."

I open my mouth to speak but he continues.

"You decide no adoption. You don't care what I think. You just decide everything. How is that being in this together?"

"It's—"

"It's not."

"I told you I'm going back to teaching."

"Yes. Because you decided. Not because of anything I said. I'd be happy to adopt. I'd love to adopt. A healthy baby. A baby who we know you won't miscarry. A baby who's old enough that she doesn't mysteriously die in the night."

He stares at me, his whole body tense. His gaze bores into mine. Christine. Of course this is about Christine, the child he lost years before he met me. How could I not have seen it? I step toward him. "Adrian, I'm sorry. I didn't think—"

"Yeah. You don't think." He stands and tosses the remote onto the couch behind him. "I'm going to the studio."

"You haven't eaten." I step after him on his way to the door. He deserves so much more than this, so much more than me.

"I'll eat there." He puts his hand on the knob. It rests there. He turns back to me. "I'm sorry, okay. I'm sorry. But this wasn't a loss. It wasn't anything. Just another cycle, another period."

"Ad—"

"It wasn't a baby, Tracey. You can't keep thinking of it as

a baby. We can't keep thinking of every late period as a baby."

"Okay." I will him to step away from the door, to hold me in his arms, to let me comfort him as he comforts me. He doesn't. Instead he leaves. I stand at the door with no idea who's hurting more. Does it matter?

I step back inside. The anger is still there, along with the sadness. He has no right to take his hurt and pain out on me. But do I have a right to force my hope onto him? Make him watch my heart ache?

This week's appointment with Saadia is in an hour. I step into the shower and make the water as hot as I can handle. I scrub vigorously, wishing I could wash away all my emotions, but when I turn off the water they're still there, clinging hard.

CHAPTER SIXTEEN

In the waiting room of Saadia's office my tension starts to dissipate. The treatments she gives are amazing, but it's also the feeling, the sense of security from being in her presence, of knowing she supports what I'm doing, knowing she gets it…cares.

For me it's more than a practitioner/patient relationship. But it's not for her. Not yet. My friends' hesitancy and Adrian's frustration comes back to me. They think I'm lying to her. The tension rises again. Am I ready to tell the truth?

When Saadia appears her smile is large. She waves me into her office and asks me to take a seat. "How were the past couple of weeks?"

I rub a hand over my opposite forearm. I'm here to talk about all that's going on, that's part of the treatment, but there's so much to tell: The fear of Christmas. The fear of Jenn's baby's birthday party. The fight with Adrian. Jojo— who I still haven't made time to talk with. My lost hope of a baby. My hope that I can one day tell Saadia who I am, who she is, without her refusing to ever see me again. "I started my period today."

"Today." She makes a note. "Later than your regular. Did you test before?"

"No."

"That's good."

"But I hoped."

She puts a hand on my thigh. "We always hope. That's

perfectly normal."

"Adrian doesn't think so." I tell Saadia about the fight this morning, about Christine.

"He's going through a lot too."

"I know. I realize that."

"But…"

"But I still need some support."

"That dinner out, finding a service to prepare meals, that sounds like support."

"It is." I know it is. "But he doesn't believe in what I'm doing."

"What you're doing?"

"The food. The meditation. You. He thinks it's just grasping at smoke."

"Why do you think he feels that way?"

"He hasn't researched it. Not much anyway, which is bizarre. He's a researcher. Yet not with this. He thinks we should be following the Western medicine route."

"And you don't?"

I rub my arm again, the question one that constantly bubbles inside me. "I'm scared."

"Because of the cost?"

"Because of everything. The cost. The pressure. The effects to my body. The incredibly low stats."

"What would be the worst thing that could happen if you did IVF and it didn't work?"

"That wouldn't be the worst thing?"

"You tell me."

I think a moment. "It working. That would be the worst. It working and then I lose the baby. Going through all that cost, all that fear, all that hope and expectation and having it realized, but only for a moment. That would be the worst."

"It's scary."

I laugh. "Of course." I rub my hands along my thighs. "Should we get started?"

"Not yet. You're tense, Tracey. Your body exudes it.

Let's work on that first. It will make the treatment better."

I smile. "You moonlight as a counsellor?"

She smiles back. "I'm not trying to counsel you. I'm just trying to talk."

I lean back in the chair. *Tell her. Are you going to tell her? Can you tell her?*

"The same thing, the worst thing, could happen with this. Your treatments, your life changes—like IVF, they don't guarantee a thing either."

"But if I get pregnant naturally, if my body heals enough for a pregnancy to occur, I figure that means a higher chance it will be healed enough to keep a pregnancy."

"Okay."

My brow furrows. "Do you agree?"

She grins. "I agree perfectly. That's why I do what I do. Could you pursue both options?"

"But why bother until—"

"It sounds as if it's something Adrian needs. There has been a lot of success with acupuncture and IVF combined. Many of my patients have chosen that route. Acupuncture and the right herbs can do wonders to maintain a pregnancy once it's started."

I hadn't thought about that. I remember reading an article about it once but didn't dig further. "So I could still come to you?"

"Absolutely."

Tell her. She's here. She cares. She wouldn't abandon you if you pursue a different school of medicine. Why would she abandon you if you told her you're her family? "I think Adrian would be even happier with adoption."

"That makes sense too. It's less scary for him." She taps a finger against her cheek. "But more scary for you, right?"

"You know what I've gone through. You know the years of feeling abandoned, of wondering who my parents were."

"It wouldn't have to be like that for your child. You could be open with him or her from the start. You could even have an open adoption."

"Even more emphasis that the child's not mine." I stop. "Not just for me. I mean for the child. And if I ever had another baby…I couldn't love an adopted child as much."

Saadia's smile is soft, patient. "You don't know that. The heart is capable of amazing things. Why put a barometer on love? Do you honestly doubt your adoptive mother loves you?"

"I know she loves me, but…" *It's not the same.* I want to scream. *Why can no one get it's not the same?* "You make it sound like it's easy. Simple. So does Adrian. But these things aren't easy or simple. Maybe the birth mother wouldn't want an open adoption. Maybe the father would be unknown. Maybe the child would live her whole life never knowing if the guy she's interested in is actually her brother, if her sister is the one taking her fare at the train station or giving her treatment in a clinic."

"Tracey, we can't live with—"

"Maybe she wants to tell her but she doesn't know how. Maybe she's spent the past months terrified if she does that sister will reject her, want nothing to do with her."

"Tracey?"

"And so she lies and lies and keeps lying and people think she's awful for it, but how do you just do that? How do you just look at someone and say," I stop, take a breath, "I'm your sister."

Saadia stands. She steps back. "Is this a joke?" Her eyes widen. Her mouth opens. She holds her palm out in front of her, as if trying to push my words away.

"No." I stand, and Saadia takes another step back. "I'm sorry. I know this is awful to just blurt out. I just…"

"That girl…ten years ago…but—" She takes two more steps back, bumps into her desk. "So there were others. He said there were no others." She lowers her head. Her chest caves in as she rests her hands on her hips. Her voice wavers. "He promised my mother. He promised us." Her head snaps up, her eyes intense yet glassy. "Are you sure? How do you know?"

"My mother told me. She said—"

"She could be lying."

"She's not lying."

"How do you know? She slept with a married man."

My voice sharpens. "She was seventeen. She was seventeen and when she told your father he had nothing to do with her. He didn't help at all. He abandoned her. Abandoned me."

Saadia sinks to her desk chair and looks at me through moist lashes. "She was seventeen and you're…" she raises her hand to her throat. "Oh, God. Lydia."

I step forward. "You knew."

"No. No. Of course not. I just—" Her expression collapses. "That poor girl."

"Then how did you—"

"Lydia and I were friends. Not super close friends but our fathers worked together. When her mother died my mother felt bad for them. She started inviting them over for dinner. We had a pool. When the weather was good Lydia would come over to go swimming. My father was always really nice to her. He was nice to all of my friends but—" Saadia brings her hand back to her throat and rubs it. "When Lydia got pregnant she stopped coming around. She stopped even talking to me. She wouldn't tell anyone who the father was. My mother was worried, but Lydia wouldn't return her calls." Saadia looks up and away. "Did he…was it…" She takes a breath. "Did he rape her?"

The thought had never occurred to me. Not since meeting Lydia at least, not since hearing her story. But would she have told me? A slight shiver runs through me. "She didn't say that. She…it seemed like it was something of a relationship anyway…until it wasn't."

Saadia's voice is a growl. "It was practically statutory rape anyway." She brings her gaze back to me. "Why didn't you tell me?"

"I didn't know—"

"You just waltz in here, making a fool of me. All this time, any day you could have told me."

"I wanted to get to know you."

"You could have gone to any naturopath. Any one."

"I know, but—"

Tears stream down her face. "Just go, please."

"But—"

"Don't pay. Just go."

"Saadia, I'm sorry, I—"

"Tracey, please."

I dash out of the office and down the hall, my pulse racing. I make a direct line through the waiting room and toward the door. "Ms. Sampson!" the receptionist calls. "You forgot to—" I push open the door. Outside the cold air blasts me. I suck it in, feeling like a fool, like the deceitful, uncaring person everyone thinks I am. I yell. A woman with her young daughter jumps and pulls the child away. That's me, a deceitful, uncaring person who terrifies a mother and her young child. This time my moan is softer. In the car I bang the steering wheel. What was I supposed to do? This could have been her reaction the first visit, the second. Maybe I never should have told her at all. Maybe I never should have stepped into her office. But I don't regret it. She's my sister. She may never see me again, but at least she knows. She knows, and I've lost arguably the best thing that's happened for my fertility. Should I even keep doing this? Any of it. Would it be better to give up? Better for me, for Adrian? My gut wrenches. I want a big vat of chocolate caramel crunch ice cream so bad it hurts. I wrack my brain for endo-healthy recipes that may suffice but can't think of even one. I blast the music and drive.

CHAPTER SEVENTEEN

When I arrive home several hours later, with almost a whole tank of gas depleted, Adrian stands to greet me. His expression is already soft, but at first sight of me his arms open. I step into them. His voice is muffled against my hair. "I'm sorry."

I tilt my head up. "No, I'm sorry." We hold each other tight.

"This is harder than I thought it would be."

"For me too."

"And Christine..." his voice catches.

"I know." I rest my head on his chest. "I want you to have everything you want. I want you to be happy."

"Tracey."

"You deserve more than this. More than me."

He grasps my shoulders. "I want you. If I'm with you I'll be happy. We don't need a baby to make us happy."

I pull away. "But what if we do? You don't know. You say this now, but in ten years, twenty, thirty? You can't predict the future." I turn from him, wishing I could turn from all of this. "I'm so sorry."

Only the sound of our breath fills the room. "Do you think I blame you?"

"How could you not?"

"Trace." Adrian turns me around.

"I'm broken. I let you fall in love with a broken woman."

"You have a disease that affects your fertility. You're not

your fertility. You're not broken."

"It feels like it."

"Feelings aren't always truth."

"It's not just the disease. I'm broken in other ways too."

"And I'm not?"

"You don't get it." I push away from him. "I'm so angry so much of the time. I try not to be but then the rage just flows through me. Rage at my own body. It's betraying me. I try to hide it, day after day." My shoulders slump. "And I'm tired. Life, existence, feels so hard. Exhausting."

He steps forward.

"Sometimes I think I'm cursed."

He takes my hands. "Then we'll be cursed together."

"Adrian."

"Your pain will be my pain. Your joy my joy."

I step back. I couldn't love him more if I tried. "I told Saadia today."

"You told—"

"That I'm her sister."

"And how did it go?"

"Not well."

He brings his hand to my head and smooths my hair. "Sounds like we both had a rough day."

I laugh.

"There are probably going to be a lot more."

I nod against his chest.

"But we'll do our best to get through this, right?"

"Yeah."

"Together?"

"Together."

༄

OVER THE NEXT FEW DAYS I can't get Saadia out of my head. I want to call her, though I don't have a direct line.

She has mine. I check my phone regularly, just in case. Every time my email pings I check that as well. She could have gotten my address from the receptionist. Thoughts of my birth father bombard my mind. Has Saadia confronted him? Is he furious? Does he deny it? If I walked right up to him, would he still deny me? After five days of this I can't take it anymore. I won't burst in on Saadia again. But her father? Our father? He's the one who created this mess. I hesitate. Me, he's the one who created me. It's time he acknowledges it. Jennifer's party is in three hours. That doesn't give me a lot of time, but it's enough.

I've stood at the door to my father's building more times than I can count. I know the way the light hits the glass as people push through. I know the scent and the taste of buttermilk scones at the lobby's café. I've sat and watched the multitudes enter and exit. I've sipped hot apple cider and cool mint tea as I scanned the faces, looking for him. But I've never gone past the lobby, never stepped into the elevator. Today I do. Today I step in and ride to the ninth floor. I expect a little more time, to pace the hallways, find the correct door, but the elevator opens directly in front of *Medina Clarke Law.*

The waiting room is stylish and modern. It has an angular, sharp feel to it, like a waiting room I'd expect from a high profile TV set. Several people sit flipping through magazines or swiping the screens of their smartphones and tablets. This is a busy law office. What was I thinking? That I could waltz in and expect to see him? I should have made an appointment, given a false name and—

"Can I help you?"

I turn to the receptionist. "Sorry." I put on a smile. "Admiring the design."

"It's nice, isn't it?" The receptionist waves me over. "Do you have an appointment?"

"Oh no," I keep my smile on, "just stopping in to, uh…see my uncle."

"Your—"

"Sebastien Medina. He's not expecting me? Saadia was supposed to let him know I was coming by today."

The receptionist clicks a few buttons on her mouse then looks to a notepad on her desk. "No, no message."

"Oh, huh." I tap my fingers on the counter. "That's weird. Saadia's usually so good about these things. Hmm, well, I suppose I could wait a few minutes." I give the receptionist my best smile. "Please tell him I'm here, Lydia's daughter, and I'll stay until he's ready to see me."

The woman looks at me curiously but then smiles back. "All right. Have a seat and I'll let him know."

About fifteen minutes later a disgruntled looking man and woman exit the doors leading to a hallway. Several minutes after that I'm told Sebastien will see me now. The receptionist tells me where to find his office, and I'm on my way. My legs shake as I walk down the richly carpeted hall. I stand staring when I reach the door with his name on it. It's slightly ajar. I debate knocking but push my way through.

The man staring out the window whips around the moment I step into the room. It's the man I looked up on the computer for the first time over a year ago, the man whose picture I've looked at dozens of times since, only he's about fifteen years older than any picture I saw. He stands tall, with the posture of a much younger man, but it's clear he's forcing that posture, that the muscles that would have held his limbs so easily in the past don't so easily anymore.

"The nerve." He spits the word. A vein in his temple bulges. "Forcing your way in here, using my daughter's name to lie your way to see me."

I stare at him, my lips firmly closed, my arms hanging loosely at my sides. A quiet rage pulses through me. "I'm your daughter too."

When the door opened to reveal my mother for the first time, I didn't know what to expect or what I wanted. The moment was full of joy and fear and uncertainty. Today I know exactly what I want, this man to acknowledge his role in my creation and the fact that he should have done more. I don't need anything else from him. He is not my father. He's nothing more than a careless sperm donor.

He takes three strides across the room and stops when he's just short of an arm's length from me. "Look at you. You look exactly like her." He hesitates. His voice shakes. For a moment I expect tears, I almost think he's going to take back his words, embrace me, and then that moment disappears. Anger covers him. "She started this, waltzing into my house and putting on that skimpy little bikini, looking all innocent and sad and in need of affection." He stops, his gaze to the floor. "The slut. The loose little slut. She started it all, made me weak for the slew of smooth-skinned women who came after her, with their tight tops and their short shorts." He glares at me, a look of disgust covering his features, as if I'm the one to blame. "I never touched another woman before her."

I keep my gaze level.

"She was probably giving it around all over the place." He scoffs. It's a pathetic sound. "I don't see an ounce of me in you." His fists ball. He turns from me, steps to his desk, and slams a hand down before turning back. "What do you want, anyway? Money? That's what she wanted. Well you're not getting a dime without a paternity test. Not a dime."

My voice is even but my body trembles. "I don't want your money."

"Then what? What is it?" He rubs a hand through his thinning hair. "Why did you have to upset Saadia?" His voice rumbles, catches—it's not all anger anymore. He's aching, and I almost feel sorry for him. "We were just starting to get along again. Do you have any idea how long it took after…after…"

I keep my stance. "I wanted to see you, to look at you, and I wanted you to see me."

"And Saadia? You know she went and told her mother.

Her brothers." His voice cracks. "If this gets out." He looks away from me. "I have a reputation to uphold. You'll ruin everything."

"I'm not ruining a thing." My voice remains firm, but inside I waver. I straighten my spine, push back my shoulders. *This is not my father. He doesn't matter.* "You did this."

"I didn't give your mother anything she didn't want. She practically lured—"

"Shut up."

"Excuse—"

"Shut up." I step forward. "I'm glad you didn't lift a finger to help her. I'm glad you didn't do the right thing. It means I didn't have to spend my whole life connected to you."

He laughs, a strained, rumbling sound. "You wouldn't have anyway. She gave you up, didn't she? That's what Saadia said. She didn't want you either."

His words hit like a punch. "She had to. She couldn't—"

"Don't defend her. If she had wanted you, she would have kept you."

My jaw quivers. Words. Just words. Words I've thought hundreds of times. Words that have kept me up nights. Hearing them from him though… My voice trembles. "If she'd had support."

"You think that would have made a difference? She didn't want you."

"She could have aborted—"

"She was too cowardly for that. That's all. She didn't want you. You were a mistake. An accident. Brought on by a stupid little girl who couldn't even remember to take her daily pill. You shouldn't even exist."

My eyes blur. I blink back tears.

"Get out of here, all right? Leave me alone. Leave my family alone. We don't want you." He brushes past me and to the door. I stay frozen. His hand lands on my shoulder as he whips me around. Our gazes connect. He pauses. "God, you look like her." He blinks. "Get out of here. Please. Go." He opens the door and pushes me forward. I shuffle over the threshold as the door shuts behind me, take several steps, then sink to the floor, weak and wounded, like a child. Something hard slams against the wall behind me. I spasm from the shock.

My phone vibrates. Adrian: *Sorry, darling. Running a bit late. Should I just meet you at the party?* I sink my head into my hands and pull my knees to my chest. My body trembles. The sound of footsteps makes its way up the hall. A figure crouches beside me. Her hands rest on my shoulders. This all feels so familiar, only this time I'm not crying. I'm furious. I lift my head to see a middle-aged woman in a business suit smiling at me. She guides me to my feet. "Divorce is hard, sweetie, but you'll get through it. You'll find love again." I let her lead me out of the office. At the door she stops. "You need to call a cab or—"

"No." I pull out the strongest smile I can muster. It's not much. "Thank you, I'm fine."

In the elevator I want to scream, to pound the walls. Of course I don't. I have a party to get to, friends to see, happiness to embrace. That man is not my father. He, and anything he says, means nothing.

CHAPTER EIGHTEEN

Once I'm outside the Tower I text Adrian back: *I'm downtown without my car. Can you pick me up? Swing by home to grab the present. We'll be late together.*

He agrees. I don't tell him where I am. That would prompt too many questions I'm not ready to answer. Instead, I tell him I'm at a store I often visit, which is about a ten minute walk up the road. Twenty minutes later, as the year's first snowflakes fall from the sky, Adrian pulls to the curb.

I slip into the seat and Adrian leans in for a kiss. "How was your day?"

"Great."

"Buy anything?"

"Not today."

"Think it'll stay?" He gestures to the snow.

"Who knows?"

I buckle my seatbelt as Adrian pulls back into traffic. He glances over. "You all right?"

I could tell him about Sebastien, but what's there to tell? It doesn't matter. None of it matters. "Just tired." I offer a smile, my father's face and words pulsing through my mind. "How was your day?"

"Amazing, actually." He grins. "One of the young women who is still in the trade agreed to speak with us on camera today. She wants out. We connected her to a shelter who helps with the transition phase. This won't just be a great story, it'll change lives."

"That's great." I glance out the window, willing myself to let go of this thick sluggish pain that seems to ooze through me. My father doesn't mean anything. And this party doesn't mean anything. Nothing bad anyway. Other people's joys do not detract from mine.

"And not even just the life of girls like this one, but women who see it too, and maybe even more support and funding for programs and shelters that—"

My chest tightens as we near Jennifer and Rajeev's place. This is ridiculous. Ridiculous. I need to focus on what Adrian's telling me, his excitement, on the joy of the babies I'm about to see. And Autumn. Autumn flew home in time for the party and the holidays. Seeing her will be wonderful.

My phone buzzes. Jojo. *What's the address again?* She's only met Jennifer a handful of times, but Neveah's less than a year older than Jennifer's daughter, so Jenn told me to invite Jojo and the kids along. And of course, despite ample warning, she's texting me after the party has already begun to ask for the address. I stifle a groan and type it in then put my phone on silent. I don't want to be interrupted during the party.

When we step inside Jennifer and Rajeev's, warmth engulfs us. The air smells of chocolate and vanilla. Balloons and posters cover the foyer walls. Clearly, Jennifer went for a dinosaur theme. Friendly looking Brontosaurus', T-Rex's, and an array of other dinosaurs surround us. When I set Mary's present on the gift table, I'm relieved to see I wasn't the only one who didn't know about the dinosaur theme. Here, Dora, Disney Princesses, and an assortment of colourfully wrapped boxes sit among the dinosaur covered gifts.

Farther in, we run into what must be all of Autumn and Jennifer's relatives, including Jennifer's father and his family, whom I've never met, as well as a number of Jennifer's friends, about eight kids, and the children's parents. The adults outnumber the kids almost three to one and it's a tight fit in this cozy bungalow. No one seems to mind though. Everywhere I turn faces smile at me, and so, of course, I smile right back.

"Adrian." Eloise and her boyfriend approach us. Eloise reaches her arms out and draws Adrian into a hug before introducing the men. "Adrian, this is Arthur. Arthur, Adrian."

"Can't believe we're just meeting." Adrian pumps Arthur's hand.

"It's been so long since I've seen you," says Eloise. "That's part of it. Has Tracey been keeping you locked up or something?"

Adrian gives a laugh, always at ease when he needs to be. "Been really busy with work."

"The sex trafficking feature?" Eloise shakes her head. "It must be rough, being so close to that."

I excuse myself to slip away in search of Autumn. She sits in an armchair in the living room with the birthday girl on her lap. "Having fun?" From behind, I give Autumn's shoulder a squeeze and kiss her cheek, just above the long scar that travels across it, a memento of the worst day of her life.

"She's so big!" Autumn's eyes go wide. "It's only been five months but she's like another child entirely."

I slip into the fold-out chair beside Autumn. "Did she remember you?"

Autumn shakes her head, her gaze focused on the child's big brown eyes. "I don't think so, but it doesn't matter. She's so friendly." Mary notices me and reaches out. "See." Autumn grins. "You want to hold her?"

Before I have a chance to answer, Autumn places Mary in my arms. "Is she talking?" I ask.

"Lots. When she wants to. Say 'hi', Mary."

"Hi, Meywee." The little girl giggles. "Down."

I release her and Mary darts through the room. "How've you been?" Autumn leans over to give me a better hug. "I wish I could have been here. I know you've been through a lot."

"I'm okay." I turn my gaze from her as Lori chases Trisa, now almost four, through the room.

"Children everywhere, huh?" Autumn follows Trisa with her gaze.

"Yep. It's wonderful."

Autumn looks back to me. "Absolutely. It is." She points to the window. "And today's the first snow. Always one of my favourite days of the year."

"You miss it in England?"

"Sometimes." Autumn shifts so she has a better view of the window. "I don't miss the shovelling or driving down icy streets."

"Who would? Is Jakob coming?"

"Not this trip."

"A whole month away?"

"We'll survive." Autumn grins. "It'll be rough, but we'll survive. I was only here for two weeks in the summer, so I wanted some more solid time this trip. Better bang for my buck too."

"Autumn!" Allison weaves her way through the other party guests and plops down in the arm chair, right on Autumn's lap.

"Oh, how I've missed you!" She squeezes Autumn, who squeezes right back. Allison feels Autumn's biceps. "All right, all right, still decent definition. Flex for me." Autumn obliges. "Not as toned as you'd be if *we* were still working out together, but it'll suffice." Allison slips off of Autumn's lap and onto the folding chair on the opposite side of her. "Business is booming, huh? We're both so fab."

I rise from my chair, leaving Autumn and Allison to talk fitness, and search for Jenn. I've been here almost fifteen minutes and have yet to greet the host. The kitchen is crowded with people, Jenn included. She waves and wiggles her way out of the throng. "Tracey, hi! Glad you could make it." She looks overwhelmed, but happy.

"Thank you for the invite."

"It's a mad house, but I'm sure we'll have fun."

"Absolutely. How's the next book?"

"Coming." She laughs. "Slowly. Mary just doesn't get it. I'll tell her Mommy needs to work and she thinks that means, 'Mommy needs to play with you, so distract her mercilessly until she will.' Oh, for the good old days of personal freedom."

"Must be rough."

"Oh no," Jenn's face falls, "I didn't mean…I'm thankful, of course I'm so thankful to have her. I would never trade her for anything or…I know how lucky I am. I know—"

"It's okay." I tense at her words. Of course she wouldn't trade Mary. I'd never think it. But she fears she's not being appreciative enough, fears in front of me, the barren woman, she's spoken too freely.

A woman I've seen a couple of times, but can't recall the name of, walks up beside us with a baby on her hip. "Oh, Tammy, hi!" Jenn turns to me. "Tracey, have you met Tammy? She's one of my oldest friends."

"I believe so."

"At a dinner a few years ago." Tammy's smile is wide and welcoming. "I'm sure of it."

"Yeah."

Jenn gets called away, so Tammy and I chat for a few minutes. "Do you know Jenn well?" asks Tammy.

"Not too well." A child runs past us, howling like a banshee. A second child is fast in pursuit.

"Today's a hard day for her." Tammy looks to the living room where Jenn laughs with another woman. "She's hiding it well."

"Sorry?"

"Her mom, did you know about Jenn's mom?"

"Oh, yes." I glance at Jenn then draw my gaze back to Tammy and her little one. "She passed away a few years ago?"

"Jenn took it really hard. She's doing a lot better. So much better. She grew a lot from the experience."

I nod. I'd only met Jennifer a few times before her mother's death and she'd been quiet, aloof, I could never decide whether she was a snob or painfully shy behind the extra pounds she seemed to hide behind. What the party has to do with her mother's death, or why Tammy is telling me this, though, I have no idea.

"Family events are always hard. I wish her mom could see her now, see the life Jenn's made for herself, the woman she's become." Tammy looks back at me. "Did you know Cynthia?"

"No, not at all."

"She was a special lady. Jenn didn't always see it then. She does now. She—" Tammy's voice cracks, as if she's about to tear up. "Sorry, I…just days like this," she lets out a somewhat forced though bubbly laugh, "and the hormones. I'm sure they're still raging through me." As if on cue, her baby starts wailing. "Excuse me."

Tammy walks away, leaving me feeling like I've been punched in the gut. There are worse things than my problems and pains. To have your mother die, to live each day wishing you'd told her when you could how much you loved her and to know nothing can change that…here I was envying Jenn, but she has her sorrows too. I close my eyes for the slightest moment. *Focus on joy. Send love and happiness out into the world, to everyone around you.* My mantras for the week. How easily I forget them. When I open my eyes Adrian is weaving his way toward me.

He cups my elbow. "You all right, hon?"

"Yes. Why?"

"You looked…" He guides me back toward the living

room. "Never mind. They're about to start a game with the kids. Let's watch."

⁕

AFTER THE FIRST ROUND of games, a taxi pulls up outside the house. Jojo and her children step out, almost forty-five minutes late. "Look." I nudge Adrian.

He turns. "That's a long drive. Why'd she take a cab?"

"I don't know." I weave my way out of the overcrowded living room and make my way to the door. I open it as Jojo approaches the top step. She holds Neveah with one hand and a huge bag with the other.

"I wanted to ring the bell." Reggie stomps his foot.

"Oh, get over yourself." Jojo looks up from her son. "Hey, Sis!"

"Hi."

Neveah pulls away from Jojo's hand and lifts her arms to me. I receive a slobbery kiss as the twins push past me.

"Boots!" Jojo hollers as she closes the door. The twins stop long enough to kick off their wet boots.

"They're so jazzed 'cause of the snow. I could hardly keep them seated in the cab. They had their faces pressed to the window. Was I like that?"

"Pretty much."

"A kid thing, I guess." She pulls a present out of her bag and sets it on the gift table. "For Mary. And," she grins, "for the adults." She passes me a litre and a half bottle of wine.

"Okay." After kicking off her own boots, Jojo leans in for a hug. Her smile is the biggest I've seen it in ages. I return the hug. "You seem pretty jazzed yourself."

"Why not? It's a good day." She laughs. Her breath is minty fresh. "Maybe it's the snow!"

"Why'd you take a cab?"

She shrugs as she undoes her coat. "Still haven't gotten

my winter tires. Stupid, I know. It's late December. But I was safe this long."

"Well," I guide her to the den, where all the coats lay on a love seat, "I guess the cab was a good idea then."

"Absolutely."

Jojo's gait is unsteady as she walks toward the noise coming from the living room. She stumbles over some toys in the hall, but anyone could. I set the wine on the kitchen counter. Jojo smiles beside me. "Should we crack that open?"

"I don't think anyone's drinking."

"Yet." Jojo searches several top drawers. She holds up a wine opener. "No one's drinking yet."

Autumn steps into the room. "Jojo!" She crosses the width of the kitchen in several quick strides. "How are you? I don't think I've seen you since the wedding."

"Probably not." Jojo's smile is easy. "Care for some vino?"

"I'm good." Autumn fills her glass with punch. "I saw those twins of yours. They're so big."

"Tyrants." Jojo laughs. "Absolute tyrants. Know where the wine glasses are? Think Jenn would mind, or should I use one of the party cups?"

Autumn points to a cupboard behind Jojo. "And Neveah, what a beauty."

Jojo reaches for a glass. "My little slice of heaven. I just wish she'd act like as much of an angel as she looks." Jojo pours a glass three quarters full. "Trace?"

"I'm good."

"Right. Your new rules."

"Rules?" asks Autumn.

I eye Jojo's glass, which in two sips is at the halfway mark. "Just trying to be more healthy."

A chorus of squeals erupts from the living room. "Shall we?" Jojo tilts her body toward the noise. Autumn and I follow.

The children crowd and jump around a clown as he shapes odd looking balloon animals. I lean against a wall and take in the mayhem. Adrian settles beside me. "A clown, huh? Jenn really went all out." He winks at me. "I wonder how much of this Mary will even remember?"

"Maybe none." I wrap my arms around my middle. I remember plenty from her age, though that's a rarity. "But the happiness will shape her. That means something."

Adrian weaves his hand behind my back. "I guess."

"Besides, it's Jenn's dad. Not a big expense."

"Oh yeah?" Adrian seems to examine the clown. "Have I met him?"

"Probably not, unless it was earlier today."

"This is fun." He squeezes my side. "It's good to get out. To laugh."

"Absolutely." I link my hand in his. He seems so at ease. My stomach clenches. He's not looking at me but at the children. And he looks so happy. How does he do it? And how long will it last? How many more years can he look at other people's joy and not hate me because it isn't his?

I look to the kids. Lulu twirls with Trisa and another little girl, both half her height. I look again to Adrian, clearly enjoying the scene. I try to follow his gaze, but it could be any number of things making him chuckle.

"What first?" Rajeev tosses Mary into the air and catches her. She clings onto his neck and squeals with delight. "Presents or Cake?"

"Cake!" a chorus of kids holler.

"Oh, no, no." Jenn wraps an arm around her family. "Presents first."

"But—"

She cuts Rajeev off. "The kids will be covered in icing, which will get on the presents."

"Presents!" Rajeev shouts. He bounces Mary up and down, getting her and the other kids excited at the prospect.

Will Adrian be such a good dad? Neveah races by and he

clothesline's her up into his arms. More squeals. More laughter. Of course he will. Adrian was made to be a parent. An all too familiar tightness rises in my throat. Unlike me. *You're healing yourself. Soon. Have patience.* My mind speaks the words but my heart doesn't want to listen. After Mary opens several presents, I make my way back to the kitchen. Jojo is refilling her wine glass.

"Another?"

She whips her head around. "I'm not driving." She moves to walk past me but I block her way. "God, Tracey. Lighten up. It's a party."

"A party for a two-year-old and no one else is drinking."

"Jenn's step-mother had some, and so did one of her girlfriends, the one with the red headed kid."

"And how many have you had?"

"This is my second. Scout's honour." She raises her hand in a mock salute.

"And before you got here?"

She pushes past me. "Tracey, relax."

"Jojo, deserve your kids."

"What?" Jojo whips around. "You think because I have a drink every now and then I don't deserve my kids?"

"Who brings wine to a toddler's birthday party?"

"I do, Tracey. Apparently. You have a problem with that?"

"I have a problem with you drinking so much you don't feel safe to drive when you're supposed to be watching your children."

"I didn't change my tires. I told you."

"Stop lying."

"I'm not."

"So you could drive right now?"

She stares at me. "I knew I wouldn't be driving so—"

"It started snowing just as you texted."

"Ever heard of a weather forecast?"

I yank the wine glass out of her hand. The drink splashes

across her sleeve.

She thrusts me against the wall. "Mind. Your. Own. Business. I take care of my kids."

"Hardly."

"Tracey, watch it." She releases the pressure on my chest but keeps her hand there. "Just because you don't get to have kids doesn't mean you can judge everyone who does. It's not my fault you're barren."

I gasp. "I'm not—"

"My kids are fine, okay. Fine. They're fed. They get to school. I don't need you—"

"And if you die? If you drive drunk and—"

"I didn't. I'm not."

"Mom said—"

"Mom's a worse worrier than you."

"Well, you're—"

She drops her hand. "Get over yourself. You're not the only one who has problems and you have no right to put your head into other people's business."

"You're my sister."

"But I'm not, right? If I were, if you really believed that, we wouldn't be having this conversation because you'd have your own child to look after, your adopted child. But you can't do that, can you, because that child wouldn't be your family," she mocks the words, "which means I'm not your family either. So don't worry about me. I'm not your concern."

"Jo—"

"Back off." She moves to the living room. I stay in the kitchen, my back against the wall, for I don't know how long. Autumn's mom walks in to put candles on the cake. When it's done, she turns and lets out a little yelp. "Tracey!"

"Hi."

"Darling, you scared me half to death. Are you all right?"

"Fine, Mrs. Caparelli."

"Okay then." She rubs her hands on her hips. "Have you

seen a lighter anywhere?"

I help her find the lighter and light the candles. The smell of smoke overpowers the sweet icing. As we light the final candle, Jenn enters the room. "You ready?" Her smile is broad. She steps to the cake. "Oh, it's perfect!" She whisks it off of the counter and is gone. Almost immediately a chorus of 'Happy Birthday' sounds. I join in the singing, just a step or two behind Jenn. My hands shake. Was I wrong to say those things to Jojo? She shouldn't be drinking around her kids. At least not that much. But is it too much? As far as I know, actually know, that was only her second. And she is my sister…more than Sebastien's my father. Sebastien. My stomach clenches. Why am I thinking of him? I should never think of him. He doesn't matter.

I try to draw my attention to the present. Mary receives her piece of cake. She smashes her hand into it and pushes the creamy mess into her mouth. It smears all over her face. Cameras flash. Autumn and Jenn's step-sister work as a team to cut the rest of the slices and distribute them around the room. I decline, just as I've declined everything offered to me today. Tammy's baby starts fussing. She coos at her and allows the baby to nurse. It looks so perfect. So natural. So right. *Believe, Tracey. Believe. With belief, there is no need for envy.*

No need. But envy washes over me anyway. If I weren't barren, like Jojo said, I'd be here with my own baby by now. If I'd actually been pregnant that day I stood in the pharmacy, terrified, I'd have a child just a few weeks younger than Mary. My mind travels back to that day, standing in front of a shelf full of pregnancy tests, fearing they'd tell me a life was inside of me… What an idiot I was.

When the cake has been served, something as close to quiet as is possible with this many children present settles over the room. Most of my friends sit in a corner. Allison waves me over. I go with a smile. The only spot open is one directly between Tammy and Autumn. I sit, keeping my gaze away from the baby and onto the animated face of Allison as she tells a story about a client she had earlier this week. When she finishes, Tammy asks Autumn how things are in England.

"Wonderful." Autumn seems to glow. "Great. The business is making more than it's costing, which is a huge plus."

"Including your salary?"

"A modest one."

"And with…what's his name? Jakob." Tammy laughs quietly, the baby in her arms now asleep. "Sorry, I'm sure everyone else is caught up, but are things going well?"

"Really well." Autumn's smile is shy. Oddly shy.

"Incredibly well." Jennifer walks into the little cluster and nudges Autumn's arm.

"I'm just starting to tell people."

My breath catches. Autumn's finger is empty, which means—

"We're pregnant."

The halted breath is sucked out of me.

"We weren't trying or anything. It just kind of happened. I don't know…a pill taken too early or too late. Or…" She looks at me. "Tracey, I hope—"

"No, no." I wave my hand. *Be happy. Keep smiling. Be happy. Be—* "So fertile. You weren't even trying. A mistimed pill. Wow." I stop. My voice breaks. "I mean, wonderful."

The faces around me stare.

I jump up, my hand to my mouth. "I'm sorry, I… Autumn." If there were a dark hole in the floor I'd gladly sink into it. "Congratulations." My voice still wavers. I scan the room in search of an escape. My gaze catches Adrian's. He rises from the group of kids around him. I turn my head. The way to the front door is practically gridlocked but I weave my way through, stepping over children and pushing past adults. Before I've escaped I hear Eloise's voice, probably directed at Adrian, "Let us."

And before I've found my jacket amid the piles of coats in the den, there she is. "Trace."

I turn. Autumn stands beside her. "I'm so sorry. Really. I don't know where that came from." I push out the littlest of laughs, but I want to scream. I know exactly where it came from, and it's still raging inside of me. "I'm so happy for you, Autumn. For you both."

Eloise steps toward me. Her hand rests on my shoulder. "Life doesn't follow the patterns we hope or expect it to, and sometimes that hurts. It really hurts. But it can also reveal amazing joy. You just have to be patient."

"That a quote or something?" I laugh again. "Listen, I really just—" my gaze darts between them, desperate. "Can you just give me some time? I just need a minute."

"No." Autumn steps closer. "We can't. I know you're hurting, but that doesn't give you the right—"

"I'm sorry, okay? I didn't mean it. I'm sor—"

"I was going to say that doesn't give you the right to treat yourself like this, to—"

"I'm not. It was just, uh…I don't know. I didn't mean it."

"You did."

"Look."

"No, you look." Eloise grips my shoulder tighter. "Look at me. My life is entirely different from the one I thought I'd be living. The life I thought I wanted cost me a man I loved. Really loved. Look at Autumn. She never would have, she never thought—" Eloise falters.

Autumn steps in. "Matt dying was the worst thing that could have happened. I thought it meant my life was over. But it wasn't. Is the pain gone? No. But the joy I feel now, I wouldn't trade it. And no matter what comes of all this, whether you get to raise your own child or someone else's or no child at all, your life will have joy. I know it."

"Of course." I smile, waving off their words. "I know. I don't need a lecture. Some days are harder than others but

I'm fine, really. Overall, I'm great."

"You haven't been fine for a whi—"

"I'm fine."

Adrian steps into the room. "Tracey?"

I grab my jacket. "I need to leave."

"Trace?"

"Now. I need to leave now."

I push past all three of them and pull on my boots. "Apologize to Jennifer for me." With my arms only half into my coat I yank open the door and step into the blowing cold. Yet again, I'm running away. I race down the driveway and up the street. I scramble in my purse for the keys then see them in my mind's eye on the hook by our front door. I walked to the Tower. Right. I brace my hands on the side of the door, the cold metal a shock, but I don't care. Sobs shake through my body, erupting from somewhere so deep within it frightens me. Like a geyser they shoot out of me. Stronger. Scarier. My body trembles. My head pounds. Still the sobs keep coming, they're accompanied with a wail that seems inhuman. I sense Adrian beside me. I'm ridiculous. This is ridiculous. Intolerable. I'm happy for Autumn. Happy. She's one of my best friends and she, maybe more than anyone I know, deserves all the joy in the world.

Adrian's hand lands on my back. It smooths a circle, the repetitive motion doing nothing to ease this shredding ache. "Shh," he whispers. "Shh."

My head snaps up, the sobs silenced. "Shh?"

"I'm just—"

"You're just telling me to be quiet. You're telling me to, 'shh'."

He stares at me. Energy seems to vibrate between us. I grab the keys from his hand. "I need to be alone. See you at home."

"Trace."

"Someone will drive you." I yank open the car door. He doesn't try to stop me. He could, of course, but he just watches. The sobs don't come back but the tears continue. The tears, combined with the snowflakes falling heavily down, blur my vision to the point where I know I'm a danger. I pull to the side of the road, kill the engine, and sit as the car grows steadily colder, as the throbbing in my head numbs the throbbing of my heart. When my body starts to shake, not from anger or sadness but from the cold, I turn the car back on and make my way home. As I walk to the door I can't tell which emotion is strongest: the sorrow, the intense frustration, or the embarrassment that travels through every vein of my being.

My chest feels weighted as I push open our door. I know Adrian is waiting for me. He always waits for me. Before I've even taken off my jacket or shoes he appears before me.

"Tracey, I'm done. We can't go on like this."

CHAPTER NINETEEN

"Done?" I sink against the wall. Adrian just told me he's done. With me? With us? With everything? Not possible. "What do you mean?"

"I mean this is wrong. It's crazy. Do you even need me anymore?"

"Adrian."

"You're married to your desire to get pregnant, not to me."

"I'm not." I stand up straight. "What about getting through this together? What about being happy with me?"

"Yeah. What about it?"

My expression falls. What is he saying?

He groans. "Let's sit."

I pull off my boots and jacket and follow him to the living room. He perches on the couch and pats the spot beside him. Anger starts bubbling within me. So I had one blow-up? So what? I sit on the chair opposite him. "Are you giving up on me?"

"No." He rests a hand on his leg, sinks his head into it. "I feel like you're the one giving up on us and, more importantly, on you. Eloise and Autumn told me what you said. The Tracey I know would never say that."

"It was—"

"Stop." He raises a hand. "It was everything you're doing. Your obsession. It's like you think about nothing else."

"I don't."

"What was I talking about in the car today, on the drive to Jennifer's?"

"Your story."

"What about my story?"

I search for the answer but it isn't there. I know what I was thinking about as he talked: My father. My fear of being around a bunch of fertile women and the proof they held in their arms. I remember Adrian's excitement but nothing more. I could lie, make up something, but what's the point? "I don't know."

"Exactly. All fertility all the time."

"It's not." My father, should I tell him about—

"I need more. I need my wife. I need my wife more than I need a child, and I would like to believe she needs me more too."

"I'm doing this for both of us. I want to give you—"

"We have other options, Tracey. Other ways. The way you're choosing, it seems like you're giving up on life. Everything you're doing, nothing's wrong with any of it, but the way you're doing it…"

"Adrian, it's not—"

"I feel like a sperm donation."

My mouth falls.

"The only real time you seem to be invested in me is when you want me to eat a certain way or take certain supplements or make the required deposit."

I look away. All the anger and frustration seeps out of me. Have I really made him feel like that? The man I love.

"I'm sorry."

"I'm glad you're sorry, but sorry means nothing, it's just a word unless change exists with it."

He's lecturing me. I hate being lectured. But maybe he has a point. "What do you mean?"

He takes a long breath then lets the air settle around us.

He's struggling, battling something inside him, deciding whether to let me in; I can literally see the instant he makes a decision. His shoulders relax as his words stream out. "I saw Julia in Toronto."

"Julia?"

"My—"

"Your ex-wife." He nods. I shift in my seat. Julia's always been this intangible being to me, no more real than Santa Claus, an entity I hear whispers about, stories, but who has no real affect on my life. "Why didn't you tell me?"

He rubs a hand through his hair, a motion that usually makes me smile but tonight seems like the action of a stranger. "You were so stressed, you had all this going on, I didn't know how you'd take it."

"Was it a run-in or—"

"No. A plan."

"You wanted to see her, you sought her out?"

He nods. "I could say it's because she had a contact I wanted. And she did. But that could have been handled through an email. I wanted to see her, to know…something. To compare maybe?" He looks at me, as if this is a question I can answer. His gaze darts away again. "When I first met Julia, when I was in the whirlwind period of falling for her, I thought that was love. Real love. She was pregnant before we'd even burned out the honeymoon phase of dating, and then we were married, and then we had Christine. Life seemed wonderful, perfect, but when Christine died Julia became this stranger. I couldn't even see the person I once thought I loved. I didn't care to see her." His eyes close. They open and he turns to me. "When I met you it was something entirely different. Deeper. More solid. I thought, 'Oh, this is love, real love, whatever I had with Julia, it wasn't this.'"

My breath catches, terror coursing through me. What's he saying? What is he about to say?

He casts a smile. "So I wanted to see her. I wanted to

know." His head drops once more. "It's not that I thought I didn't love you anymore, not at all. I just…I wanted to see if after the pain of Christine, after our raging grief had settled, I could look at Julia and remember any spark of what we once had compared to what you and I had, because I thought I was losing that with us. You were starting to feel like a stranger too."

I swallow, my breath small and tight.

"I needed to know if it was the same." He stops, and though it lasts only seconds, hours seem to pass between us. "It was nothing, Trace. The way I felt for her was nothing compared to what I feel for you—even now with all the frustration and pain and the fear that I'm losing my wife. What I feel for you, it's strong. You're what I want."

I lean back. Betrayal seeps through every pore of me, but relief too, and maybe the slightest bit of understanding. "But not like this?"

"I want you no matter what. But like this," he shakes his head, "like this I'm not happy, and I don't think you are either. If you were, I think I could be."

A weight pushes into my chest, my throat tightens.

"So far it's been all your choice. And I get that it's your body, but we're supposed to be in this together. So my thoughts should matter too."

"They do."

He smiles, but it's not comforting. "You say that, but they're just words. Just like these are words I've told you before. And they haven't changed anything. I need them to change something."

"Change what?"

"I want us to make a decision to try another way. Keep up with your pursuit of health and healing as much as you can while still being you. That's fine. I know you're not one to give up, but you can do that and also try IVF, or put our names on an adoption list. That's what I need. I need something I can believe in. I can't go on like this."

"Believe in me."

"I do. And you need to believe in me too. You need to trust that what I think feels right for us has value."

I stare at him. "Or what?"

"I can't go on like this. I'll have to stop."

"So you'll leave me?"

"No." He lets out a firm breath. "I'm not leaving you. But I need a break from trying, from this madness, this obsession."

"A break from trying? So you'd refuse—"

"Maybe. And maybe if I did, just for a while, we could get back to us, maybe you could get back to the person I married. You don't feel like the person I married."

"Who am I then?"

"I don't know." He hangs his head. When he looks up, his eyes are moist. "I really don't know. But you're more than this. This passion for a child, it's only one part of you, but you're making it everything."

"Adrian, I—"

"You need to make a choice." He stands. My gaze follows him but I stay seated. "We can take a break, or we can try something I believe in. Our name on the adoption lists, IVF—"

"It's so expensive."

"We'll figure it out. You just…I just can't go on like this."

"So you're giving me an ultimatum."

He wears a look on his face like he thinks he's awful. "Yeah. I guess I'm giving you an ultimatum." He pulls out his phone. "I have to go. I'll be back in a few hours. I'd stay but this young girl, the one I was talking about earlier, she agreed to speak with me—on video. If I'm late she may change her mind."

He's leaving? Now? "Adrian."

"Maybe it's good, give you some time to think. Think about who you want to be, who you want us to be, and what you're willing to sacrifice, 'cause right now, you're sacrificing too much."

CHAPTER TWENTY

Adrian walks out of the apartment. I stay on the couch, staring where I last saw him. An anvil to the chest couldn't hurt this much. He says I'm not me anymore. Says I'm obsessed. Am I? I'm focused. Driven. Passionate. I'm not teaching anymore. I go back next semester, but I didn't have to wait that long. I haven't seen the Aspire girls. The things I used to love more than anything, I've abandoned. And he's right, I have no idea about the details of his story. Despite his disbelief in my health practices, he knows exactly what I can and can't eat. He might not know the ins and outs of why, but at least he's paying attention. Still, an ultimatum. He's making me choose a path I don't want, that terrifies me, just to make him more comfortable. I grab a pillow and squeeze it hard. He'll refuse me? Stay out of my bed—metaphorically speaking? I drop the pillow.

He feels like I could exchange him for a sperm donation. Of everything he said, that's what hits me the most, what makes me wonder if I really am obsessed. Having a child, my own child, is only part of the dream. I wanted a family, a family that includes the man I love. Eloise and Autumn's words come back as shame and embarrassment settles over me like a shroud. That's not who I am. I'm a person who loves her friends, who sees their joys as my own.

I already apologized, but it's not enough. I'll need to make it right with them. Somehow. I need to make it right with Adrian too. The options he gave float through my mind. I don't want any of them: To stop trying, it'd be like giving up. It would make all the pain and fear of the surgery seem pointless. It can't have been pointless. To adopt? The same result, essentially. But it's so much more than that. I can't adopt. I want to believe I could love a stranger's child as much as I would my own, but what if I can't? I won't take that risk. I won't do that to a child… I know what it feels like. Which leaves IVF. I've been over the reasons it terrifies me dozens of times, but it is a chance and everything I've been doing, everything I've obsessed over, could improve the odds of that chance. And with Saadia's help…or the help of an acupuncturist who would take me, the chance would be even greater. It could work. Outside of leaving Adrian, letting go of my dreams entirely, it's the only option I can even consider.

As night creeps its way into the room, I go over these thoughts, wanting Adrian to return, willing him to return. At last, I hear his keys jingle at the door and flip on the light so he won't know I've been sitting in the dark. "How did the interview go?"

"Good." Adrian sinks onto the couch. "Rough. But really good."

Focus. Be engaged… Is the fact that I have to tell myself to be this way a signal that he's right about me? I lean forward. "Rough in what way?"

He looks exhausted: physically and emotionally. "Just these girls' lives. It's hard to see. But Trace," the slightest smile graces his face, "it makes me think what a wonderful thing adoption is. How it's an amazing way to give a child a good life who may otherwise have a horrible one. To stop the cycle."

"Adrian."

"I want a child, Trace. I'd be a great father, better than before even. I've grown. Christine helped me grow, and Julia too. I'm not as selfish. I know how to step outside of work and be present. And until…until all of this struggle, you knew too. If the child we parent is ours by genetics, wonderful. Amazing. But if not, I truly feel that's okay. It's better than okay." He rubs his hands, his eyes watching the motion. "This girl I was talking to today, her father was a drunk. He killed himself and her mother in a car accident when she was six. She had no family who wanted to take her and so she spent the next decade being bounced from foster home to foster home until finally she left at sixteen. Sixteen, Tracey." He shakes his head. "She went to the streets. She was stuck in a broken system and she escaped it only to fall into a broken life. She's too scared to leave her pimp. She won't let us use her name, her face, only her story—to help warn others. She's not pregnant today, but one day it'll probably happen. Will she keep that child? Maybe, maybe not."

He scooches forward, pulls me over to the couch beside him. "Your parents did an amazing thing adopting an older child. Few people will. If they hadn't, that girl could have been you. You could have lived a completely different life."

"I never—"

"You don't know that. You can't know that. I know you've had a lot of anger; I know you think they weren't perfect, but they gave you a much better life than you could have had."

"So you're saying I'm a charity case who should just be thankful?"

"No, I'm saying you're a human being who deserved a good, loving life. And it may not have been one hundred percent the life you wanted, but your Mom and Dad, they gave you that."

Now I look to my hands. He's right. I know he's right. That girl, from foster home to foster home, old enough to understand it all…the fear that consumed me, the abandonment, the imagining I wasn't good enough, it must be nothing compared to what lives in her.

"We could help a child like her, like the child you could have become. And we could do it soon, too. We wouldn't have to wait eight to nine years for an older child."

"There's a reason for that, Adrian. They're damaged." I shift away from him. "Trust me. I know. Maybe you don't mean to but you're talking about these kids like they're a cause. I don't want a cause. I want a son or a daughter. My son or daughter. Maybe this girl you talked to wasn't, but we could be adopting the child of an addict, a child who was abused and will never, no matter how much we try to love them, get past that pain. We could—"

"We could stop the cycle."

"Why us? Why does this have to fall on us? You're making it sound like I'm selfish and heartless for not wanting to save the children, well no one else is expected to." I grit my teeth. "I can't do it. I won't have a child in my home feeling like second choice."

He sits back. The disappointment in his eyes makes me want to scream. "Just because you felt like second choice doesn't mean another child would. Think of it the other way, maybe they'd feel so happy that we chose them. Your parents chose you. Yes, they wanted their own child, but they decided that child didn't have to come from them, and then they chose you. There were lots of other children they could have chosen, but it's you they wanted. You they love. You they'll always love."

My eyes blur. It sounds so simple when he says it, but there's nothing simple about it. I want to believe him, but some hard, rough thing within me won't allow it. Still, I have to give him something. "I'll do IVF."

Adrian pulls away from me. "What?"

"You said I had to make a choice. That's my choice. We can do a cycle. I'm going back to school for the next semester. I already told Sally, just like we talked about. She's ecstatic. So I'll go back to school, I'll do better at being present for you—engaged in our life—and I'll try one cycle." I pause. "Is that enough?"

He stares a moment. I imagine all the fears that stream through his mind, the same ones that stream through mine. IVF is a risk, a huge risk. His eyes cloud with that fear. Is he thinking of seeing the heartbeat, holding onto hope, and then losing a child all over again?

"I don't understand. Why is this the better option?"

"It wasn't just the babies today, Autumn's pregnancy, it was more than that."

"Trace?"

"Before you picked me up, I wasn't shopping. I went to see Sebastien."

"Oh." Adrian leans forward. I give him a brief account of our exchange.

"It doesn't matter what he said. I know it doesn't matter. But it shook me. It…anyway," I look away, "I wouldn't want a child I raise to ever have to go through that, to look into the eyes of the person who abandoned her and—"

"Trace, it's not like that for everyone. Think of your first meeting with Lydia."

"I know."

"And the child would have the experience anyway one day, whether they lived with us, someone else, or grew up a ward of the system. At least with us they'd be with good people, have a stable family, we'd give them love and—"

"I said I'd do IVF, okay. Accept that. Be happy."

Adrian searches my face before responding. "This isn't just because of your father? You won't change your mind tomorrow or—"

"No."

"Okay." He takes my hand. "We'll try IVF. We'll take a leap." He draws me to him. "And if it doesn't work?"

"We're not going there."

He squeezes me tighter and whispers in my ear. "Good plan."

My stomach rumbles and Adrian releases me from his embrace. I pull out my phone to see what time it is and see several missed calls and texts from Eloise and Autumn. The screen lights up with another call. "It's my mother."

Adrian leans back. "Take it."

"But—"

"Take it." He stands.

I answer the call and brace myself. More about Jojo, most likely, and after today, I'm in no mood to hear it.

"Hello."

"Hi, sweetie."

"Hi, Mom." The line stays silent. "Mom?"

Her words rush out in a long breath. "How are you?"

"I'm all right."

"I don't think you are."

"What?"

Another sigh. "Eloise called today."

"What!"

"She says she's really worried about you. They all are."

Now I'm silent.

"I've been so focused on Jojo, honey. So worried about her. You always seem to have it together and honestly, well, I simply haven't wanted to talk about what you're going through. It hits too close to home. It brings back all the sorrow, all the fear—"

"Mom, you don't need to talk about anything. I'm fine, I—"

"No, Tracey. I haven't been a good mother to you lately. With you going ahead with the surgery and then having Lydia take care of you and even just, even just how much it hurts that you're feeling this pain." She stops. "When I saw you in the group home, so tiny and delicate, I wanted to protect you from any more pain. I thought you must have been through so much and it simply didn't seem right. I wanted to protect you and now here you are, all grown up, and I have no idea how to take your pain away."

"It's not your job to—"

"It is my job. You're my daughter. It'll be my job, to try at least, till the day I die."

A lump rises in my throat. "Mom."

"I don't want to talk to you on the phone. I thought…I thought coming to your door would be…I was scared. I've been so uninvolved and…I'm at the café on the corner. *Mimi's*. Will you come meet me?"

"You drove all the way here?"

"And chickened out half a block away."

"Just a minute." I put my hand over the phone and search out Adrian in the den. "Mom's at *Mimi's*. She wants me to come join her."

He raises an eyebrow. "So go."

"But we were—"

"It's fine. Go."

I draw my hand away from the phone. "I'll be there in five minutes."

CHAPTER TWENTY-ONE

utside, the world is brighter than it should be. Street lights reflect off the snow, casting a diffused light that isn't day, isn't night, but something in between. I glimpse through *Mimi's* front window. The café is bustling. Mom sits in a corner with a cup of something warm in her hands and another mug sits at the seat across from her. Slow tendrils of steam rise from both cups. Mom looks into the distance, her expression pained but expectant. She turns her head and I can see the exact moment when I become not some stranger standing in the street, but her daughter. She stands and waves. A jingle sounds as I push open the café door.

"Hi, darling."

"Hi." Her smile doesn't hide she's been crying. After we hug, I take the seat opposite her and reach for the mug.

"Hot cider. I know you've always loved it, and since it's late."

"Thanks, Mom." I try to turn off the warnings in my mind. *This probably has loads of sugar in it. Could be nothing but artificial flavouring and syrup.* "It smells great."

"They make it right here with real apples, so I thought…well, you're trying to be healthy, right?"

"I'm sure it's perfect." I take a sip. It definitely has sugar but is not pure syrup either. It's delicious. "So Eloise called you? What did she say?"

"She told me about the party. How you've been

incredibly distant lately, that she was worried. She also said you didn't answer her or Autumn's calls, and Adrian wasn't answering his phone. She just wanted to make sure you both were okay."

"We're fine…it wasn't a big deal."

"You're right." She nods and sips her cider. "It's not a big deal to feel the unfairness of all the women who get pregnant so easily, without even trying, who seem to take this crazy, seemingly impossible miracle for granted. Thoughts like that are inevitable. They're normal." She pauses. "It makes sense they'll slip out every now and then. Your friends don't know that though. They have no idea what it's like to live the life you're living. They can imagine, but they don't know." Mom takes another sip of cider. I stare at her. She lets out a little smile. "Your 'outburst', as they called it, sounds like nothing compared to a few I had in my day. Very mild indeed."

I can't help but laugh. "You had outbursts?"

"Oh yes." She chuckles. "It's not funny, really. And I don't mean to minimize the pain you felt today, the pain I imagine you feel a lot of the time. But the wife of one of your father's employees was over one day. She had four kids. And she knew we were trying. She announced she was pregnant again and said she'd trade me any one of her children for a day to herself, just one day to herself. I threw my coffee in her face."

"Mom!"

She laughs again. "I was horrified that I did it. But it also felt good. I'm just glad I was using creamer. I might not have forgiven myself if I'd scalded her. As it was, she *maybe* got what she deserved. Or at least that's how I felt at the time, though I now know she meant no harm. People simply don't understand."

I gaze at my cider. "Autumn's been through so much. She must think I'm a bitter, horrible friend."

"She's just worried about you. That's all. She knows what

it is to let pain change you."

"How would you—"

"She told me, or, rather, Eloise did. Autumn was there. She knows you're happy for her."

"She said that?"

"No. But she knows. She knows you, sweetie."

My lip trembles. "How'd you get through it? It seems like it's on my mind almost every waking moment. Every twinge and pain of my body I'm reminded. When I'm near my period, every time I go to the bathroom I have this fear…and then when I'm late." I rub my hands on the rim of the mug, watch the steam rise. "How did you get through it? I feel so broken."

"Oh, baby." Mom stares at me with more compassion and empathy than I've ever seen, and in that moment I have more compassion for her than I've ever felt. She knows. It's been less than three years for me, it was thirteen for her. Fifteen if you count the time to Jojo.

She gets out of her seat, crouches beside mine, and reaches her arms around me. "You just get through it, day after day, it's the only thing you can do. You try to focus on the good you do have. Everything you're feeling is normal. You're not broken. As much as it feels like it."

I look away. "Adrian says that. Everyone seems to. But it's not true. My body is against me, against my biggest dream. You know. You know what it's like. And don't tell me I should just adopt."

"I won't." She leans back. "I'm not going to lie, sweetie. I wanted my own baby. And I understand that you do too. If anything, it makes sense that you want your own child even more than I did. You lived your whole life not knowing your biological family. And blood means something. It does. But it doesn't mean everything."

"If Jojo had come first you never would have taken me."

She looks at the floor, gives the slightest of nods, then raises her gaze back to me. "That might be true, but I would have missed out on what I never could have imagined. I know you don't believe it, but in my heart, one hundred percent, you are just as much my daughter as Jojo." She grips my shoulder. "Just as much. And if Jojo hadn't come after you, we would have been satisfied. You gave us the family we wanted. You were the child we'd dreamed of. We stopped trying after we had you. I stopped even hoping. I didn't need to hope. You were my baby. You were my daughter."

"Mom, that's not true."

"It is true. Was I elated when I found out about Jojo? Did I see her as a miracle? Yes, absolutely. But that didn't take away even a smidgen from the miracle it was to find you."

A torrent of emotion rushes through me. I let out a half scoff, half gasp, then look away from the few stares of the other customers taking refuge from the cold. I'm transported back to the house I grew up in. I stand outside the door where Mom's ladies' afternoon is taking place, wanting to feel a part of them, eager for the day when I'll be old enough to join, and then I hear it, Mom's voice full of laughter: *'All those years everyone said stop trying, relax, it'll happen. It infuriated me. And then we found Tracey. We relaxed. She was our child. She made us parents, and then,'* Mom's voice swelled with joy, *'it happened. Our little miracle.'*

I *was* their child. Was. Until Jojo became their miracle. "But you said…"

"Said what?"

"Nothing." I shake my head. "Would you really have been satisfied with just me? Would I have been enough?"

Mom's smile blossoms. I'm not sure if I've ever seen her look so beautiful. "Yes. Now that we have Jojo, I would never trade her for the world. I would never trade either of you. But yes, you would have been enough. More than enough."

Such simple words. Words I've rejected so many times.

Today I let them settle over me.

"Adrian wants us to adopt but I…"

"It's okay, Tracey. I know."

"We decided to do IVF."

Her mouth forms a little 'o'. She returns to her seat. "Really?"

"Yeah. What do you think?"

"It's risky…I mean a gamble. But you know that."

I nod.

"A lot of people have great success with it."

"But not you. You never mentioned…did you even—"

"No." She wraps her hands around the mug. "It wasn't even an option. Not at first. Just a couple of years before you came along we heard about it. And then we didn't need it." That blossoming smile returns. "It's wonderful, sweetie. Absolutely wonderful. I'll be sending out all the hope and belief I can muster."

"Thanks." I wrap my hands around my mug, enjoying the warmth. "There's a huge chance it won't work though, and that terrifies me. It'd be my body failing one more time, only this time it would cost thousands."

"You can't think of it like that."

"How can I not?"

She's quiet. "I don't know."

"We planned for this. It won't all have to be on credit or anything. That's why the wedding was so low-key."

"Tracey," my mother tuts, "that's why? You should have told us. You said you just wanted something small and intimate." She shakes her head. "I should have questioned. You'd always had such dreams for a big wedding and then—"

"It's fine. Our wedding was beautiful. Perfect."

"It was."

"So we have most of the money, but that money could also go to a down payment on a house. I'm not saying a baby's not worth more than a house to me. Not even close.

If it were a guarantee..."

"But it's not. I know, sweetie."

"You think it's the right thing to do? Not frivolous? A person with my condition has an incredibly slim chance, and that's just of a confirmed pregnancy, not a live—"

"Tracey." She raises her hand to cut me off. "It's not frivolous, and a chance is a chance. If this is what you've decided, you need to go for it and not look back."

Go for it and not look back. Can I do that? Do I even want to?

CHAPTER TWENTY-TWO

By the time we leave the café it's too late for mom to drive home, so she stays the night and leaves early the next morning. A few hours later, she calls. "How are you feeling, honey?"

"All right. Good. Fine."

"Good." Silence. "It was great talking with you last night, spending some one on one time. We don't do that enough. I'd like to do it more."

I could brush away her words, come up with the excuse of time or how far we live from each other… I no longer want to. "Yeah. That'd be nice." Silence again. I can almost see the smile that probably covers her face.

"This isn't about that specifically, and I know that Christmas is coming up soon, so lots of visiting, lots of travelling, but your father and I would really like you and Adrian to come for dinner beforehand. Just the four of us. This weekend. I'm not sure if we've ever had a dinner with just the four of us."

We haven't. "This weekend?" My mind goes to all the items on my schedule. But I can fit this in. Balance is what I promised Adrian. Dinner with my parents would be a perfect place to start. "How about Saturday night?"

"Perfect."

My full list of off-limit foods would overwhelm my mother, so I choose the most important. "If it could be a meal without dairy or red meat that would be great."

"Done. Six o'clock? We'll have some dairy and red-meat free appetizers and then dinner at seven?"

"I'll have to check with Adrian, but I imagine it'll be fine."

"Yes, yes, check." The awkwardness between us grates like a knife. Even after last night, one of the closest moments I've ever shared with my mother, it's still there.

"The drink. I had a talk with Jojo but—"

"I shouldn't have asked that of you. Especially with all you're going through. Your sister is not your responsibility."

"She's going through a lot too."

"I know." Sadness falls into my mother's voice. "I'd take it all away from both of you if I could. You have no idea."

I'm quiet for a moment. I believe her. "Thanks, Mom."

✦

FRIDAY AFTERNOON THERE'S a knock on my door. Eloise.

"Hi." I pull open the door.

"Can I come in?"

"Yeah. Of course." I open the door wider and step to the side. She passes through. Her hands stay at her side. She clutches her purse against her. "How are you?"

She bites her lip as she smiles. It's weird to see her like this: Hesitant. Uncertain. Eloise is the woman on fire. The woman who always knows exactly what she wants and how she wants it, yet she stares at me like I'm a puzzle, or something broken she's not sure how to put back together.

"I called your mom."

"She said."

"I've been pretty angry at you lately."

My brows raise and my mouth opens, but no words come out.

"You've been so involved with you. Obsessed. And I get that you're sad. Or focused. Or whatever. I know you've always wanted to be a mom."

I nod.

"But that can't be all you want. It isn't all you want. You have other things you're passionate about. You always have. All those years of the wretched guys, of the fear you'd never get your dream, it's the students who kept you grounded, who gave your life meaning."

I scrunch my brow, waiting for her to continue.

"And those girls. They love you, Trace. Really. You're a mother figure to some of them. You know that, right? Jayden asks about you every session." Eloise taps her purse against her thigh then takes a deep breath. "Her mom's in rehab now."

"No." I lean against the wall. "What's she—"

"Jayden's with her grandma. And she's still so fantastic. She's handling it all like a champ."

"I had no idea."

"Of course you didn't. You haven't been there. And I admit, I've been judging you for it." She gestures to the living room. "Let's sit."

She follows me and we sit across from each other on the couch, something we've done a thousand times before. "Being a mom, it can't be everything."

"It's not."

"Right now it is. And maybe right now it needs to be. And I can get that. I can understand, or at least I can try. But the other day, that wasn't you."

"I know. I'm happy for Autumn."

"Of course you are." Eloise laughs. "Sorry. I feel like I'm botching this."

Botching what? I want to ask, but I just keep silent.

"Don't pull away, okay? Do what you have to do but keep us a part of it. Let us in. Let me in."

"El—"

"And come out with me tonight. The Aspire Christmas party is starting in an hour. The girls would love to see you.

You don't have to explain anything, just come. It'll be good for them. They've been dying to see you. They've been worried. It'll be good for you too."

"Okay."

Eloise's brow raises. "What?"

I shrug. "It'd be good to see them. It'd be good to see more of you too. I left too early the other night."

Eloise bites her lip with a smile. "Let's get you out of those sweats and into something fabulous."

THE PARTY IS IN THE workspace the Aspire program has used the past two summers. A large open area that adds a sense of class none of the high school gymnasiums could have given. It's a spectacular event, and all the students seem to be glowing, proud as anything to show off the semester's projects to their parents and siblings. Various stations are set up around the room. One group of girls started making and selling their own handbags. Another set up an after-school tutoring program. A third took their term project online and partnered with an organization that sells environmentally sustainable water bottles and worked with them to set up a system where every time one of the girls prompts a sale, the company donates a gallon of water to communities where clean drinking water is scarce. A dozen other projects are on display, each showcasing the business skills this program is developing.

As I peruse the stations, I'm interrupted every minute or two by students wanting to talk to me, wish me well, and ask when I'll be back. It's not until I have the girls from my core program around me—the ones who were there when Aspire was twelve of us in my classroom instead of the almost seventy-five students it's grown to—that I realize just how much I've missed them.

"So for sure, for sure?" says Jayden, her finger twirling in her hair like it always does. "You're coming back next semester? You're okay now? You're healthy?"

I grin. "I'm coming back next semester."

Jayden looks to the ceiling. "Oh my gosh, that's so great." She laughs. "I was seriously scared you wouldn't be back."

"We couldn't graduate without you," says Jolie. Unlike the other girls, she hasn't grown in the past months and looks even more petite than I remember. "You've been our teacher pretty much forever."

"I'll be there." I promise.

Sherry smiles. Jayden wraps her arms around me. "I've missed you Mrs. S. Like seriously missed you."

I return her embrace and squeeze this girl who no longer has a mother at home. "I've missed you girls too." Eloise smiles at me from across the room. "It'll be good to be back."

❧

THE NEXT NIGHT ADRIAN and I are quiet on the drive to my parents' house. When I got home from the party the previous night we had what could easily be called a fight about IVF—him wanting to make an appointment and get the process started, me suggesting we wait until I'm back teaching for a few months, recoup some of the savings we've depleted since I've been off.

"Don't bring it up in front of Mom and Dad," I say as he pulls the car into their drive.

He sends me a look, which makes it obvious he knows exactly the 'it' I'm referencing. "Thanks for that. It's nice to know you think I'd try to use your parents' influence against you."

"That's not what I—"

"We're here."

We knock and wait. It's our first visit since the surgery. Over three and a half months. Not ridiculous considering the two hour drive. And we saw them once at the twins' Fall recital, but still, I won't be getting any daughter of the year awards.

My father answers the door with a huge grin. "My girl!"

"Hi, Dad."

"Look at this." He kicks his leg forward and back, side to side. "As good as new."

"You heading up ladders yet?" Adrian asks as he and Dad shake hands.

"Of course." Dad laughs. "I was back to it the day after they removed the cast.

"Good man."

"Come in, come in." We step through the foyer. As always, the smells that greet us are amazing. Tantalizing.

"H'ordeuvres?" My father waves a hand toward the trays lining the coffee table.

"Looks good!" Adrian grins.

A shuffle of footsteps announces Mom's entrance. After another round of greetings, we gather in the living room. Adrian catches Mom and Dad up on the status of his documentary and Dad catches us up on his latest project.

"Your mother nearly threw a fit when I said I wanted to finish the deck, what with the snow coming on, so I'm building shelfing in one of the basement rooms instead.

"Didn't you do those a year ago?" I ask.

"But not shelfing." Dad grabs a goat cheese, pecan, and honey covered cracker. It looks delicious. "The shelfing is brand new."

"For all the books he reads, I suppose." My mother laughs.

"I read."

"You do not." She turns to Adrian. "He opens a book, turns a couple of pages, and then falls asleep. He reads the same book for a year."

"A page a day is still reading. I absorb the words and then contemplate them in my slumber."

"Sure. Sure." Mom smiles at him and in her eyes it's clear, even after all these years and all the frustration he causes her, she loves him. I look to Adrian. Will we still love like that forty years from now? Do we love like that now? He notices my stare and casts a little grin. He's glad about my decision to do IVF but wants more than that. He wants me open to adoption. If the procedure doesn't work and I still refuse, he'll probably stay, but he may never fully forgive me.

Dad looks to Mom. She nods. "Your mother filled me in on some of the things you've been doing." He gestures to the appetizers. "Food. Yoga. Meditation." He smiles. "That's my girl. Taking control, making the best of a bad situation."

"I'm trying."

"She also told me your decision. To pursue IVF."

Adrian takes my hand. "We are."

"That's a big decision. I'm sure you both thought long and hard about it."

Adrian again: "We did."

"And you're sure this is something you want to do? One hundred percent. You've decided. You're willing to put in the money. You're willing to take the gamble, knowing it is a gamble, but with hope for the best."

Adrian. "Yes."

"Tracey." Dad looks at me. "Honey, you're ready for this? It's a big step. A big commitment. It puts a lot on a woman, in a multitude of ways."

I look to Adrian, confusion spilling over me. Do my parents not want me to do this? The other night Mom seemed fine. Supportive even. And am I one hundred percent committed? The prospect terrifies me. Completely. The cost. The uncertainty. The potential heartache. But I promised. I decided I'm not looking back. "I'm committed to it."

Dad grins. "Good then. You're not backing out. We needed to hear that, that you'd decided, that no matter what, you're not backing out."

"Okay?"

Mom wears a coy smile. Dad's face is stone serious. "We're paying for it."

"What?" Adrian coughs. "No. We can't let you do that."

"It's done. It's decided."

"No turning back now." Mom does a little bounce in her chair.

"Save your money for a house with enough room for your baby, or babies. Twins are really common with IVF, right?" Dad laughs. "Could you imagine—two sets of twins in our little family?"

"I'd have offered on the spot the other night, honey, but I thought it only right to confirm with your father."

I look between them, more afraid than excited. "Mom, Dad. You can't."

"We can and we will."

"Consider it an early portion of your inheritance if you want," says Mom, "if that makes you feel better."

"It's too much," I plead. My chest tightens. It's far too much.

"It's nothing." Dad grabs another goat cheese covered cracker. "We have the money. It's just sitting in investments going up and down by the day. Let's put it to use."

"Dad." I turn to him. "Do you know the statistics for someone with my condition? The chance is small. Really small."

"But there's a chance." He rests one of his large hands on my knee. "And if that chance means a happy ending for someone, why not you?"

"We love you, Tracey. We love Adrian. We want to see you both happy and fulfilled. We know the past year has been rough." Mom turns to Dad, her expression intimate. "We've been there. Everything you're going through is stressful, and if we can take away one level of that stress, well, it would be a gift to us, to know that's off of you. It's selfish too." Mom laughs. "I want more grandbabies. Jojo's are getting so grown up."

The old familiar argument bursts within me—they won't be her grandchildren. Not really. But for my parents, technically, there'd be no difference whether the children I raise are mine or a stranger's, as far as blood is concerned. I look away, my brow furrowed and my lips pursed.

"Tracey." I look up. Mom leans forward. "You want your own children and if we're able to do anything to help, that would be a gift to us. I know you're hurting. I know you've been hurting for years but let us do this. Whether this treatment works, whether you adopt, any child you have will be ours, because you're ours."

"It's too much." My voice catches. "And if it doesn't work—"

"Tracey." Dad stands. "Come with me. I have something to show you."

I look to Adrian.

"Just you, sweetie." Dad offers his hand. I take it and follow him to the basement, through the large rec room, and into the storage room. He walks to the corner, lifts several boxes, and pulls away a sheet. Underneath it sits a rocking chair with a small cradle attached. It's the exact replica of one I cut out for the little hope box of baby items and ideas I'd started years ago. I run my hand over the smooth wood.

"How?"

He smiles and rests a hand on my shoulder. "I saw you looking at it and I thought: I can make that. So I did."

"But when?"

He laughs. "Two thousand and four."

"More than a decade."

"Well, I wasn't sure how things would go with your

college beau. Wanted to be prepared."

"You've had it all this time?"

"Of course. It still needs to be painted or stained. I wanted to let you choose the colour."

"It's beautiful."

"It's been here waiting for you. For your child. This is what you've always wanted. I saw it in you when you watched movies featuring children and families, the way your face lit up around babies. Ever since you were a young girl, I know you've longed for your own family. That's your dream. And you'll be an incredible mother." The corners of his eyes crinkle. "You're sweet, and caring, and thoughtful. Your children will be lucky."

"Dad."

"Being a mom has always been one of your dreams, even the fact that you became a teacher—it's worked out so well because you love children and they love you. I know one way or another your dream will come true. The world wouldn't be right if it didn't. You'll be a mother." His shoulders rise and fall. "Maybe through this procedure, maybe naturally, maybe another way. But if this is the route you're trying right now, your mother and I want to do all we can to make it the most stress free journey possible. Let us do this for you."

"Dad." My throat tightens.

"Will you let us?"

I can't say yes. It's too much. I can't get out the words. But I nod. And that's enough. Dad wraps me in his arms. "That's my girl."

CHAPTER TWENTY-THREE

With the issue of cost erased, my argument to wait until we've rebuilt our savings before going ahead with the IVF procedure is erased too. Less than a week after dinner with my parents, Adrian and I leave the fertility clinic and get in the car for the two hour drive back to Mom and Dad's for their annual Christmas Eve's Eve party. Adrian turns the ignition and puts the car in gear. Before pulling out of the parking lot, he looks at me. "How's it going?"

"Good. Great." I offer a smile.

"Trace." He glances over as he eases out of the lot. "You seemed tense in there."

"It is nerve-wracking."

"The clinic has a great success rate."

"I know. Absolutely."

"And the timing is working out really well: start in the new year, transfer at the middle of the month, and you'll know whether it worked or not before school starts."

"I know. It's great." I draw my gaze away. It is great. It's the best timing I could have asked for. The new semester starts in February, so I won't have to take any additional time off of teaching for the transfer. I'll have all the time I need to focus on creating the most relaxed, healthy atmosphere I can for the fertilized egg to take root, and whether it does or it doesn't, I'll start teaching just days after I get my answer: a healthy distraction.

"You're not having second thoughts?"

"No, I am not."

"Good." Adrian pulls onto the highway and we drive in silence for several minutes.

"What about you? Do you feel good about it?"

He sighs. "I'm nervous." He taps his hand on the wheel. "I don't even know if that's the right word. We both know this is only one step in a multifaceted process, but I think we're doing the right thing, being proactive." He looks over. "Not that you haven't been proactive. I know you've been doing so much. But for me, this is more tangible."

"I get it."

"The best thing both of us can do is try to relax, like the doctor said. We'll follow everything they say medically, and outside of that we can just let nature take its course."

He makes it sound simple, seems so calm and sure, but I know he's not. His hand grips the steering wheel, his jaw twitches. He's thinking about Christine. Already, fear of the new pain that may greet us is probably coursing through him.

I rest my hand on his leg. "I'm sorry I'm putting you through this. I'm sorry—"

"Hey," he grasps my hand, "you have nothing to be sorry for. This is not your fault."

Not my fault, no, but because of me... "I just wish—"

"Tracey, I want a baby with you, I do. And I know you think... I mean, I've said how scared I am, how I don't know if I can handle more loss, but I can. Despite the risks, this is worth trying. A child is worth fighting for."

"I know. Anyway," I squeeze his leg, "are you looking forward to the party?"

"A room full of people I don't know, most of them several decades older than me? Yes, please!"

I laugh. Most people would be saying those words sarcastically, but for Adrian the prospect is practically like candy—a room full of people means a room full of potential stories. "I love you, you know."

"Oh, I know." He winks. "You're practically my biggest fan."

"Practically?"

He nods, completely straight-faced. "I'm sorry, but my mom would more than give you a run for your money in that department. You love me. She adores me."

"Which explains that big head of yours."

He raises his hand to pat the top of his head and then the bottom of his chin, as if determining the size. "Guess it does. Always wondered about that." He looks over at me again. "And you? Will you stick to your meal restrictions?"

"Yeah."

"You don't have to. I'm pretty sure all diets get a free pass during Christmas."

"If only my body knew that!"

He chuckles.

"It'll be a bit rough but if Mom and Dad can chunk out that kind of cash, I can definitely keep doing what I'm doing, try to make my shot the best it can be."

We drive with only the sound of the wheels on the pavement and the wind rushing around the car for several minutes. "You know, wife of mine, you're a pretty spectacular person."

I stare ahead. This is the first time he's really commended my efforts. My gut reaction is to dismiss his words or compliment him. Instead, I accept. "Thank you."

When we exit the highway and begin the long road leading to my parents' house, Adrian turns down the radio. "I didn't even think to ask, but this will be the first time you've seen Jojo since the birthday party, right?"

"It will."

"Nervous about that?"

"I don't know. We've fought before." Her words never hurt like they did that night, but if I was wrong, if I accused her of a problem she doesn't have, my words were just as bad.

"Think she'll have her drink on?"

I turn my head. "It's not a joke."

His smile vanishes. "I know. I know it's not." He taps the wheel. "Do you really think she has a problem though, or was it an isolated incident or two? I mean I know I've self-medicated with alcohol more than once, or even just to blow off steam during rough times. Jojo has definitely been going through rough times."

"I hope that's all it was. Probably that's all it was." Which would mean more than her, I was in the wrong.

Several minutes later we step into the party. All the regulars are here, people who've watched me grow from a young girl. Less than five of the thirty or so faces are unfamiliar. We make the rounds, greeting and catching up on each other's lives. After about the eighth person asks when Adrian and I are going to start a family (always phrased some witty way) I'm about ready to throw my drink in the next curious person's face.

About an hour into the evening, I find myself in the kitchen alone. I brace my hands against the counter and gaze at the burgundy-tiled back splash. The questions are wearing on me. It's okay, I repeat for maybe the tenth time since we've arrived, they're just words, well-meant words.

"Tracey?"

I jump and turn at the sound of Jojo's voice.

"Hi." She raises her glass. "Merry Christmas."

"Merry—"

"Don't worry. It's just egg-nog. The kid approved one."

"Christmas." I step toward her. "It's a party. Drink what you want."

"Trace—"

"Yes?"

She approaches, her movements hesitant. Jojo is never

hesitant. "I'm really sorry about a few weeks ago. What I said."

"Jo, I—"

"No. I shouldn't have been drinking like that at a kids' party, and with my kids around. And to call you barren…"

I clasp my hands in front of me, not knowing what else to do with them. "Technically, you were correct. I am barren."

"Only so far. That could change anytime though. Maybe really soon, right?"

"Maybe."

"Mom and Dad told me you're doing IVF." She moves to the kitchen table and pulls out a chair. "That's great. Really great. I hope it works out for you."

"Us too." I stay by the counter. "I'm sorry for what I said. I didn't have a right to call you out like that. I know you take care of your kids."

"Not as well as I should." Jojo's head falls into her hands. "I'm really messed up. I'm not doing so well."

I join her at the table. "Damien?"

"Yeah, Damien. And life. I love my kids. I definitely love my kids. But I'm so tired all the time. I hardly have a minute to myself and if ever I do, I'm too exhausted to enjoy it."

"So you drink?"

"Damn, Tracey." She pulls her head up. "You know how to cut right to the chase."

"Is it a problem, Jo?"

"No." She places both hands flat on the table. "I don't know." She chuckles. "Could be better. Could be worse."

"If it is a problem there are places that can help. Programs or—"

"Damn." Jojo pushes back her chair. "I'm not in need of AA or anything, k? I just wanted to apologize for the way I spoke to you. I'm okay. I'll be okay. I probably drink too much every now and then, but I would *never* do anything to jeopardize the safety of my children."

Mom's frantic call, when Jojo wanted to drive the kids home after a night of drinking, pops into my mind. It would do no good to bring that up. "What about jeopardizing your own safety? That would hurt your kids t—"

Jo stands. "I was trying to be nice. Trying to smooth things over, but you've always got to pour your holier-than-thou, Miss Perfect Tracey Sampson opinion over everything. Maybe it's best if you deal with your problems and I deal with mine. We'll cross paths when we have to."

I stand, flabbergasted.

"Mommy!" Neveah's voice squeals from the other room.

Jojo walks past me. "Looks like I'm needed. Lovely chat."

"There you are." Adrian enters the kitchen as Jojo leaves it. "You and Jojo having a tête-à-tête?"

I step into his arms. "Something like that."

Adrian drapes an arm over my shoulder. "I was just talking to your Dad's friend, Frank. Did you know he once met Princess Diana? Not just saw or had a single handshake but actually ate a meal with her? Before she was royalty, of course."

"Oh yes," I push my emotions aside and wrap my arm around his middle as we rejoin the party, "I've heard all about that one."

"I told him a bit about my story too. He was pretty interested. He kind of invited himself to the viewing party."

"Oh yeah?" I turn to him. "That's at Jim's bar, right?"

Adrian's smile fades. "Yeah. It's at Jim's bar. You remember when, right?"

"Of course." I smile and search my mind for the date. It's in my phone. It has to be in my phone. I'll check when he's not staring at me. Still, how could I forget?

For the rest of the party—and the rest of the holidays—I do my best to be attentive, present—with Adrian and with the friends and family who surround us.

❧

JUST AFTER NEW YEAR'S I get a clear sign of ovulation and head to the fertility clinic to start my injections. Dr. LeBlanc told me the drugs shooting into me will give the doctor in charge of my case complete control over when I ovulate next. This is truly happening. No turning back.

As we pull into the clinic parking lot Adrian squeezes my hand. "You excited?"

"Sure." I offer a tight-lipped grin. "You?"

"This will work, Tracey. I can feel it."

"And if it doesn't?"

"Then we regroup. We decide what we really want and what we're willing to do for it."

I squeeze his hand back and take a breath. "We won't think of that. We'll stay positive."

"Yeah."

Positive. Positive. Stay positive. The tightness in my chest that's become so familiar squeezes again. I have to believe. I have to erase from my mind that what they'll be putting inside of me is actually a baby, our baby. Almost a handful of times in the past couple of years I've suspected I've conceived, only to lose it before implantation, but this time I'll know. I wouldn't be losing a potential pregnancy; I'd be losing our baby. But I won't lose it. Positive. Positive. Hopeful.

"You ready?"

I look to Adrian. "As I'll ever be!" No more fear. No more worry. It ends today. In the doctor's office I rub my hands together. The bloodwork is good. We're doing this. Our doctor, Dr. Chen, says she'll help us with the first injection so both Adrian and I know how to do it.

"Tracey can do them herself," she says, "but it's more affirming if this is something both of you participate in.

"I'm happy to." Adrian laughs. "Not in a sadistic way or

anything."

"Of course not." The doctor looks to me. "Are you ready?"

I nod. She positions the needle. "Right here. You got it?"

"Yeah."

"Adrian, would you like to do the honours?"

"Sure, okay." He takes the needle from Dr. Chen's hand. "I can't mess up? I won't hurt her."

"It'll hurt. But no, you've got it. Just push down fully."

He does and the pain shoots through me. It's not fun, but nothing compared to the pain I live with regularly. "Like that?" he asks.

"Just like that," says Dr. Chen. "So you're on the short, stimulated procedure." Dr. Chen turns to me. "It means more effect from the drugs, but we find the success rates highest. So normal for you is normally day nineteen?"

"The most normal."

"We're aiming for day fourteen of your treatment cycle, which means your body will go through the process faster than usual and you'll be producing multiple eggs. We'll be monitoring you closely to make sure this process all goes smoothly and to watch out for ovarian stimulation. You remember what—"

Dr. LeBlanc told me all of this before sending me to Dr. Chen. Going over it again only makes me nervous. "I remember."

"We're giving you the highest chance we can."

"I know. We want our highest chance."

"And we'll freeze any high quality fertilized eggs we don't use for future potential use."

Frozen babies. The thought makes me shudder. But I can't think of it like that. I won't think of it like that.

"Of course," Dr. Chen smiles, "let's hope we won't need them."

"And you don't implant more than one?" asks Adrian.

"No, no more than one. But the others will be there if

you decide to go through this again. If you need to. And at a much lower cost." Dr. Chen turns to me. "Tracey, once your period starts you'll be in for more tests: blood work, ultrasounds. If all is good, then another round of injections that will help you produce those multiples."

It's all happening so fast. Dr. Chen hands me a paper with a list of dates. "If all goes well, that's when you'll come in." Dr. Chen passes Adrian another page with the date he'll need to come in for his sperm wash. "No fun time for at least two days before. That's important."

"You're saying if all goes well…what are the chances it won't? Does that mean we may not even get to the transfer?"

Dr. Chen pauses a moment. "The best thing to do is operate with the mentality that all will go well."

Adrian rubs my arm. "Is there anything else we need to be doing during this time, or should be doing?"

"Just relax." Dr. Chen tilts her head. "As much as you can. This procedure, the whole experience, can be stressful, but try to go about your normal life. Pursue all of your normal activities, at least before the transfer. Until then, life as normal."

I give Dr. Chen a smile. Life as normal. I can do that. We can do that.

CHAPTER TWENTY-FOUR

After leaving the clinic, Adrian suggests we go to lunch at the vegetarian restaurant that's now become one of our regular spots. I glance at my watch. "I thought you had to get back to the studio. Isn't it crunch time?"

"I can take another hour off. Today may be the start of our new life." He grins. "Let me correct myself. I believe today will be the start of our new life. We should celebrate."

"Okay." I take his hand. "Let's walk." The snow falls gently around us, coating the world in pristine white. Adrian wraps his arm around my waist and draws me close. We're in this. Together.

The next day I'm back online, searching for naturopaths and acupuncturists. It's unfortunate that I'll have to go to two practitioners, but treatment matters now more than ever. Just as I reach for my phone to call one of the acupuncturists, the screen lights up. Saadia's clinic. "Hello?"

"Good morning. Is Mrs. Tracey Sampson there?"

"Speaking."

"Great. Tracey, Saadia asked me to follow up with you to see if you'd like to book your next appointment. You left last time without re-booking and as it's been several weeks—"

"Is this standard?"

"Pardon me?"

I take a moment to compose myself. "Is this a standard procedure when a patient doesn't return? Do you normally call after a certain amount of time?"

"No." The receptionist sounds flustered. "Saadia specifically asked me to call you. She said she was certain you still wanted treatment and wanted you to know she was eager to continue as well. It's actually," the woman pauses, "well, it's not standard at all."

"Oh." I lean back in my chair.

"She said she has an opening this afternoon if you happen to be free or she could also fit you in Thursday morning at ten a.m. or Friday at two."

"This afternoon." My body tingles. "What time?"

"Three fifteen."

Two hours from now. I'll have to reschedule a tea date with Eloise, but she'll understand. "I'll take it." I grin, nervous but excited. This couldn't have come at a better time. "Thank you." I end the call. Saadia wants me back. She's willing to take me back. This could be nothing but professional honour, a practitioner not wanting to give up on her patient, but it could also be more than that. It has to be more than that. My sister is reaching out.

IT'S BEEN OVER THREE WEEKS since I've sat in the waiting room of Saadia's clinic. It feels good to be here, to give the eggs maturing within me and the eventual fertilized embryo Dr. Chen will implant the best chance to survive. I try not to think too much about the other side of it, whether or not this will be the start of a relationship.

Saadia walks into the waiting room. She greets me as if nothing has changed. "Hi, Tracey. Come on in." I follow her. Once the office door closes, she gestures to the chair I always sit in and pulls up a stool.

"I'm sorry." Her back is rigid, her expression calm. "I didn't handle your announcement well."

I swallow. "It's understandable."

"Yes. It is. But that doesn't make it right. I was so focused on my father, on what it meant for our family, the lies, that I didn't think at all about you, how hard it must have been, how scary." She looks down. "But I'm glad you told me. I'm glad I know."

"I went to see your father."

She nods. "Our father. He told me. It sounds like he was horrible."

I let out the smallest smile. "It wasn't the best day."

"I guess the apple doesn't fall far from the tree." Saadia shakes her head. "I hate clichés, but sometimes…"

"You were nothing like your father. Our father." I stop. "I can't think of him as my father."

"I understand." She lets out the slightest laugh. "There were many years when I didn't like to think of him as my father either. When I wished I was adopted, or that my mother had been the one to cheat and there was a decent man out there somewhere just waiting to call me daughter." She rests her hands on her lap. "That's not entirely fair. He always provided for us. When he could, he went to my school events. He didn't support me through all of this," she waves her hand to indicate her office, "but I know it's partially because he wanted the best for me—a secure life, a stable and respectable career." Her gaze wanders away. "Also because he wanted those things for himself, to brag to his colleagues about his successful children." Her gaze returns. "Anyway, I'm sorry. It was a shock and I reacted badly. I hope you can forgive me."

"I don't think there's much to forgive." I lean forward. "You should have seen the tantrum I threw a couple of days after I met my birth mother. Your response had nothing on that."

Saadia grins. A real, genuine grin. "Well, we all have tantrums from time to time. I understand, too, why you held off telling me. To just walk in here and say that, it would have been an incredibly hard thing to do."

"I didn't know how to do it. And I genuinely wanted…needed treatment. I still do. Besides, you're the only acupuncturist who's also a naturopath in the city. I probably would have chosen you even if you weren't my sister."

Saadia rubs her hands on her pant legs. "And I'm happy to treat you." She pauses. "I don't know if I can offer more than treatment quite yet. This is a painful time for my family. My father denies it, but we know. We all know. My mother cared for Lydia. She welcomed her into our home as a place where a hurting girl could find comfort and security, and my father abused that." Saadia looks away. "When I told my mother about you, about Lydia, how she had no support when her father died, how she gave you away because of it, she nearly broke down. It's as if she feels she's partially to blame."

"She's not."

"I know." Saadia takes a deep breath. "I'm hesitant to ask this, but my mother wanted to know if you could get her Lydia's contact information. She wants to talk to her, to apologize."

"Really?"

"That's what she said."

I hesitate. Is that what Lydia would want? "I'll call her. I'll ask if I can give it."

Saadia nods. "Thank you. If she's able to talk to Lydia, to express her remorse, it could be helpful. My mother and father have had a lot a trouble throughout the years and because of her beliefs my mother has stuck with him through it all, but I don't know if they'll last through this. I feel almost certain they won't. Maybe that's a good thing."

"I didn't mean," I hesitate, "I never thought—"

"This isn't your fault. None of this is your fault. There was another time he…probably more than one, I think I mentioned it?"

"You did."

"And it almost destroyed them then. It could have destroyed my father's image, maybe even his career. He had to stop teaching after that. But besides that consequence it was all very hush hush. My mother now thinks that was wrong. She knows it wasn't a one time thing. But to let her friends know and—"

"I won't tell anyone."

"Thank you. That means a lot to my family." Saadia offers a tight-lipped smile. "When my brothers and I get together in the future…it'll take time, but I hope one day you'll feel welcome, that you can meet our extended family too, and that they'll know who you are."

"Brothers?"

"Patrick and Adham. Patrick may take a while. He's more traditional, believes family must fall under certain structures and doesn't believe you fall under those structures. He's angry about the whole thing. He actually defended our father. It's ridiculous. He may come around. He may not. He's too much like our father. But Adham's excited to meet you. He's closer to your age. He would have been five when you were born. My parents' accidental baby."

I consider Saadia's words. I know all about structures. It's been a problem my entire life. I believed family meant a certain thing—a mom, a dad, and children, all connected. Blood connected. I see my father standing in the basement, his pride over the gift he'd made so long ago, the love in his eyes. I see my mother sitting across from me in the café, my sorrow her own, and then the joy she held at being able to offer me the gift of this procedure. If that's not family… "I knew about Patrick. A friend has worked cases against him. That's actually how I found out about you. But not Adham.

I knew another child existed, but that's all I knew."

"He's the legitimate doctor. After I gave up on traditional medicine I don't think he had a choice." Saadia smiles, a full one this time. "He's a good kid." She laughs. "Man. He's a good man."

"I'd like to meet him too. Both of them." Adham and Patrick. My big brothers. "You said you're still willing to treat me. So this appointment, it's about more than talking things out?"

"If you'd like, absolutely."

"Then I need you now more than ever."

She raises an eyebrow.

"We're doing IVF. I had my first injection yesterday."

"Okay." Saadia draws her stool toward me and takes a hold of my wrist. "Tell me more."

Over the next fifteen minutes Saadia takes my pulses and checks my tongue. I fill her in on all the information about my IVF procedure. When I get up on the table in preparation for my acupuncture treatment she takes my hand. "I want you to come twice a week. We're going to turn your body into the most nourishing home we possibly can. We'll give your baby the best chance. And it's on me."

"Saadia, no."

"There will be no argument." She squeezes my hand. "Think of all the birthdays and Christmases I missed. It's the least I can do for the baby sister I never had a chance to spoil." Her eyes glisten. She gives them a swipe with the back of her sleeve and lets out a small laugh. "I know we're not *there* yet, but I always wanted a sister."

❧

BACK AT HOME, I DECIDE TO call Lydia. If I don't, it will be just one more thing to weigh on me, to create stress where I want relaxation. We've exchanged calls every few weeks since she left and an email or two, but we've talked mostly of surface things: Her travels. My yoga and the new recipes I've found and loved. She knows nothing of the decision to do IVF and nothing of Saadia. She answers on the third ring.

"Tracey, hello!" Laughter sounds in the background. The kids?

"You're back home, now, aren't you?"

"Yes. Just after Christmas."

"That's great. Feel good?" My voice sounds robotic, fake.

"It does." Lydia must hear it. She murmurs something to someone then returns to the phone. "I'm in a quiet room now. What's going on?"

I chicken out. "I decided to do IVF. We decided."

"Wow." There's a slight thump. Has she sunk to a chair? "Well, that's wonderful. Very exciting."

"Yeah. Scary. But exciting too."

"Well, we'll be thinking of you, Westin and I, when's the—"

I take a deep breath. "That's not actually why I called."

"Okay."

I've been pacing the living room floor, but now I sit. "The naturopath I told you about, who does acupuncture too…"

"Yes?"

"It was Saadia."

"Saa—"

"Medina."

"That's uh…wow." Her words come out tight. "So you've met Sebastien then?"

"I have. Just recently. Months after meeting Saadia."

Silence. "And?"

"I finally told Saadia who I was, just a few weeks ago. Then I met Sebastien."

"Okay."

"And Mrs. Medina, she…she wants to talk to you."

A deep intake of breath.

"Lydia?"

"Why?"

"I don't know. To apologize? To—"

"It's not her fault."

"I said I'd ask."

More silence.

"Lydia, are you okay?"

Several breaths.

"I think it's important to her. It's fine if you say no, but—"

"It's fine. Yes. Give her my number. Or email. Whichever she prefers."

"Are you sure you're okay?"

"It can't be easy, learning that about your husband."

"No."

A few more breaths. "Let's talk about you. What made you decide on IVF and how are you feeling, really feeling?"

I smile at the warmth in her voice, the genuine interest. She's just had an emotional bomb blasted at her, and yet she's more concerned about me. I can scarcely believe it…how good it feels.

CHAPTER TWENTY-FIVE

Almost a month later, it's the morning of the embryo transfer. I open my eyes feeling nervous but surprisingly energetic, considering I probably didn't sleep more than three hours. I lie in bed, contemplating what's still to come and what's already transpired on this journey. The past two weeks have been intense, with trips to the clinic—ultrasounds or blood tests—almost every other day. After the transfer, however, there'll be the lull…the wait. So far, every test I've taken has been just as it should be. That, in itself, says Dr. Chen, is reason to celebrate. Many women, especially women in my situation, don't even get this far in the process. But I have. The eggs collected were healthy…all nine of them. Five were successfully fertilized and are dividing and growing well. The healthiest will be chosen today. Dr. Chen grinned when she passed on the news. 'You must be doing something right. Whatever it is, keep it up.'

So I do just that. After a glance at Adrian, who lies against his pillow with the ease of sleep drawn across his face, I turn on to my back. I take a moment to appreciate the warmth of the covers, the softness of my sheets, and the comfort of this space. Then I close my eyes. Due to my cysts and other potential issues with inflammation and scar tissue, the doctor told me she'll do a mock transfer of the chosen fertilized egg before the real one. I asked her to walk me through it all. With patience, she did. Holding Dr.

Chen's words in my mind, I start today's visualization, imagining each step the doctor and I will take: me walking into the room, hoisting myself up onto the bed, placing my feet in the stirrups, then leaning back and feeling the coolness and pain of the speculum, followed by the catheter. Next, Dr. Chen will do the mock run, where she finds everything to be clear and ready. I'll smile at this, as relief and certainty run through me…everything is as it should be.

The actual transfer will begin. With as much detail as I can muster, right down to the paint on the walls and the colour of the tiled floor, I bring to life each moment and send out thoughts of protection for the child that is little more than a conglomeration of cells. The embryo will be inside of me. And then I'll wait. I take the visualization even further, relying on videos I've watched on YouTube. I see implantation happening. I envision that embryo dividing, growing, and transforming from a mass of cells into a perfectly formed human being. I skip over the labour, right to the moment when I hold our child in my arms.

After my visualization, I rise from the bed, shower, get dressed, and head across town to Saadia's clinic. She opens the clinic doors then locks them behind me—the office doesn't open for another half hour. She pulls me into a quick hug then steps back. "How are you feeling?"

I undo my coat, my fingers shaking with each button. "Nervous. Excited. Hopeful."

She squeezes my shoulder as she guides me to the treatment room. "Just as I thought you'd feel."

"Thank you again—"

"Stop." She waves a hand. "This is as much selfish behaviour as it is a favour. I would be thrilled to have another niece or nephew around, and," she stops at the door to her office, "my daughter Natalie is great with kids. I'm sure she'd love to babysit one day."

"How was her recital?" I hover by the desk.

"Wonderful. She plays like an angel."

I step to the bed and pull off my boots. It's only been in the past few weeks that Saadia has told me about her family. Her two girls, Natalie and Kaitlyn, and her son, Patrick Jr. I've yet to meet any of them but from the way she talks, I almost feel as if I have. "And Patrick Jr. has a big game this weekend, right?"

"His skates are sharpened and he's rearing to go." She steps out of the room and I undress. When Saadia returns she does her needle magic then steps to her stereo. "I prepared something special for you today. It's a forty minute guided meditation specifically for IVF transfers. A friend of mine made it."

A sliver of resistance runs through me. This wasn't part of my plan. I imagined the music I always listen to here, had already gone over the mantras I planned to use...but I push the resistance away. Today is all about being open. "Sounds wonderful."

Saadia is about to start the track when she stops. "My mom said to say thank you for Lydia's number. She called her."

"Yeah?"

"It was helpful, being able to talk to her. She said Lydia was wonderful, so gracious."

"She can be."

"Thank you for setting that up. It meant a lot to Mom, to be able to apologize...Lydia was a guest in her home."

I nod, not knowing what else to say. Saadia starts the track and backs out of the room. Within minutes the core of my fear and nervousness has softened. The peace and hope the track brings rests inside me like a ball of energy. If I can hold on to this feeling throughout today, throughout the next two weeks, I know all will go well.

Of course, the minute I step into the fertility clinic the ball of peace seems to dissipate. Adrian squeezes my hand. I squeeze it back and hope and pray that this time, this one time, my body will not fail me, and I won't fail the people I love most.

The whole process goes almost exactly as I imagined it, everything as it should be. And then Dr. Chen says goodbye. Time to wait.

✧

A WEEK AFTER THE TRANSFER I'm practicing yoga when, in the middle of sun salutation, a cramp radiates through my lower abdomen. I stop, frozen, waiting for another, wondering if it was real or an imagined nothing. I keep my breath even, willing it to be nothing, willing everything to be fine. Another cramp pulses. Every fear of the past week, of the past year, rushes through me like flood waters. I sink to the couch.

I close my eyes and breathe in, out, in. This pain is not as bad as the worst pain. Not even close. I try to assess it, think critically. Is it the same pain I often get as notice that Aunt Flo is approaching? It's similar in intensity, that's for certain, but is it the same?

With my eyes still closed I lean against the seat cushions, waiting to assess the next cramp, but hoping that moment never comes. Several minutes pass and I'm just starting to relax when there it is, a radiating pulse of pain and discomfort. It could be different. Maybe it is different, the pain of my uterus prepping to expand, or the convulse of the little embryo, my baby, fighting to burrow itself deeper into my endometrium wall. How many times have I held these same fears, ruminated over these same questions? I've read the forums. Many women have thought for sure their period was coming based on pains that seemed like their normal cramping. Nature's cruel joke. Eve's consequence, perhaps. So maybe that's all this is. Maybe. Probably. I ease the tension in my clenched jaw and relax the vice grip of my hand on the throw cushion beside me. This could be nothing. Better than nothing. It could be the sign I'm hoping for…or the one I dread. Either way there's nothing I can do, nothing I should do, except relax. I stretch out on the couch. But what if I can do something? I reach for my phone and dial Dr. Chen's nurse's line.

"Hello?"

I press the phone to my ear, hating the way my hand trembles. "Hi, I'm Tracey Sampson, one of Dr. Chen's IVF patients. Is she available?"

"No, and probably not for several hours. Is there anything I can help you with?"

I explain my symptoms.

"Oh, hon, it could be nothing. And Dr. Chen already has you on progesterone cream, correct?"

"Yes."

"Then there's nothing else to be done."

"But—"

"If you're nervous, take it easy. Relax. Watch your favourite movie or read your favourite book."

"So there's nothing—"

"Honestly, go about your life as normal. No heavy activity, nothing that will have you straining or bouncing around, but beyond that light activity can be good. Try not to stress."

"But you just said to relax. To lie down."

"Relax your mind. Do things that help you not to stress. If that's lying on the couch to watch a movie, fabulous. If it's taking a nice walk with your hubby, all the better."

"Could it be safer to lie down?"

"Hon," the nurse's voice is strained, her patience worn thin. "If you'll feel better lying down, then lie down. Rest. Try not to worry. That's the best thing you can do."

"Okay. Fine. Thanks." I end the call feeling no better. Do what makes me feel most relaxed? In this moment, I can't see how anything can. Thousands of dollars, months of effort, and the hopes of a multitude of people rest on my ability to relax. That seems like the perfect set-up for intense stress. I go back to the yoga mat and try to finish today's routine. I get through the moves, but they're nothing more than that, moves. When I finish, my body feels tighter than when I began. Tight and angry. With all the technological advances humanity has made, it's ludicrous they don't have this down yet. They can clone a sheep, but they can't facilitate with any certainty the most important process to ensure the success and continuation of the human race.

I pace up and down the hall from the living room to the kitchen. These thoughts are stupid, pointless. Narrow-minded. The continuation of the human race does not rely on this procedure, only the continuation of my genetic line. Toulouse scampers by my feet. I scoop him up and nuzzle my face against his soft, purring body. He nuzzles right back and I hold him tighter. My phone rings. Jojo. Instantly any anger that had dissipated returns. Jojo, who's been taking the privilege of being a mother for granted, who has no idea how lucky she is. I set Toulouse down and answer the call. "Yes."

"Oh, great. Trace, hi."

"Hello."

"Would you mind watching the kids this afternoon? I've had a crazy week at work and Mom and Dad are busy. I need some time for myself."

"I'm busy." Focusing on needing to relax may not exactly count as busy, but Jojo doesn't need to know that.

"Hey," Jojo's voice is easy, charming, "I know we had a little bit of a ruffle at Christmas, but Reggie was sick last week then Lulu and Neveah caught it. I just really need some time to relax, de-stress, you know?"

"What, by getting drunk?"

"No." Jojo sounds as if I've whipped her. "No. You were right, okay? I was self-medicating I guess, but I thought about what you said, what Mom and Dad said, what one of my co-workers said…I was going a tad overboard.

I'm not anymore. I promise. I just…well," she pauses, "I wasn't planning to tell anybody, but I'm training for a half-marathon. And with the kids sick, I'm way behind on my training schedule. It's so nice today, I thought I could get a run in outside, with the snow and the cold lately, well, I want to take advantage of good weather. I need this. I need the motivation and—"

"I never took you for a liar."

"What?"

"Irresponsible. Rude. Childish. But an out and out liar?"

"Trace." The line goes silent. "Why is this so hard to believe? I did one in high school."

"Yeah. And I haven't known you to run since. This is really low, Jo, lying to get your way, to—"

"Never mind."

"Yeah, never mind. Isn't it you who said it'd be better if we each kept to our own problems? Let's do that."

More silence. "You're right. I'm sorry, I…sorry to trouble you. Have a good night." The line goes dead and I stare at the phone. I'd expected retaliation, even begging. Not that. The fight drains out of me. If I were looking at myself in a mirror right now, I'm sure I wouldn't like what I see. I set the phone down and slump back onto the couch. I still don't believe her, but for maybe the first time in our relationship, it's me who feels like the child. I curl up, hating this new part of me, wishing I was the person I always thought I was—a person full of compassion, love, patience. The person I'd always presented myself to be. Instead, I'm angry. Bitter. Selfish. Maybe I don't even deserve to be someone's mother.

⤱

I HAVE NO IDEA HOW much time has passed when Adrian rouses me. "Hey, sleeping beauty. We've got to go soon.

Get dressed."

I stretch and yawn. "Go?"

"The showing. My doc." He grins. "Tonight's the night!"

"Your?" I sit up. "Oh. I thought that was tomorrow."

His smile drops. "No. It's tonight. I told you."

"I know you did, I just…" I rub my cheek, trying to infuse life back into my face. "I thought it was tomorrow."

"It's tonight." He sits beside me. "Hey, have you been crying?"

I shrug.

"What's up?"

Do I tell him about the cramps? Worry him tonight of all nights? "It's nothing. I'm fine."

"Trace."

"Really."

"Okay, well," he shifts to the edge of the couch, "you need to get ready then. We have to leave in fifteen minutes or we'll be late."

"Babe." I let my hand fall on his knee. "You mind if I watch it at home? I won't ask you to, I know you'll want to see it with the crew, but I need to take it easy tonight."

He stands. "Are you sick?"

"No, but—"

"Tracey, I've been working on this for over two years. It's the biggest story of my career."

"I know and I'll watch it. I'm excited to—"

"I need you there with me."

"Adrian." My smile comes out sad. "I've got something really big going on right now too."

He crosses his arms. "And how exactly will coming out tonight affect that? The doctor said—"

"She said I should try to relax. And it's at a bar. It'll be loud. Everyone will be drinking. I've had a stressful day and—"

"No."

"What?"

"No. You're coming. You've known it would be in a bar for weeks and you never said anything before. You're my wife, and you're going to be there."

"Excuse me?" I sit straighter. "I'm going to be there? Are you commanding me?"

"Damn." He steps away then turns back. "Don't pull that on me."

"I'm not—"

"Our lives are not exclusively about you, and they're not exclusively about trying to have a baby either. This is our life. Tonight is our life. And tonight is about me. It's not about you. It's not about the cluster of cells inside of you—"

"It's not a cluster of cells. It's our baby."

"Not yet."

"Adrian!"

"Okay, if that's our baby, what are the frozen embryos in some clinic somewhere? Are they our babies too?"

"We can't think like that."

"I know. And we can't think this is our baby yet either. It's not. It's the hope of a baby, yes. But only a hope. And you're doing everything you can and should do. More than that. You've been amazing, really, inspiring in your commitment, but staying home won't improve anything. Tonight is not about procreation. It's about me."

He steps back, his hands extended in supplication. "Just one night. That's all I'm asking. One night." He sits again. "I need you there. And maybe this sounds selfish, but it's not. You sitting in a bar, whether it's noisy or people are drinking or doing back-flips or whatever, will not harm your chances. You may think it will, but it won't. And if it stresses you out, that's on you. That's you letting yourself be stressed."

"Adrian."

"Listen, I put up with a lot. And for the most part I'm happy to. I love you. And I want what you want. But this wait we're on, it's only one step. Even if you get a positive next week, it doesn't mean we have a baby."

"I know." My voice rises. "Don't you think I know?"

"Then act like it. You can't spend the next nine months avoiding every possible, potential risk. You still have to live. We have to live." His voice cracks, whether from anger or sadness I don't know.

"I'm trying my best. Everybody is counting on this working and—"

"No. No one is counting on it working. I'm not. Your parents aren't. You shouldn't be. We're hoping. Hoping. But it's out of our hands." He drops his head. "Just have a little peace."

"I'm trying. That's why I want to stay home. I told you, today was rough and—"

"No. You need to come for me, and you need to come for you. You need to do something other than wait for a baby that may never show up."

"Everyone will question. Your family will be there, your friends and—"

"And maybe they'll question and maybe they won't. If they do, you politely say we don't know yet but we're hoping, and you leave it at that. You deal with it." He looks up at me. "Get this through your head, with all respect, you have to understand tonight is not about you. This procedure, this wait, isn't even about you. It's about us and our potential family. And tonight, I'm asking you to do something for our family. Give me your support. Give me your attention. More than anyone else, you're the one I want to see this. And I want to be sitting beside you as you do."

I'm shamed hearing him, my own husband, begging for a little attention. He's right, too, any stress tonight brings will be stress I allow. "I'm sorry. Tonight's about you. I'll go get dressed."

CHAPTER TWENTY-SIX

The pub is crowded with people, the air warm, and the atmosphere festive.

"Adrian!" A beautiful woman steps into his arms: Maesa, the anchorwoman I was jealous of last year. "And Tracey," Maesa offers her hand and I take it, "it's so nice to see you again." She grins. "You're looking lovely, as usual."

"Thank you."

With a smile, Maesa holds my gaze a moment longer then leans in toward Adrian, her body inches from his. "The network execs are very pleased. They had a screening this afternoon." She lays a hand on his arm. My body tenses. "This will be a game-changer for you. I heard whispers of a permanent position."

"And give up free-lancing?" Adrian practically glows. "I don't know about that."

"Well," Maesa's voice reminds me of a bubbling brook, "you'll have options, anyway." She waves and steps away as someone catches her attention.

Adrian squeezes my shoulder. "I know exactly what we're going to see. I know it's one story among hundreds of stories, but—"

"It's an hour and a half feature documentary. It's more than just a news story. This is big."

Adrian nods. "Yeah." His grin still makes my stomach flutter. "And it's important, too. If the right people see this, or if it inspires others to act, it could change lives."

"Exactly."

Adrian's oldest brother, Ricky, clamps a hand down on his shoulder from behind. Adrian turns and they embrace. His brother laughs. "From print to the big screen, huh? Quite the leap."

"It's not the big screen."

Ricky points to one of the large flat screens above the bar. "Looks pretty big to me."

Adrian chuckles. "I guess."

"Now, don't tell me all of these people are here for you." Ricky gives Adrian a light shoulder punch.

"They're here for the doc."

"Well, you drew a crowd."

"Journalists love to drink."

"But," Ricky grins, "look, even Ma came. Ma in a bar, can you believe it?" Ricky gestures to a booth across the room where their mother sits with Adrian's Dad and Ricky's wife. Adrian excuses himself to say hello.

Ricky turns to me. "And how's my favourite sister-in-law?" He gives me a squeeze.

"Are you allowed to say that?"

"Of course I am. Just don't tell the other one."

"Oh, I see."

"You pretty proud of that man of yours?" He looks toward Adrian.

"Of course."

"He's something else." Ricky turns to me. "As are you. After…well, we weren't sure Adrian would get out of the slump he was in. A justified slump, don't get me wrong, but then he met you."

"He certainly didn't seem in a slump when we met. I don't think I—"

"No. You did. Adrian's, well, Adrian. He's the proverbial golden boy; he puts on a good show. Everyone loves him and he knows how to stay loved. In public. But he was not doing well, then you snapped him out of it."

"Ricky—"

"Maybe I shouldn't talk like this but none of us had huge love for his first wife. Julia was a nice enough woman I guess, but she wasn't right for Adrian. They met young, it was fast and furious, and then she got pregnant. I'm not saying they didn't love each other, in a way, but it wasn't like with you. I never saw Adrian look at Julia the way he looks at you."

I rub a hand along my neck, remembering Adrian's visit, his need to compare his love for me to his love for her. "I'm causing him a lot of pain too."

"Nah," Ricky gives my shoulder a squeeze, "circumstance is causing you both pain. It's not you."

I look to Adrian, who has his arm around his mother, who looks so happy. Ricky's words are only partly true. Yes, it's circumstance, but it's also me. Selfish, one-track-minded me, who's been so wrapped up in her own wants her husband had to beg her to come out on a night that means so much to him.

"Hey." Ricky jostles me. "Trust me. Not once has that man regretted you're the one he chose. Despite all you're both going through, not once."

"Thanks, Ricky." I smile up at him. "I hope you're right."

"Oh, I am." He looks at me straight-faced. "I'm never wrong. That's my best quality."

I laugh and we walk over to Adrian and his parents. Adrian spends the next twenty minutes or so weaving through the room as he chats with more family, friends, and colleagues.

Eloise, Allison, and Sheila show up about ten minutes before show time and I quickly catch up on what's been going on with them. Eloise flashes a ring and grins. "We decided."

"Congratulations!"

"Just last night. We're going to keep it all very low-key."

I wrap my arms around her and probe for what details she can quickly give, but as the documentary's about to start and there are no seats near us, I have to wave goodbye as they head to a table across the room.

A minute before the doc starts, the owner of the bar makes an announcement and turns up the volume on the TVs. About five are dispersed throughout the space. Several minutes later, Maesa's voice announces the upcoming feature, warning that viewer discretion is advised due to mature and potentially disturbing content. And then it's Adrian's voice over the video of a young girl walking in a sketchy part of lower downtown. The girl looks like any other. She's wearing skin tight skinny jeans with flat-bottomed sneakers and a purple t-shirt. Her hair is pulled back in a high ponytail and her makeup is evident, though not overdone. She doesn't look like a prostitute. She looks like a girl I could find sitting in one of my Advanced English classes. Eager. Hopeful. A bright future ahead of her. Adrian's words tell another story.

This is Melinda. She started working as a prostitute when she was fourteen. It was a better option than living on the street, afraid of being raped or beaten every day, afraid of starving or freezing to death once winter hit. Today she's seventeen. She's not on the streets anymore. She's not being raped. She's not being beaten. But the life she was thrust into is one she'll never fully escape. Last month, the same month she came to a shelter looking for a way out, the same month she decided she wanted to turn her life around and put all she's been through behind her, Melinda learned she is HIV positive.

The image pans out and morphs into another where a cluster of girls sit in a classroom. I recognize the room, it's one of mine. I glance to Adrian. When did he go into my school? Who did he talk to? How did I miss this? Or did he tell me? He could have told me. I scan the faces. None of them are ones I recognize.

Melinda's story is just one story. Thousands of girls in this country have similar ones, and the majority of them aren't on the streets. They don't need to be. All they need is a camera, a skimpy outfit, and internet access. They may have a pimp directing their every move, or they may have figured out the system for themselves. Neither is a safe scenario. They could be sitting beside your child in school. They could be your child.

The camera pans away from the pseudo students to the window. A girl stands outside that window, Melinda, looking in. The camera focuses on her, leaning against a tree, looking like her life is not one she wants to be living. And then we have the voice of Melinda. She tells her story. Her dad died when she was seven. Her mom couldn't handle it. Went heavy on the anti-depressants. Stopped really being a mom. Then the boyfriends came. The fourth one raped her. At eight. When her mom found out, she overdosed. Instantly, Melinda had no one. She bounced from foster home to foster home until, at fourteen, she'd had enough. She ran away for good, crossed half the country to do it, and met her pimp. She didn't know that's what he was at first. He was someone to take care of her, to make her feel loved, special. Until he decided it was her turn to support him. She hardly saw a dime of what she made. But what did it matter? What did any of it matter? Sex wasn't sacred. Her mom's boyfriend had taught her that. And her new boyfriend made sure she never forgot it.

Her words sound like a stereotypical story, only it's not at all, because it's hers. And it's real. Seventeen.

I used to be so afraid I'd get pregnant out there, she says at one point in her story. *I'd seen it happen to other girls. My guy would warn me about it all the time. But condoms break. Pills aren't one hundred percent effective. It was a fear. I saw girls get pregnant. Some tried to keep those kids and it was a bad scene. It was funny, not haha funny, but weird funny. The ones heavy on the drugs were always the ones who wanted to keep their babies. Most of the other girls knew better. They gave them up. And I didn't want to get pregnant because I knew I'd have to give my baby up too. But what if he or she got put in a crap home? What if she was in no real home at all, in the system like I was? What if my life became my child's? And now.* Melinda looks away from the screen. Her jaw is clenched tight. *Now I don't have to worry about it. I'll never have a kid. How could I?*

The documentary cuts to social workers, shelter workers, women who've gotten out of the trade and are trying to help those still in it. Some who've gotten out just try to forget: their faces are blurred, as are the faces of several other underage girls still working. Their stories are told in snippets, not the full detail of Melinda's, but each is heartbreaking. Each seems impossible.

Adrian interviews politicians and judges. He talks to several men with blurred out faces or altered voices he's contacted by posting fake online ads using terms such as young, fresh, and innocent: codes for underage. The stats the documentary delivers for the number of girls living this life, the number of estimated men supporting it, and how little the country is doing to stop it, is staggering.

But my mind keeps going back to Melinda and the child she'll never let herself have, to all those other babies who, hopefully, will find families worthy of them. And Melinda, what if, when she was eight, the right foster family had come along? Or what if loving people had stepped up to adopt her? People who could have given her an entirely different life, helped her deal with the trauma inflicted by her parents' deaths and that scumbag of a man who tore her childhood away? Surely her face wouldn't be on the screen before me now. Surely she wouldn't have, if not a death sentence, a life and disease no young girl should have.

I draw my eyes away from the screen. What would have happened to me? I've told myself my life wouldn't have turned out like this if Mom and Dad hadn't taken me in, but it could have. I have no idea what could have happened. An overwhelming urge to call my parents, to thank them, bubbles within me. I could have been her. So easily, I could have been her.

"Are you okay?" Adrian whispers in my ear as he takes

my hand.

I look over at him and, in that moment, realize I'm crying. "Yes. Sorry. Yes." I wipe the tears away and squeeze his hand. "This is really good."

"Thanks." He kisses my temple and we both turn back to the screen.

As the documentary continues, I do my best to pull away from thoughts of myself and the life I could have lived if Mom and Dad hadn't walked into my group home. This night is about Adrian and the incredible thing he was instrumental in creating. People will be moved, convicted. Funding will flow in to support these girls, to help them find another life. Regulations may be changed. The piece is hard-hitting yet full of heart. It's amazing. And I knew so little about it. I squeeze Adrian's hand again and he glances over with a smile. I've been so wrapped up in my own life and problems. How many times has he come home eager to talk, and I've only half listened? How often has he put his excitement or frustration aside to comfort or support me?

Melinda appears on the screen once more. She has her own apartment. She's taking GED courses. So far, the meds are working well. She has hope. Next, we see the director from the shelter and transition house. Funds are waning. The wait list for the program is ridiculous. She's angry, and, as far as I can tell, justifiably so. *Some of these girls end up in prison.* Her look is scathing. *They're the victims.*

It's at this moment that I realize the bar is silent except for the sound coming from each of the TVs. Everyone is riveted. They have been since it started. And I almost didn't come. When the credits roll my grin is so big it almost hurts. Adrian and his crew stand to a round of applause. Joy and pride burst through me. How did I not see how amazing this husband of mine is, how important, the potential he has to spread good in the world? I knew it once. But how could I have forgotten?

And then it hits me. I forgot because this side of his life

has nothing to do with us making a baby. It has nothing to do with me being broken. Neither has this night…and I've loved it. It's been wonderful. Being with Adrian, his family, his friends, and, for the most part, not thinking about my lack of a baby, has been wonderful. It's felt like life again.

Eloise rushes over to us. "Adrian, that was phenomenal."

"So crazy." Allison sidles up with Sheila by her side. "So tragic. I mean you hear about these things, but I didn't know it was happening here."

"Too many people don't know," says Sheila, "but way more will."

Adrian nods. "Thanks, again, Sheila, for connecting me with that judge. She really rounded out the piece."

I raise my eyebrows. "And the classroom?"

"That was me." Eloise lifts a hand.

"How did I not know this?"

Eloise shrugs. "You've been busy. Preoccupied."

I'm about to reply when Maesa and a couple of people from the camera and editing crew come over. Adrian thanks the girls for coming and for their help, then turns to chat to his colleagues. I watch him a moment before turning back to my friends—friends who've apparently spent more time with my husband than with me in the past few months. "Okay." I let my curiosity about how I missed so much fall away. There's something more important to be curious about. I focus on Eloise. "Tell me about this proposal. I want every detail."

I listen intently as Eloise, her face lit with excitement, tells the tale. I smile and nod and ooh and ahh. It feels good. It feels normal. This whole night feels like normal life again. I guess because it is… I didn't realize how much I missed it.

CHAPTER TWENTY-SEVEN

Outside of the owners and staff, Adrian and I are among the last to leave the bar. We step into the softly falling snow. On the two block walk to the car, Adrian wraps his arm around my shoulder and draws me close. "So what did you think?"

"It was amazing."

"Complete honesty here. If it was lacking something I want to know. That way we can do better next time."

"It amazed me. And it's important." I give him a squeeze. "I'm proud of you."

A smile breaks across his face as he looks to the sky. "I feel this huge release, you know? I mean, off and on, that was over two years of my life."

"I know."

"And now it's done."

"And you'll be on to the next incredible story."

He laughs. "I actually already have an idea for the next."

"Really?"

"Yeah. I like the news pieces, writing's great—digging for a story, having that sharp deadline, pulling it all together. It's a rush. But this," he shakes his head as if amazed, "this was so much more. I was able to dig so much deeper, meld things together, and working with the crew, getting feedback from other journalists, it felt so much more important."

"It was important. It is."

"I know. I mean fewer people actually watched it tonight

than would have watched a fifteen minute news segment, but this has more permanence. This will last."

"Did I mention I'm proud of you?"

He pushes aside my furry winter hat and kisses my forehead. "You did. You may not know it, but I was pretty nervous leading up to tonight. I needed you here." That grin again. "Thank you for coming."

I stop and step over to a bench then perch on top of it. Adrian follows. "We need to talk."

His brow furrows. "What's up?"

I take in the white world around me, the chill in the air, the way the snow mutes all the sound around us. "I owe you an apology." I turn to Adrian. "Tonight made me see that in a way I couldn't before. I've been selfish and entirely focused on me. I was holding up having a child as the most important thing—for me and for you. You've told me it's not. You've told me you could be happy either way. But I didn't believe you." I smile and shrug. "I couldn't believe you. I do now, or at least I did tonight. I can't promise I won't slip back into…well, how I've been."

"Trace—"

I raise a hand. "Let me finish. I can't promise that, but I promise I'll try. I'll try to be the woman you fell in love with. The woman you deserve."

Adrian's face softens. He wears the look of a man in love. "You're more than I deserve. Do you have any idea how much I admire you?" He steps forward. "Your determination. Your drive. You're already a better mother than millions of women out there. You've done so much to become one."

"But not enough to be a good wife for you." I reach one of my gloved hands to Adrian's cheek. "I want to change that. You've told me we're stronger than infertility, stronger than whatever fears may plague us. I finally believe it. We can make this work, child or no child."

"Of course we can."

"And we're a family. You're my family."

"Yeah." He lets out a chuckle. "We are."

"There's something else too."

He leans back. "What?"

"If this doesn't work, I'm not saying we stop trying, but maybe we'll put our names on that adoption list."

His mouth opens with a silent laugh of excitement.

"We're good people. Not everyone is."

"No. They're not." His smile fades to seriousness. "Is this about the doc? I don't want you to make a decision you're not sure of just because—"

"Yeah. It's about the doc. But it's more than that. Melinda's story opened my eyes to what my life could have been, but it also opened my eyes to the lives of all the children out there who need someone to love them. And who knows, maybe we're meant to be those people."

"We could be."

I bite my lip, hardly believing the words coming out of my mouth, words I thought I would never say. "I was given a family. I didn't always see it like that, I focused on what I didn't have, what was taken away, but my parents are my parents. Just as much as Lydia is, more. More than Sebastien." I pause. "He's not my father, he's—"

"A sperm donor."

I laugh. "Yeah. Exactly. Nothing more." I look to the ground, then back at Adrian. "This procedure may be my only chance at a genetically related child. I can't lie and say I don't still want that more, but it's not everything. It's not the only way to have a family."

Adrian pulls me from the bench, spins me in his arms, then rests me back down. "I was worried you'd never get there, babe. I gotta tell you, at times I was worried." He hops up beside me. "Don't get me wrong, I want this baby."

"Me too. I still feel I need this baby."

Adrian takes my hand again.

"But I know if it…if he or she doesn't come, we'll be

okay." A dash of fear and nervousness threatens to slither over me, but I push it away. "Eventually, ultimately, we'll be okay."

He rubs his thumb against my hand. The silence of the night surrounds us as we sit, each in our own thoughts. The words I've spoken spill through my mind. Some terrify me, but they're true. All of them.

Adrian nudges me. "My butt's starting to freeze."

I hop off the bench. "Mine too. Besides, we've still got a bun in here trying to cook. I'm supposed to keep it warm."

He draws me to his side and wraps his arm around my middle as we walk the remaining block to the car. "This help?"

I nod and snuggle into him.

EXHAUSTION WEIGHS ON me like a cloak by the time we step through our apartment door. It's still early, but I head right to bed. Some time later I'm roused as Adrian settles in beside me. He stretches out his arms and draws me close. Our bodies nestle together as if they were made to fit that way. I drift back into sleep. It's the dream I've been waiting for. I'm holding a baby and somehow I know it's mine. I draw my finger across the child's cheek and she coos. She smiles and gurgles and I can sense she's hungry. Without an ounce of fear or hesitation at the prospect of feeding this baby with my own body, or concern of how to actually go about doing it, I take out my left breast and the child latches on effortlessly. She's sucking, and it's one of the strangest, most incredible things I've ever experienced. But then the baby lets go. She whimpers. I try to guide her mouth back to my nipple, but she won't latch on. She screams. Louder and louder and nothing I do stops her. It's heartbreaking. It's terrifying. I try to speak, to sing, to do something to comfort her, but no words come. She keeps screaming. Blood curdling cries. I jostle her and the screams get worse. It's like nothing I've ever heard.

My eyes whip open. My body is drenched in sweat. I'm shaking.

"Trace, it's just the phone. It's okay."

"What?" I turn to Adrian. What is he talking about? What? The phone. Our land line. It rings again and again. No one calls the land line.

"You okay?" he asks.

I nod.

"All right. I'll go get it. I'll be right back."

I grip his arm. "No."

"It's okay. You must have been having a dream."

"No. I'll get it." I step out of bed. The ringing stops. I look to Adrian. "I'll see if there's a message." Before I've finished my sentence, the phone rings again. I dash to the living room and answer the call.

"Tracey?"

"Mom? What—"

"It's Jojo."

CHAPTER TWENTY-EIGHT

y mother starts rambling things into the phone. She's crying and choking over her sobs and I only pick up pieces. Jojo. Hit. A car.

Fear and anger overtake me. "Was she drunk? Was she driving drunk?"

"I don't know." My mother wails. "They won't tell us anything. No one is telling us anything."

My father's voice. "Tracey, honey, it may be bad." Silence. "How soon can you get to the hospital?"

My blood runs cold. It's not just an expression. I can literally feel a chill flow through me. My throat tightens. "Daddy?"

"Hopefully it's not. Hopefully…" his voice trails off. "Are you coming?"

"Yeah. Yes. We're leaving now." I drop the phone and return to the bedroom. I flip on the overhead light, pull out the first pair of pants I see, and reach for a sweater.

Adrian scrambles out of bed. "What's going on?"

"A car accident. Jojo. They don't know how bad it is." Adrian steps toward me and pulls me into his arms. I push him away. "There's not time."

"Okay."

"I have to get to the hospital."

"I'll take you." I stop—one sock on, the other in my hand. Adrian reaches into the closet and brings out a bra. "You might want this."

I take it from him and sink to the bed. My hands shake. Jojo. "I yelled at her this afternoon. I—"

"Don't worry about that right now, okay? Finish getting dressed."

In the car I stare out the window, words rotate in my mind like a mantra: *Let her be okay. Let her be okay. Let her be okay.*

❦

AT THE HOSPITAL, ADRIAN and I are directed down a hall I've never walked. Through a glass walled room I see my parents. I push through the doors and step into their waiting arms. My father holds me so tight it's hard to breathe. Flashes of Dad's accident this summer rise to the surface, but I know without being told this is worse. Much worse.

"Any news?" asks Adrian.

"She's still in surgery," my father's eyes look vacant, "but they said her condition is stable."

Mom grasps Dad's arm. "What was she doing running at this hour? Why would she—"

"What?" I snap. "She was running?"

"Yes. Running at eleven at night. Why would she—"

I collapse into a chair.

"Tracey?"

"Nothing, I—" The words close off in my throat.

Dad sits beside me. His voice sounds vacant, too. "The driver was drunk. Drinking. Past the limit. If he hadn't realized…if he hadn't called."

I look at my father.

"A nurse said one of the EMTs said there was no way she would have made it if the driver hadn't called 911 when he did. Three more minutes and—" Now his words cease.

"He should go to prison," Mom clenches her teeth, "anyone who—"

Adrian steps forward. "Where are the kids?"

"At their house." My mother's voice is shrill. "We had no idea about that either. We didn't know if the kids were with her or…" she lets out a little moan. "When I heard I thought…I thought maybe she…and the children."

"But the kids are fine." Dad stands and pulls Mom to his side; he seems to regain an aspect of himself. "One of Jojo's high school friends is with them. Apparently Jojo is training for a race and asked the friend to stay while the kids slept."

"A race." Mom scowls. "Why so late at night?" She looks at all of us, as if expecting an answer. My head hangs. Words from this afternoon trail back to me…

"We don't know, sweetie." Dad pats Mom's hand, fully the father I know once again. "When Jojo didn't come home when she said she would, the friend started calling."

"Thankfully someone was smart enough to bring Jojo's cell phone in. If they hadn't—" Mom stops. Her eyes widen. She steps out of Dad's arms. I turn my gaze to see a young man in a white coat approach. I stand.

Dad speaks first. "What's the word?"

The doctor takes us all in before answering. "She's still stable. For now. We'll be monitoring her closely."

"Is she awake? Can we see her?" Mom.

"Let the man finish." Dad.

"A few more hours." The doctor. "She's still in surgery, but things are going well."

"Going well? It's already been hours." Mom. "Is she okay? Will she be? What—"

The doctor raises his hand. "She's had extensive damage to her leg and arm on the right side. She's getting a rod inserted to stabilize her femur now." The doctor pauses as a strangled breath escapes my mother. He clears his throat. "Her lungs have severe bruising. Several ribs are cracked. We had to remove a kidney."

"What?" Mom shrieks. Adrian holds me tight.

"Joanna." Dad's hand falls on Mom's shoulder. "It'll be

okay, sweetie."

"You don't know that!" Mom crumbles against Dad. "Doctor, is——?"

"All of those injuries should heal. Given time." He looks at his chart. He's stalling. He knows what comes next. I want to shout, 'get on with it,' but this can't be easy for him either, so I keep my mouth shut. "Right now, honestly, my biggest worry is the hit to her head. She's showing signs of severe concussion, but we haven't been able to wake her up yet due to the immediate need for surgery. She'll need to be watched closely."

"But she'll be okay," I say. "Eventually, she'll be okay?"

"Hopefully. As I said, we haven't been able to wake her up yet. Once she's out of surgery we'll try. Then we'll know more."

"She has three kids," says Mom.

The doctor angles toward my mother. "We're doing everything we can. We always do everything we can for each patient."

"Of course." Dad draws Mom back to his side. "Thank you, doctor."

We stand in an awkward little cluster after the doctor leaves.

"A kidney." Mom seems shorter. Smaller.

"So the kids," my voice is weak, "they don't know any of this happened?"

Dad shakes his head. "We asked the friend if she'd stay for now. They're sleeping. But she mentioned she has to work tomorrow. She didn't say it, but——"

"Who can we send to be with them?" asks Mom. "Beverly. Maybe Beverly. She and Gerald live near Jojo."

"I'm sure my parents would go," says Adrian.

I shake my head. "The kids don't know any of them." It'd be scary, terrifying, to wake up and have a stranger…and then to learn… "Besides, don't you think Jojo will want to see them when she wakes up? We should bring them here."

"I don't know," Adrian looks at me cautiously, "to wake them up in the night and—"

"No." Mom stops him. "Tracey's right. It'll be scary bringing them here, but it would be scarier sending someone they're not familiar with, and Jojo will want to see them, need to see them."

"Do you think they'd even let kids in recovery?" Adrian questions. "If she's pretty banged up, that could be worse for the kids."

Mom's face falls. "I didn't think of that." Her expression turns to one of resolve. "We'll figure that out later if we have to. At least the children will be with family. No matter what, that'll be better."

"All right," Dad reaches for his coat, "I'll go get them."

"No." I step forward. "We'll do it. You stay here with Mom."

"Oh!" Mom waves a hand at me. She looks to Dad. "What did the EMT say? About the letter?"

"Right." Dad turns to us. "He said before Jojo lost consciousness she kept saying something about a letter. Repeated it over and over. That we had to get the letter with the birth certificates."

"Do you think it's a will?" asks Adrian.

Mom's face pales. "No, I…maybe."

"If she thought she was dying…" Dad's voice trails off.

"Well, don't worry about it then." Mom reaches into her purse. "Here are her spare keys, so you can lock up after."

"Are you sure?" I ask. "I mean if Jojo wanted it?"

"She's not dying, so she doesn't need a will."

❧

ADRIAN AND I ARE QUIET on the drive to Jojo's. The night is so silent. It's been several years since I've been on the road this late. I look at the clock. 3:05 a.m.

"How you holding up?"

I turn to Adrian's voice. "Fine. 'Cause she will be fine."

He touches his hand to mine. It's so warm. My fingers are freezing.

No lights shine out of Jojo's apartment windows. The whole building seems asleep. Once inside, we make our way to Jojo's door. "Should we knock?" asks Adrian.

"It could wake up the kids."

"We have to wake them up anyway."

"Yeah, but I want to be with them."

"Just walking in could scare Jojo's friend."

"She'll expect someone's coming." I take out the key and open the door as quietly as I can, then switch on the hall light and travel to the living room. A sleeping form rests on the couch. I tiptoe over, crouch down, and put my hand on her shoulder. She whips around with a start. I recognize her. It's one of Jojo's friends from high school. Melanie.

"Hi, uh…" she rubs a hand over her eyes and sits up. "Jojo. Is she okay? Will she be okay?"

"She's in surgery." I step back and take a seat on the coffee table. "The doctor says there's reason to hope she'll have a full recovery."

"Good. Good." Melanie stretches. "Scary. At first I was mad and then… Wow. Just wow. I never expected—"

"I know." I touch her knee. "Thanks so much for staying. We'll take the kids now. You can go."

"You'll let me know, uh…I mean, I'm worried and—"

"Your number's in Jojo's phone?"

"Should be."

"I'll send you a text when I learn more."

"Thanks." She stands. "Good to see you, Tracey."

"You too."

As Melanie heads toward the door, Adrian steps beside me. "I thought you'd want me to wait."

"Yeah. Thanks." I push myself up and give his hand a

squeeze before walking to the twins' room. A night light casts a soft glow. Reggie's blankets are in a twisted mess at the foot of his bed. In a flannel-hooded monkey onesie, so only his hands and face are exposed, he lies half on his side, half on his back, his limbs spread in every direction. His pillow is on the floor, but besides that, the room is clean. Lulu sleeps the exact opposite. Her body is curled up tight, fetal style. Her blankets are tucked around her and only the top of her head peeks out through her covers. How do I wake them? Who first? I step toward Lulu and perch on the edge of her bed. I lay a hand over her hair and smooth the strands. She stirs, then settles back into a sound sleep.

"Lulu, sweetie." I stroke my hand again. After several tries her eyes blink open. She scrunches her face. "Auntie Tracey?"

"Yeah. It's me, honey."

"Where's Mommy?"

What do I say? Why didn't I think of something to say? My mind searches for the right words…could anything be right? "She's not feeling so well so I came to get you. We'll go see her and—" Can they see her? Eventually, but—

"What happened?"

"She had an accident."

"I want to see her."

"I know and…well, you remember when we saw Grampie in the hospital, right?"

Lulu nods. Reggie brushes by me and crawls onto Lulu's bed. He rubs both fists in his eyes. He looks so young. It's as if time has spun back three or four years. Sitting there like that, he could be a toddler. "What's going on?"

My words catch in my throat. I glance back to the door where Adrian stands. He walks toward us and settles on the bed beside Reggie. "I need you two to pick out some of your favourite clothes, a few good books, and two toys each. Can you do that?"

"My play station? That's kind of a toy."

Adrian smiles at Reggie. "Just toys that can fit in your school bag. Each of you can fill anything you want into a school bag as long as you have one outfit and a few books in there too."

"Can we take Mommy's iPad?" asks Lulu.

"Yes. Great idea." Adrian turns to me. "I'll supervise. Why don't you get Neveah?"

I nod and make my way out of the room. Jojo has to get better. She will get better. Neveah sits in the centre of her bed, a thumb stuck in her mouth. "What happening? I heared voices but is night." She points to the window. "I no allowed to leave until is no night."

"I know." I pull her into my arms. "And you're such a good girl for staying here."

"Why you here?"

"We're going on a trip."

"Where?" Her eyes light up. I groan inwardly, the smile still pasted on my face. Getting her excited is the last thing I should be doing.

"Mommy had a little accident."

"A booboo?"

"Kind of."

"Kiss it!" Neveah shouts.

"It's a little bigger than that, and so she needs a lot of rest to get better. She needs doctors helping her and—"

"Did she get needles?"

"Probably."

"And now she gets lollipops."

My smile wavers, but I draw it back. "She's sleeping right now but when she wakes up she'll want to see you, so we're going to go wait with Grammie and Grampie and make sure we're there when it's time to see Mommy."

"Okay." Neveah crawls out of bed. I help her get dressed and pick out some toys and books. When the bag I found in the closet is almost full, Adrian steps to the door with the twins beside him.

"Hi," I give him a smile of thanks, "you mind getting them dressed for outside and into the car? I'll put together a few things of Jojo's she may want."

"Sure."

In Jojo's room no clothes lay on the floor. Her bed is made. I haven't seen the kitchen, but no take out containers were strewn through the living room like last time. I walk to Jojo's closet. I know exactly where the birth certificates will be, in an old shoebox she's had since middle school. It's where she keeps everything that's precious. I remove the lid and right on top of all the mementos is an envelope. It has my name on it. As I hold it in my hand, the paper shakes. I rifle through the box. There are other letters, but none in envelopes. None sealed. I glance at a few of them: Love notes. A recommendation from her favourite high school teacher, the one who tried to encourage her to go to University. A notice saying she was accepted to Mount Saint Vincent University…dated the same month she found out she was pregnant with the twins. I close the box, stare at the envelope in my hand once more, then stuff it in my sweater pocket.

A duffel bag sits on the closet floor. I grab it, empty the contents, and refill it with items: sweatpants, her favourite cozy sweater, warm socks, her toothbrush and toothpaste. I look at the two books by her bedside table: *How to Recover from Loss* and *The Successful Single Mom: Get Your Life Back and Your Game On*. My hand hovers over them then moves away. Jojo would not want me to see these. She wouldn't want anyone to…I stare at the books for a moment longer. My sister. My sister I've hardly made time to really know…but who I love more than I realized. *Let her be okay.*

I step away from the table and scour the room. After I've added a few more items, including a framed photo of her and the kids, I rush to the car.

"Sorry I took so long."

"No problem." Adrian gestures to the back seat. "Two

out of three are gone already."

Only Lulu's eyes stare into mine. "It's okay, sweetie." I reach back and squeeze her knee. She offers the smallest of smiles.

✒

THE KIDS CLUSTER AGAINST me as we step through the hospital doors. Neveah reaches up. "I'll take her," says Adrian. He scoops her into his arms before I can answer. The twins, each holding one of my hands, sync their steps with mine. No running ahead like usual. They're quiet. Unless a screen's in front of their faces, these two are never quiet. When Adrian opens the waiting room doors, Lulu and Reggie release my hands as if on cue and bolt toward Mom. Neveah yells, "down," to get out of Adrian's arms and chases after them. Mom huddles the kids around her, kissing and squeezing and kissing again.

I sit across from Dad. "Any news?"

"She should be out of surgery soon." Dad's shoulders are slumped. He looks old. Older than I've ever seen him. "The doctor said once she's out it could be up to thirty minutes until the anaesthesia wears off, and then they'll try to wake her."

"Wouldn't sleep be good?" asks Adrian.

"Not with a concussion. Not yet at least. They need to make sure she can wake up." Dad turns his face away. His Adam's apple bobs. "She might not wake up."

"She'll wake up."

His voice is so soft I can hardly hear him. "But she might not."

"No. She will wake up."

His head falls into his hands. "But what if she doesn't?"

"She will." I pull one of his hands away and grasp it. I'm not lying. I can't be. I look to my mother. She's smiling.

Lulu tells her a story and she laughs. It's convincing. If one of them were to fall apart, I thought it'd be Mom for sure.

Dad wraps his other hand around the both of ours. "I can't lose another one," he whispers, "not like this."

What is he talking about? The miscarriages? "Dad?"

He looks up at me. "It's nothing, sweetie. I'm just worried. We can't lose Jojo."

"We won't." I smile at him then turn my gaze back to Mom.

Her voice trembles as she responds to Reggie's question. "Mommy's taking a nap right now, to help her get better."

"But can't she nap at home? I don't like it here."

"Oh, it's nice." Mom leans in with the smile she always wore when trying to convince Jojo or me something not at all pleasant was actually wonderful. "They have a play area and—"

"Yeah. For babies like Neveah."

"I not a baby."

Mom cups Reggie's chin. "And you have your iPad and books and, well, just about everything you need."

"When can we see Mommy?" Lulu tugs on Mom's hand.

"I'm not quite sure." Mom pulls Neveah onto her lap. "Why don't you all curl up and try to get some sleep. "Maybe when you wake up Mommy will be awake too." Mom looks to me. "You brought blankets?"

"Yeah."

Dad releases my hand and I stand. Adrian offers to find some pillows. Within fifteen minutes all three kids are spread out on play mats in the corner, their arms and legs intertwined, fast asleep. The hours pass slowly. Around quarter to eight a doctor returns.

"She's out of surgery. It went longer than expected—"

"Why?" asks Dad.

"Some complications."

"What—"

"She's breathing on her own. A good sign. We woke her

once, but she slipped back into sleep again fairly quickly. It could be the concussion, but her body also needs the rest. As long as we can wake her up for at least a minute or two every hour we'll take that as another good sign."

Mom stands. "Can we see her?"

"Yes. But one at a time would be best. Two at the most. There's a lot of machinery. And try not to wake her. But next time we do, we'll make sure one of you is with us."

"Henry?" Mom turns to Dad, a hand pressed to her throat.

"You go, Jo. You first."

Mom nods. The doctor rests a hand on her shoulder. "You need to be prepared. You all do. It's not pretty. It will be shocking. She's badly bruised. Badly swollen."

"What about the children?" Mom gestures to where they still lie, piled together.

The doctor presses his lips together. "That's up to you. Maybe up to Jojo once she wakes up. I wouldn't take them in unless she's awake. Seeing her like that and not being able to talk to her, it could be traumatizing."

Mom blinks. "She'll want to see her children."

"We'll let her decide."

Mom isn't in the room for long. Seven or eight minutes at most. When she comes out she practically falls into my father's arms. She clings to him in a way I've never seen. It's terrifying. "Our baby," she cries into Dad's chest.

"It's all right, sweetheart. You heard the doctor. She'll be all right."

Dad's turn is next. I sit with my arms resting on my knees, my hands clasped. Adrian smooths a circle over my back, again and again. Every few seconds I glance up to see if Dad has returned. When at last he does, I bolt out of my seat.

"It's a sight, honey." Dad cups my cheek. "But she's breathing. Her vitals are good."

Adrian stands beside me. "You want me to go in with

you?"

"No," I turn to him, "the doctor said it was better one at a time."

"Okay."

Room 337. The hall is long. I pass six rooms until I get to Jojo's. A steady beeping sounds from behind the partially open door. I stand frozen. But I have to move. I have to step inside.

CHAPTER TWENTY-NINE

When I enter Jojo's hospital room the smell is the first thing to hit me: a mix of fresh blood and some kind of antiseptic. The beeping of the monitor feels deafening. It fills the room. It should be a comfort, that strong repetition. Instead, it's the first indication of how frail my sister is. She needs a machine to let us know she's still alive.

I step further in and pull back the curtain hiding her from view. Her arm and leg are in casts. The leg hangs suspended in the air. The cast is more complex than Dad's. Pins stick out of it. I step closer. It's her face I can't look away from. Abrasions cover the left side of it. Her eye is so swollen I can't imagine it'll open. The skin is a motley mix of red, purple, and a blue as dark as midnight. I sink into the chair beside her and continue to look at that face. It shouldn't be my sister's face. I take her free hand and hold it gently. At last my gaze falls away.

The beep, beep, beep, sounds like a talisman. With each pulse my guilt increases. If I hadn't been so angry, if I'd just gone and watched the kids, she'd have run in the afternoon. If I weren't so selfish and bitter and petty, she'd be home in bed like she should be. I know that drunk driver being on the road is not my fault, not at all, but still…

I pull the envelope out of my sweater pocket and rest it on the edge of the bed. I can't open it. Whatever's inside I'm not meant to know. Not yet. Hopefully, not ever. I rest my head beside our hands. My eyes peer at the envelope. After a while I let them close. The constant beat of Jojo's heart throbs through me. *Live.* The words trail over and over again. *Be okay. Just be okay.*

"How long have I been out?"

I snap my head up.

"Whoa." Jojo lets out a noise halfway between a moan and a chuckle. "I must look shitty. You should see your face. Or is it the prognosis? Am I dying?"

Stop, I want to say. Don't. But that's not what Jojo wants to hear. Not what she needs. I push out a smile. "My face? You should see yours."

"That bad, huh?" Jojo's words come out slow and warbled. "Looks like my arm. My leg. My side hurts something fierce. There a nurses' button or something? Whatever drugs they have me on, they're not enough." She pauses, takes a shaky breath. "A gal wakes up like this, she has a right to be high as a kite." She attempts a laugh, but it quickly turns into a groan. A tear rolls out of her swollen eyelid. I search for a call button. When I find it I reach out, but Jojo's free hand stops mine. "Nah. Not yet. I need to be lucid a bit longer."

She draws her gaze to the ceiling. "I remember running. And then bright lights. And then," she pauses, "pain worse than this. Sirens. More lights. It kinda stops there."

"You were hit."

"By a car?"

I nod.

Her eye closes. "And I made it out alive. Jojo Sampson against the machine." She's quiet for so long I think she's fallen asleep. But then her eye flashes open. "Was he drunk? Or she? Was the driver drunk?"

"Yeah."

Jojo lets out a choked laugh. "What irony, huh? I decided last week I was done with the drink, at least until I could have a glass without wanting another and another. You were right. It was getting to be too much."

"Jo, I—"

"No. You were right. Mom was right. Or at least on the road to being right." She stops and stares at the foot of the bed. "It was turning into a problem. One night a week or so ago Neveah woke up with this raging fever and I needed to go to the pharmacy. We were all in the car and then I remembered—I'd had a few before bed. More than a few." Her jaw clenches. Waves of pain roll across her face. "I almost drove with them." Her eye closes again. More tears dribble out. "I was drunk and I almost drove with my babies in the car. They were buckled in and everything." She opens her eye. "So I took them all back inside, called a cab and decided it had to stop—this drinking to numb the pain." She smiles. "Back in high school, remember how good I was at track? How I ran the half-marathon? I was so good."

"You were amazing."

She smiles. "I know. It's 'cause I took all that teenage angst out on the field."

"All of it?" I grin.

"A lot of it." She chuckles. "It could have been way worse. You have no idea." She looks to the ceiling. "Really great move, though, right? I decided to run a half-marathon. Do something positive with all this angry energy. Run my pain away instead of drinking it. And yet the drink still wrecks my life."

I squeeze her hand. "Your life's not wrecked."

"Really? Seriously, Trace, by the look of you, I'm pretty sure I only have hours to live."

"You've got tons of time."

Her face starts to smile, then a look of panic flashes across it. "The kids. Are they—?"

"They're in the waiting room. They're fine."

She visibly relaxes. Pain, not fear, defines her features. "Yeah. Of course they're fine. Of course. I just...I couldn't remember for a sec where they were or what..." her voice drops away. Another long pause. "So what happened? How long have I been here?"

"Just the night."

"And what's wrong with me?" Another moan/chuckle. "Or should I ask what isn't?"

I turn my head to the door. "I should get the doctor. And Mom and Dad, now that you're awake—"

"No." She taps my hand. "No. It can wait."

I bring my gaze back.

Jojo reaches for the letter. She grimaces with the effort. "You read it?"

"No."

"It's for you."

"I thought…I thought maybe it was only if…"

"If I died."

I nod.

"That was the idea. I'm not going to die, right?"

"No. Absolutely not."

She shifts and pushes the letter toward me. "That's good. Read it anyway."

I rub a hand along my arm. "Now?"

"Good a time as any. They *say* I'm out of the woods, but what do they know?" She tries to wink, but the bruises and swelling make it an awkward affair.

The envelope's seal breaks easily. I pull out a piece of torn notebook paper.

"Not fancy, I know. I was planning to do it up better. Thought I'd have time."

I look to the page.

Hey, Trace,

I guess if you're reading this, things haven't turned out too well with me. It's okay, though. I've had some good moments. Some INCREDIBLE ones really. So that's something. I know I haven't always been the most responsible person, not like you…okay, I should probably erase that. What is it, passive aggressive or something? But I won't. Anyway, not sure if I've ever said it, but as much as I hate how perfect you are, I also admire it. And I KNOW you're not perfect. I can almost hear you denying it. But you come damn close. Look at me rambling.

Down to business. I want you to take care of my kids.

I look up from the letter. "Jo?"

"You don't read that fast. Keep going."

I open my mouth to say something more then let my gaze fall.

Their good-for-nothing bastard of a father would probably forget to feed them, if he's even anywhere to be found. Mom and Dad are too old. Mom will probably fight for them, but don't give in. They've raised their children. They're done. But it's more than that. I know as much as I've ever known anything that you'll love them like they were your own and do everything to give them the best life you can. I haven't looked into the legality of all this, but if Damien comes back and says he wants them, fight him too. He doesn't know how to be a dad. To him, the kids are little more than ornaments. He's abandoned them. At the time I write this letter it's been over four and a half months since he's made any real effort to contact them. A few measly post-cards. That's it. He's provided little to no financial support in close to a year. That is not a father. Show the judges or whoever makes the decisions this letter. Show Mom and Dad too. Fight for my babies.

Do this, okay big sis? I know I should talk to you in person, get it all figured out and written up pretty, but I'm chicken-shit. Even this is the weirdest thing ever—writing someone else, asking them to raise your children. But if it can't be me, it should be you. I love you. Love them.

I stare at the letter a moment longer, then lift my head. "Why'd you want me to read this? Now, I mean."

Jojo takes a long breath. "If you knew how I felt, you would not be so confident these aren't my last hours."

"Jo—"

"No, seriously. I should have talked to you about it, like I wrote, not just wussed out and put it in a letter. We should have talked about a lot of things."

"The doctor said you need rest."

"I'm lying down. I'm resting. Listen, I haven't been supportive about your issues lately. I'm not used to being supportive with you. And honestly, it made me kind of angry how set you were on *not* adopting. It's like each moment of obsession over having your own child was another moment of you rejecting me. To me, you've always been my sister, but I know I haven't been to you."

"That's not true."

The smallest smile passes over Jojo's face. "Trace, I'm banged up. I'm not stupid. On some level you think I'm not your sister. You think it's not as real just because…well," another strained laugh, "trust me, no one but a sister would talk to me the way you do. Sometimes, you know, you treat me like garbage. Like I'm this stupid screw-up."

I bite my lip, wanting to defend myself, but if this is how she feels…

"Not all of the time. Not even a lot of the time. But sometimes. You wouldn't if you weren't my sister. You wouldn't care so much when I make stupid choices." She takes a long, shattering breath. "I really hope the procedure works. I hope you get your own child. But if you don't, you need to get it through your head that you'll still have a family. A real family. You always have."

"I know."

Jojo's one good eyebrow raises.

"I didn't. But I do now." Her skepticism remains. I let out a little laugh. "It's a recent development."

"Well, good."

Her eye closes again. She speaks with both shut. "Will I be here for a while?"

"I'm not sure." I start to rise. "I'll get the doctor. He should—"

"Chill out, okay?" Jojo's voice cracks. "Sit here another minute, two maybe. Then everyone can pile in. The doctor, the kids, Mom and Dad. And they can give me more drugs. Not yet though, all right?"

I lower into my seat. "All right."

With her eyes still closed, my sister squeezes my hand. I haven't lost her. She's still here. She's still Jojo. I squeeze back.

I sit for several minutes, until Jojo's breathing is so rhythmic I know she's fallen asleep. I slip my hand out of her grasp and slowly rise from the chair. Jojo has always been one to drop into sleep. She sleeps heavy, soundless, motionless. Today though, her body seems to quiver with the slightest of motions. Her one good eyelid flutters from time to time. Every now and then murmurs escape her lips. Five minutes must pass before I've realized I'm still standing there, staring.

How long has it been since I left? Will my parents be worried? I step into the hall. Probably not too worried, or someone would have come.

CHAPTER THIRTY

Mom pops from her seat when I step back into the hospital waiting room after visiting Jojo. "How is she?"

"She woke up."

"We know."

My eyes ask a question.

"I went down there," says Dad, "when it was taking so long. I saw you two talking, so I slipped away."

"Oh." I make my way to the closest chair.

"Is she okay? What'd she say?"

"Umm…" I look up. I open my mouth then close it again. Jojo's words were for me, not them. "She wanted to know that the kids were okay. I told her they were."

Lulu, who I thought was still sleeping, raises on her forearms. "Mommy's up?"

"She's sleeping again."

"But soon she'll be up again?"

"Yeah. Soon, sweetie."

Mom sits beside me; she keeps her voice low, low enough that the children can't hear. "Did she say anything else? And did she seem—" She glances to Dad, her face a vision of distress, then back to me. "Did she seem okay? Lucid."

"Yes." I smile. "Same old Jojo."

"Was she giving you lip?" asks Adrian.

"You could say that."

"Does she want to see the kids?"

"The doctor said she needs to wake up every hour, so maybe at the next wakeup?"

"Why don't I take them for breakfast?" Adrian motions toward the children. "Probably by the time we get back Jojo will be ready for another visit." He looks to Mom, Dad, and me. "Would any or all of you like to come, or what can I bring back for you?"

"I'll stay with Mom and Dad."

"No." Dad shakes his head. "Get out of here, hon, get some warm food. Help Adrian with the kids."

"It's fi—"

"No," says Mom. "Your father's right. We'll be fine." She pauses. "Everything will be fine."

It takes several minutes to rouse the children and get meal orders from Mom and Dad. We bundle the kids up and, to kill time, go to a family style restaurant up the street rather than the café style restaurants in the hospital lobby. Lulu and Neveah hold my hands. Reggie walks in front of me, stoic and brave.

"What about school?" asks Lulu. "Aren't we supposed to be in school?"

"You can skip it for today." Adrian tousles Lulu's hair. "You're smart enough anyway."

Neveah starts crying. "I want Mommy."

Reggie turns to her and crouches down. "It'll be okay, Nevie. Mommy's going to be okay."

Neveah nods, a thumb stuck in her mouth.

Reggie stands and looks to me for confirmation. I nod and smile, hoping my assurance isn't a lie.

When we return, the doctor says Jojo's lucid enough that we don't need to worry about the one visitor rule, but not to crowd her.

He looks to the children, a comforting smile on his face. "She's asking to see you."

Reggie steps forward. "Okay."

Mom and Dad, who've just come from talking to Jojo, take the food Adrian passes them. "You go in, sweetie," says Dad. "We need some nourishment."

Adrian rests a hand on my shoulder. "I'll sit with your parents."

I nod and usher the children down the hall toward Jojo's room. Neveah, in my arms, keeps her head pressed against my shoulder. Outside the door I motion for Lulu and Reggie to stop. "Mommy's going to look a little scary. She's hurt badly, but she's still your mommy." Lulu's eyes widen. I do my best to keep my voice steady. "Be very gentle. Very slow. She has wires and…just be careful."

"Can we touch her?" asks Reggie.

"You can hold her hand." I smile. "If more than that she'll tell you."

Neveah pulls back to look into my face, hers full of alarm. "Mommy no wants hugs?"

I jostle her higher on my hip. "She wants them. Of course she wants them. But hugs may hurt her."

Neveah's brow furrows in confusion. "Hugs hurt?"

How do I answer that? How do you make a two year old understand? I open my mouth to speak but nothing comes out. I step into the room. Jojo's lips quiver as the children step into her line of vision. Her one visible eye brightens and mists.

"Hey, Rugrats."

"Mommy?" Lulu stops about halfway between the door and Jojo. Her little body shakes. Neveah, after a quick glance in the direction of her mother, turns her face into my shoulder and whimpers.

Reggie walks right up to Jojo. He takes hold of her hand and presses his head against it. "Hey, Mom."

"Hey." Jojo pushes out a smile.

They stay like that for several breaths. At last Jojo raises her arm and motions for Lulu. She skitters toward Jojo and presses up against Reggie. "You're hurt real bad?"

Jojo grins. "It's not too bad."

Lulu places a hand on Jojo's wrist, just above Reggie's. Jojo stares at her twins. She looks up. "Neveah?"

Neveah pushes her face deeper into my shoulder and squirms so her whole body angles away from Jojo. Reggie turns. "Nevie, come to Mommy."

"No!" Neveah's voice is muffled.

Jojo smiles. She pats Reggie's arm, her eyes full of pain, more than just the physical. "It's okay," she says. But it isn't. She wants to hold her baby in her arms.

&

THAT NIGHT MOM AND DAD camp out at the hospital while Adrian and I take the children to our place. All three share a bed in our spare room. I lie down, my back propped against the headboard, and they cuddle around me. We read three Dr. Seuss books. They laugh and giggle at the crazy pictures. To practice their reading, Lulu, Reggie and I read alternate pages on the second and third book.

"Another," says Neveah around the thumb in her mouth. She can barely keep her eyes open. She snuggles into me.

Lulu pulls Neveah's thumb out. Reggie shakes his head. "What about one of our books?"

"No." Neveah says. "Not enough pictures."

I close the final book and set it on the bedside table. "I think that's enough for tonight."

Reggie grumbles.

"And tomorrow night we'll start earlier. Dr. Seuss for Neveah and," I glance at the cover of the book in Reggie's hand, "*A Series of Unfortunate Events* for you and Lulu."

"Fine." Reggie sighs, but it turns into a yawn. I hug and kiss each of them. Lulu's arms linger around me after I let go. "Mommy's going to be okay, right? She's strong?"

I nod. "She's very strong."

Once the light is out I stand by the door, staring at my nieces and nephew. My heart swells with love. This is what I wanted—a home full of children. But not like this. Definitely not like this. I close my eyes, thanking God or the universe that Jojo survived. I jump as a hand grazes my arm.

"Sorry." Adrian whispers at my ear. "You're tense."

I lean into him. "It's been a long day."

He kisses my temple. "You haven't had dinner."

I turn to him. "Haven't I?"

He shakes his head. "You fed the kids, not you." He smiles a sheepish grin. "I made that apple pie oatmeal you like. I know it's not really dinner." He shrugs. "It's easy."

"Thank you."

"Have some then go to bed, okay? I also called that lady who prepares the meals. I told her your restrictions. She'll put a rush on it, but it'll still be two days."

I look to the floor. "It's fine. It's not important."

He rubs his hand along my arm again. "It is important. I'll do my best until then." He draws me to him. His arms feel safe and warm. I want to stay in this moment, in the security of his arms, and believe everything's all right. But it's not. My mind travels back to Jojo—hooked up to machines and IVs—could she really be okay?

CHAPTER THIRTY-ONE

The next morning it's back to the hospital. And the day after that, and after that. The doctor tells us Jojo's coming along well, that she's strong. But she doesn't look it. I know my sister. I know the brave face is just that. A face. I see the way the sides of her eyes flinch as she's trying to mask the pain. By the fourth night, when the swelling in Jojo's eye has gone down enough that she can open it fully, Neveah shuffles over to her mother. She won't touch her at first, but she giggles when Jojo tells a joke.

"You've been a good girl for Auntie Tracey?" asks Jojo, her eyes and her strained smile on Neveah.

"Uh huh." Neveah pats her mom's hand. "When we go home?"

Jojo takes a deep breath. It's shaky. "You don't like it at Auntie Tracey's?"

Neveah looks at me before turning back to Jojo. "It's nice. But I wanna go home with you."

"Soon, honey. Soon." Jojo's face looks flushed. She reaches to rub Neveah's cheek and the jolt of pain sends out a groan before she can stop it.

I step toward her. "Don't move, Jo."

"It's fine, I—" Her eyes go wide. Her lashes flutter. "Trace…ee…I…fine."

I press my hand to her cheek. It's on fire. Before Jojo can protest, I press the call button. Neveah looks up at me, her eyes now wide. I ruffle her hair, amazed how so quickly she can sense my fear. A nurse comes in. She motions for me to clear her path and I take Neveah into my arms. We exchange some words as the nurse takes Jojo's temperature then lifts the dressings covering her abdomen. As she presses them back down, a terrifying moan escapes my sister. The nurse calls for a doctor. Adrian, who was at the lobby getting snacks with the kids, approaches. I pass Neveah to him. "Take them to the waiting room," I say, my voice as calm and even as I can make it. "Send Mom and Dad." He nods.

The doctor arrives. Now the nurse and he exchange words as Jojo insists she's fine through almost incoherent mumbles. I'm not sure what's dangerous, but the temperature they mention seems high. The doctor's face as he examines the wound sends a shock of terror through my heart. Jojo stops her protests. Her eyes roll back in her head and she starts seizing. I lunge toward her but am held back, am told to leave. The nurse and doctor's words swim in my head. Fever. Infection. Possibility of staphy-something…of toxic shock…I don't know what either is, but they sound bad.

Mom and Dad rush up the hall as I stumble down it. Mom looks past me while Dad holds her back. Medical staff run toward Jojo's room. Mom clutches my arm so tight I know I'll be bruised.

There's nothing we can do but wait. After what feels like an eternity but can't be more than a few minutes, a doctor approaches Mom and Dad. Jojo needs surgery. Immediately. Mom and Dad insist it's best for me to take the kids home. They promise to let us know the instant they know more, then leave with the doctor to sign some forms. I stand watching, helpless.

❧

AFTER WE GET HOME IT takes some cajoling but, eventually, all three children fall asleep. I stand at the spare room door again, a sense of déjà vu falling over me. Only this time, it's not thanks I'm offering up. It's a plea.

Adrian draws me away and into the living room. I sink onto the couch, my hands in my lap. I flick and twist my wedding and engagement rings, watching the light shimmer.

"That call is going to come any minute."

My head still down, I offer a smile. "I know."

"Infections happen sometimes, but the doctors, they know what to do."

"Of course."

He's quiet. I feel his gaze on me. I look up. He gives a half-smile. "Are you okay?"

"I never told you about the letter."

Adrian sits beside me. "The one Jojo was talking about at the accident?"

I nod. "I took it from her house that first night. It was addressed to me."

"Oh?"

"I didn't open it, not at first, but once she woke up she asked me to. I read it with her." I take a breath. Adrian says nothing, waiting. "She wants me to take the kids if anything were to happen to her, if—"

"She's fine, Tracey. Everything is—"

"I know… Probably." I look back to my hands. "But a second surgery. Internal infection." I twist the rings. "The night it happened I had a dream. I was so happy. I had our baby and was nursing her in my arms. The baby was ours and alive and well and I thought: My life is what it should be. My life is complete. And then the baby started crying. Started crying and—" My words stop.

"Trace?"

"It was the phone ringing. It was Jojo. I wanted a baby so much. I thought that's all that mattered. I wanted it and…if I hadn't, if, Jojo wouldn't have been running at night and—"

Adrian rests his hands on my shoulders. "You're losing me."

"Sorry." I give myself a shake. "Jojo wanted me to watch the kids that afternoon so she could go running, but I said no," I stop, my teeth clenched, "because I was angry, angry at her and how without even trying, without even wanting them, she got these three amazing kids, and she wasn't taking care of them the way she should have been. I thought she was lying. I thought she wanted to drink. And I didn't want to do a single thing for her that would jeopardize the chance for me."

Adrian sighs. "You don't think it's your fault?"

I shake my head. "No. No. Of course not. I know it's not my fault. It wouldn't have happened if…but no, it's not my fault. A drunk driver's at fault."

"Exactly."

"It's just weird you know, though. Funny. I want…" I lay a hand on my abdomen, stare at it. "But Jojo. Jojo needs to get better. Jojo needs to raise her kids."

"She will."

I stare at the phone. "Shouldn't we have some news by now? She should be out of—" the phone rings. I pick it up without looking at the screen. "Mom?"

"No, uh…" A pause. "Saadia, it's—"

"Oh," my breath releases, "Saadia, hi."

"Is everything okay? You missed your appointment today."

I apologize and fill her in on the events of the past few days. I try to dissuade her, but she insists on coming by tomorrow after work to give me a treatment at home. I thank her, then end the call. Jojo still on my mind, I stare at the phone, waiting for it to ring, willing it to ring.

CHAPTER THIRTY-TWO

Moments after I disconnect the call from Saadia, my phone rings again. This time it's the call I've been waiting for. Jojo is out of surgery. She's responding well to the antibiotics, which is the most important thing. It'll be a longer road ahead than expected, but the immediate danger is likely past. After the call I collapse into Adrian's arms. I wake up the next day, snug and secure in our bed, with those arms still around me.

After a quick visit with Jojo in the morning, at her insistence, I drive the twins to school and Neveah to preschool. Neveah only lasts two hours before the teacher calls, telling me she's too upset and I need to pick her up. The twins make it through the day.

In the evening we return to the hospital. Jojo, looking even stronger than she did just hours before, somehow dregs up more energy and smiles than seems possible. The children laugh with her. Neveah crawls up into the bed, cautiously, to give hugs and kisses. Smiles abound when the doctor tells us Jojo should be free to leave within the week so long as she has sufficient home care. Mom and Dad assure she will.

When it's time to leave, the children come back home with Adrian and me for another night, one of their last. Next week I'll return to teaching, and the kids (and eventually Jojo) will set up camp at my parents' house.

At dinner, I eat one of the meals prepared by Adrian's

mystery chef—it's delicious—while the children and Adrian set up their plates of pizza in the living room in front of a movie. Saadia arrives at seven o'clock, exactly when she said she would. After introducing her to Adrian and the kids—I tell the children she's a friend—we make our way to the bedroom.

"How've you been holding up?" Saadia asks before inserting the needles.

I smile, for some reason feeling more vulnerable and exposed here, in my own room, than I ever have in her office. This is not normal clinician/patient behaviour, her coming to my home. This is something more.

"Busy." I breathe in and out, willing my body to relax. "Jojo's been through a lot. The kids. Mom and Dad."

"But you," she caresses my shoulder, "how are you doing? How are you feeling?"

I take several breaths before answering. Outside of the worry, I'm good. Surprisingly good. It's busy, it's tiring—I'm doing everything I can for Jojo, the kids, Mom and Dad, while still trying to make time for Adrian, who's been doing all he can to support me. For the first time in months I'm focused on people and events outside of myself and my own body. When people tell me things, I remember them. And all of it—being needed, fulfilling the need, letting someone else help when I need it—makes me feel like me again. I look up with a smile. "Good. I'm feeling really good."

Saadia has another visualization tape prepared for my treatment. I try to think back to the last time I visualized the life I hope is growing inside of me—the day of the showing, the accident, almost a week ago. I sink into the words, the music, and feel no fear or stress. Hope. And nothing more.

When Saadia returns to take out the needles she hesitates after removing the last one. She stands at the foot of the bed, her hands clasped in front of her. "My daughter, Natalie, was saying last night that she thinks it's about time they meet you. I know you have a lot going on but maybe in a week or two, once things have settled," she pauses, smiles, "maybe you and Adrian would like to come for dinner. Meet my husband and the kids. There's a chance Adham would come too."

A thick ball of emotion wells up in my throat, making it impossible to respond right away. Once it dissipates, I nod, my eyes moist. "That would be great. Wonderful actually."

Saadia gives my foot a squeeze and smiles back. She steps out of the room, leaving me to get dressed. I take my time, savour these few quiet moments in a week full of more activity and noise and sadness and joy than I've experienced in years, perhaps than I've ever experienced.

Eventually though, I follow the sound of laughter. In the living room Saadia is stretched out on all fours with Lulu, Neveah, and Reggie crowded around her. The laughter bubbles up over a game of Twister. Toulouse prances among the tangled hands and feet, creating even more giggles. Adrian spins the wheel and calls, "Left foot green." More chuckles and maneuvers. Reggie, stretching his body in a way that hardly seems possible, catches sight of me. His face lights up. "Auntie Tracey, come play!"

My throat tightens again. My chest feels full. "Next round." I grin. "I'll take on the winner."

TWO DAYS LATER I WAKE to the sound of Neveah crying and Reggie groaning.

"She wet the bed!" Reggie shouts as I enter the room.

"Oh, sweetie."

Neveah's lips tremble, her cheeks wet with tears. I lift her off of the bed then urge Lulu and Reggie to get off too.

Lulu stands in her underwear, holding her pyjama bottoms out with an outstretched arm. "She peed on my pants."

"And you'll get new ones."

Reggie holds out his arm. "My sleeve's wet."

"Come on." With Neveah in my arms, I motion toward the twins. We make a parade to the bathroom where I strip Neveah down and tell the twins to get undressed.

They splash and laugh in the tub. I hold a finger to my lips. "Uncle Adrian's sleeping."

Lulu giggles. "Whisper splash party."

Giggles turn into boisterous laughter in minutes as the splashes get bigger and bigger.

"All right, all right." I grin during the first major lull, unable to keep my own laughter at bay. "It's time to get back to bed. It's hardly morning."

Neveah gets the honour of pulling the plug. She watches with focus as the bubbles swirl away. I offer each of the twins a towel and swaddle Neveah in one. As the twins dry off, get dressed, and then, under my guidance, help Neveah into new pyjamas, I strip the bed, put on new sheets, and usher them all back under the covers.

Once the final giggles have settled, I make my way to the kitchen for a glass of water. As I lean against the wall my gaze falls to the calendar hanging beside the fridge. A bright red circle is looped around tomorrow's date, marking my appointment to have a blood test at the clinic. Over yesterday's date are the words: *Do I dare?* Yesterday. I step forward. Fourteen days past embryo transfer, the day I would have been booked to go to the clinic for my pregnancy blood test if it hadn't fallen on a Saturday. The day I could have tested at home, not that the doctor recommended I test at home…a blood test is more accurate. Still. Today marks fifteen days past transfer. The possibility of a test giving a false negative is extremely slim.

I grab my phone to make sure I'm not confusing the date. No. Today is Sunday. And yesterday I forgot? I lay a hand on my abdomen. I haven't been doing my meditation, my yoga, with the exception of Saadia's visit, no visualizations. I certainly haven't been resting—I've had other priorities. I close my eyes. I haven't been cramping either. Hope springs. Of course, this cycle was forced, not a regular one, so who knows what lack of cramps means?

In the bathroom I open the drawer I've gone to dozens of times in the past two years. Do I check? If I don't, it's like Schrödinger's cat—as far as I know, a baby is growing inside of me. But once I open up the lid of that box…

I want the answer I've always wanted, a bright and strong positive, yet I'm less scared than I've ever been that I won't get it.

I do what I need to do, dip the stick in the little container I keep especially for this purpose, set my phone's timer, and close my eyes. If I look at the stick and the answer is negative it just means this route, this time, will not result in my child. It doesn't mean I'm broken. I've repeated these words, this idea, so many times before: I'm not broken. Adrian's documentary and all it taught me, Jojo, and the intense love I've realized I have for her, for her children, float before me. The students who, despite months of abandoning them, still embraced me with love. At last I believe the words. One part of me may not work the way it's supposed to, but that one part isn't me. I'm not broken.

I can't lie to myself and say the result on that stick doesn't matter. Of course it matters, but it's not everything. A negative won't define my life. It won't define me. And whether a life grows inside me now or whether one never will, I already have what I've longed for all these years, as complex as it is.

A fist bangs on the door. Reggie. "Can I have some juice?"

My voice is soft. "It's not really morning yet."

"But I'm so thirsty."

These kids, Jojo, Adrian, Mom and Dad. I take a breath. Eloise, Autumn, Allison and Sheila, they're my family—no blood connection needed—my real family. A smile blossoms on my face. And now Saadia and Lydia too, maybe Saadia's kids one day. Her brothers. And if it's the road I take, just as Jojo's my sister, my true sister, an adopted child would be my child—my family. I glance at the timer. "I'll be out in a minute, sweetie." I still want my own child, one with a biological bond. That hasn't changed. Maybe it never will. But I don't need that child like I did, not to be happy, not to feel fulfilled. There are multiple roads to happiness, multiple avenues to express that mothering love I've always yearned for.

I wait.

"Is it a minute yet?"

My phone beeps. "Yeah, it's a minute."

I take a deep breath, open my eyes, and look down.

A NOTE FROM THE AUTHOR

Thank you for taking the time to read *Whispers of Hope*. I hope you enjoyed it. If you've travelled through the stories of all the women in my *A New Start Series*, this is the end…for now at least. Who knows, perhaps one day I'll write some spin-off novellas or even a spin-off series about this group of friends. The characters have worked their way into my heart, and I hope they've worked their way into yours as well.

To those readers who may have been a bit disappointed you didn't find out whether or not Tracey's dreams of having a child are fulfilled, trust me, it was not an easy choice! I debated long and hard about whether to include that piece of information. The thing is, a positive pregnancy test wouldn't necessarily mean a live birth for Tracey—it would only be the first step in an uncertain journey. But it's more than that—the truth is, for Tracey's story, that's not what really matters.

To me, what's most important is the emotional journey she went on, the realization that having a baby doesn't have to define her life or her happiness, that she can choose a life fuelled by joy. Whether Tracey holds a baby who shares her DNA, one she takes into her life the same way she was taken into her adoptive parents' heart and home, or, perhaps, whether she never raises a child at all, she can still be happy.

I'll trust for her, just as I must learn to trust for myself, that, if we're open to it, life has a way of working out and happiness is so much bigger than our limited ideas of what our happiness should look like. To any readers out there who've been through a similar journey or may encounter it one day, I hope Tracey's story opens your heart to that same truth.

Tracey's journey was one I needed to explore not just for my readers, but for myself. That's largely why it ended up expanding over two books. As I had Tracey work through some of her issues and fears, I found myself working through some of mine. Every book I've written has taught me things, but Tracey's two, more than any others, has changed me. I know the pain of infertility, as well as the feeling that your body (and in a sense your life) is broken.

Endometriosis is one of the 'invisible' diseases and over 176 million women suffer from it every day—often with no idea this disease is the cause of their pain. I went seventeen years before a doctor even brought up the word to me. It took two more years before I was diagnosed. While researching for these books, I've learned that's a common occurence.

The average time from complaint of symptoms to diagnosis is seven to nine years—far too long. It is my hope that any woman reading this who thinks there may be something wrong with her menstrual cycle or reproductive organs will take the time to research the disease and talk with her doctor. There are many more possible symptoms than mentioned in these pages. It's also my hope that for any woman experiencing the isolation that can stem from endometriosis, infertility, or any disease affecting the organs 'people don't like to talk about', this story has helped you feel less alone.

If you've enjoyed this story it would mean so much if you took a moment to leave a review on your retailer of choice and/or Goodreads. Your thoughts matter and could help a fellow book-lover discover a story to enjoy.

If you want to know when I release other books, please sign up for my newsletter at charlenecarr.com. For a limited time, you'll also get a free novella, *Before I Knew You*. Don't worry, I won't flood your inbox. I rarely send newsletters more than twice a month.

Feel free to jot me a note if you have any questions or if there's a character from the *A New Start Series* you'd like to hear more about. No guarantees, but your suggestion could prompt another tale!

You can also learn about my new books and promotions by following me on BookBub. And if you've read *Whispers of Hope* as part of a book club, you can visit my website for a Book Club Discussion Guide.

Again, thank you for taking the time to read my work.

Read on, my friend,

Charlene Carr

OTHER BOOKS IN THE A NEW START SERIES

When Comes The Joy
Book 1

Jennifer's not perfect. Not even close. But she may just capture your heart.

At 27, Jennifer's out of work, her mom just died, and despite stellar qualifications, every job interview ends in rejection.
Haunted by the teasing, taunts, and fat jokes that defined her childhood, Jennifer blames her unhappiness on her ever-growing waistband.
And she's ready for change.
Messy and real.
Beautiful and harsh.
When Comes The Joy (previously titled Skinny Me) explores one woman's journey along the road of forgiveness, healing, and strength.

By What We Love
Book 3

**Sometimes getting exactly what you want is the
worst thing ever.**

Dream job? Check. Man to make every woman you know stop and turn? Check. But when having one means giving up the other, what's a girl …excuse me, *woman* to do?
Eloise Grant, a successful and driven Public Relations Consultant, has worked her whole life to make sure she never has to depend on anyone but herself.
But when she's offered a promotion she feels she can't refuse, depending on herself means leaving her friends, her family, and the man she loves behind.
Whatever choice she makes, it seems like Eloise's life is about to unravel.
Smart and engaging.
Heart wrenching and unpredictable.
By What We Love, book 3 in the *A New Start* stand-alone series, is the story of a woman desperate to have it all, while battling with memories of a past she'd rather forget.

ACKNOWLEDGMENTS

I would like to thank my wonderful beta readers who gave generously of their time and provided invaluable feedback. It amazes me, the little nuances you are able to see that help me make these stories so much more than what they were. I would also like to thank my editor and her keen eye.

BOOK CLUB DISCUSSION QUESTIONS

1. What did you think of the way Tracey connected with Saadia. Was it understandable? Or do you think she was entirely out of line?

2. If you were in Tracey's position, would you have met your birth father? What were your thoughts while reading that scene? How would you have reacted in the same situation?

3. Tracey goes all out in her efforts to conceive. Did that seem a healthy reaction? What did it tell you about her character?

4. Jojo had a lot of issues growing up too, and seemed to think that she was not loved as much as Tracey. Do you think the birth position in any given family (first child, middle child, last child) has a lot to do with the feelings of confidence, loneliness, or security?

5. Tracey seemed to partially blame herself for Jojo's accident. Do you think that played a role in her decision to watch Jojo's children? Was that reasonable with all she was going through at the time?

6. Would you have been upset or annoyed to find that your spouse looked up and actually met up with his or her ex and

didn't tell you about it? Or considering the circumstances did it seem reasonable?

7. We don't learn whether or not Tracey became pregnant. Do you think knowing would have added or detracted from the overall story? Why?

If you have any questions about the discussion guide or would like a chance at having Charlene visit your bookclub through a webcall, email contact@charlenecarr.com

ABOUT THE AUTHOR

I'm a lover of words. Pursuing this life-long obsession, I studied literature in university, attaining both a BA and MA in English. Still craving more, I attained a degree in Journalism. After travelling the globe for several years and working as a freelance writer, editor, facilitator, and starting my own Communications business, I decided the time had come to focus exclusively on my true love - novel writing.

My goal is to write books that are almost impossible to put down, not because of some great mystery, or high-speed chase, or sexy scene, but because they're full of characters who enrage and delight you; Imperfect people in circumstances that could hit any one of us.

Characters full of human frailties who make awful, sometimes stupid choices …

But who don't give up when they're knocked down. Who struggle and fight and come out on the other side stronger, braver, ready to live a life of their own making.

Read more at www.charlenecarr.com/books

www.ingramcontent.com/pod-product-compliance
Lightning Source LLC
Chambersburg PA
CBHW061621190726
48288CB00007B/2414